# PopularMMOs

HEY GUYYYYYS!

DUDES!

Jen and I are about to take off on another Popular MMOs adventure, and we want YOU to come along!

As you know, every Pat and Jen adventure starts with awesome gear!

And sweet swag! And that's where YOU come in!

Turn the page and let's get started!

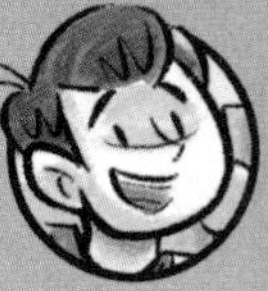

Before we get started, connect the dots to help me get my **BATTLE GEAR** ready!

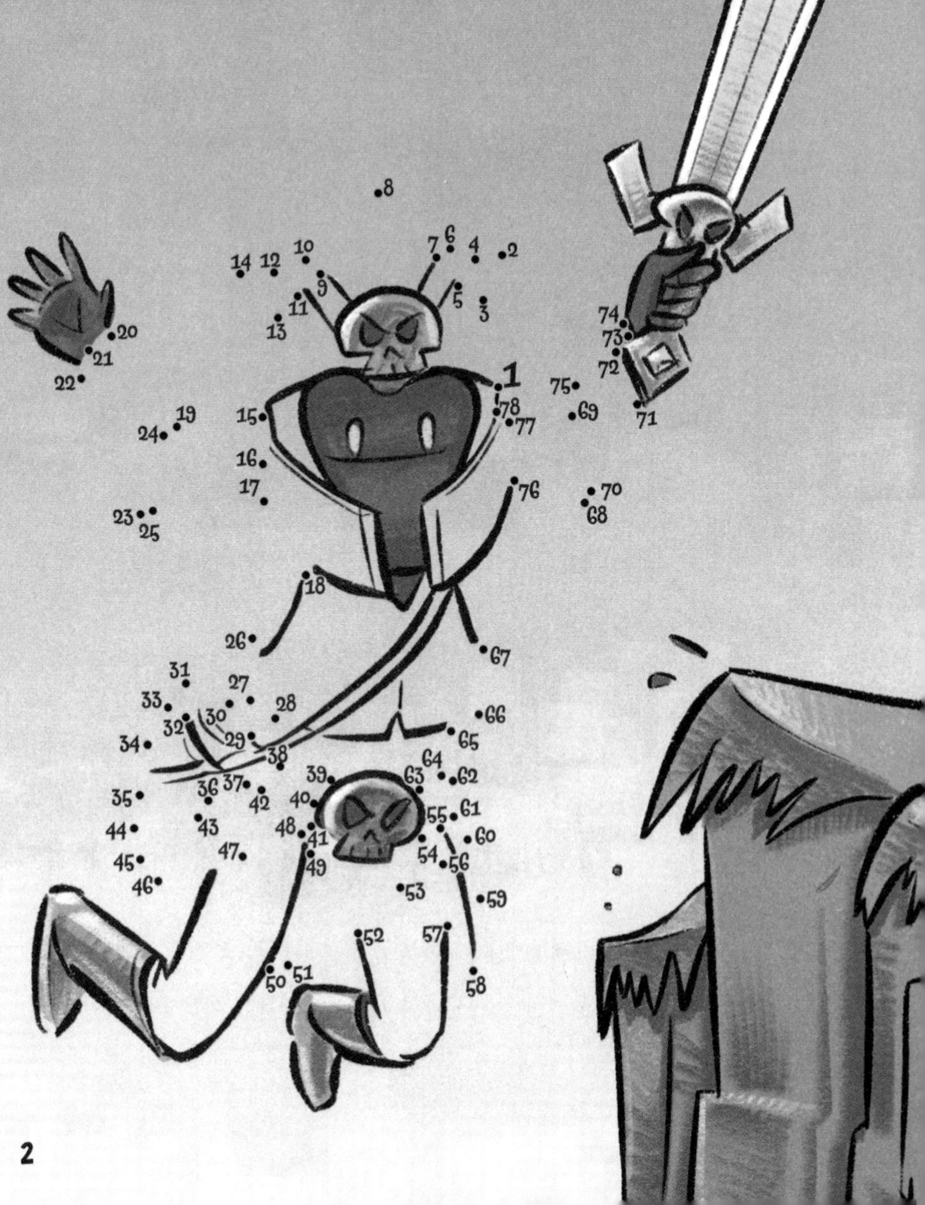

And DRAW a sword in each of my hands so I can defend myself against any spooo-kay ZOMBIES!

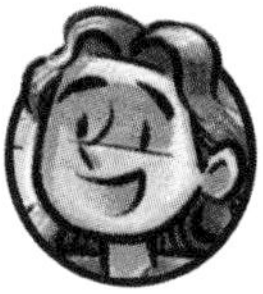

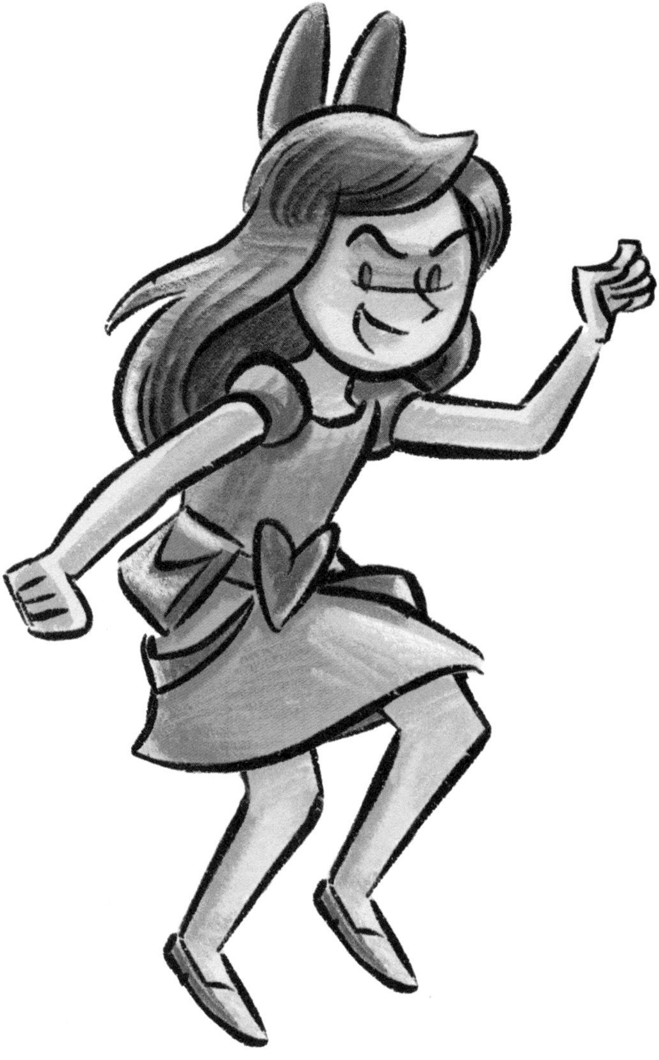

Now tell us all about YOU! Write your first name on the top line . . .

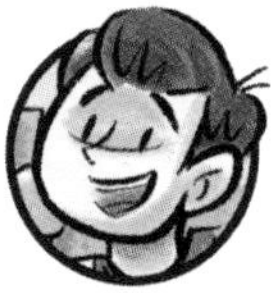

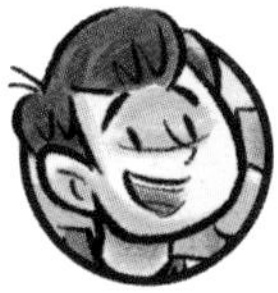

. . . now use each letter in your name to start a new word that tells us something about you!

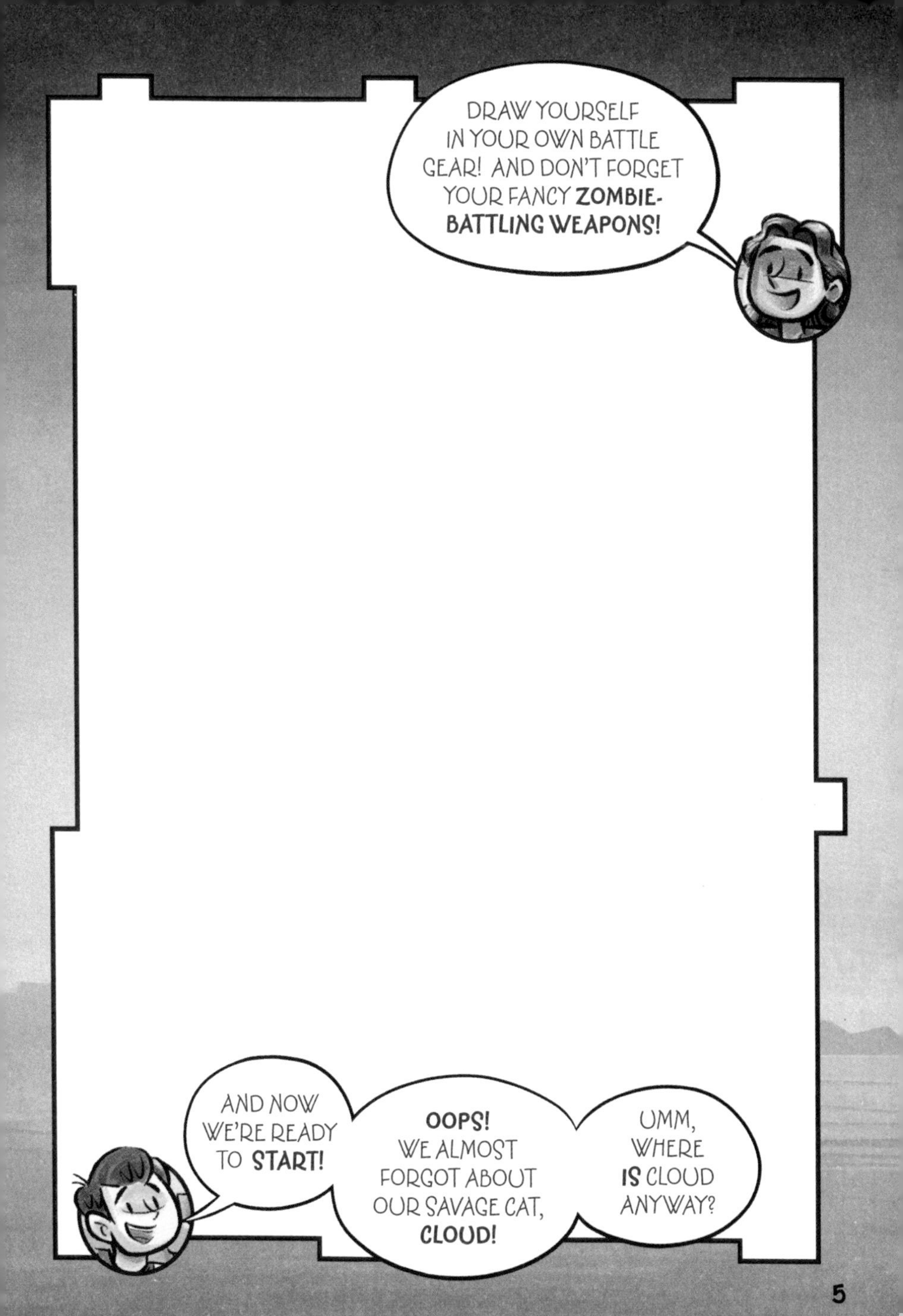
DRAW YOURSELF IN YOUR OWN BATTLE GEAR! AND DON'T FORGET YOUR FANCY **ZOMBIE-BATTLING WEAPONS!**
AND NOW WE'RE READY TO **START!**
**OOPS!** WE ALMOST FORGOT ABOUT OUR SAVAGE CAT, **CLOUD!**
UMM, WHERE **IS** CLOUD ANYWAY?

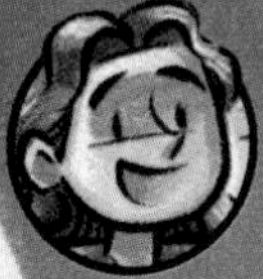

Oh no! CLOUD'S GONE MISSING! We have to find him! Help us to describe him by unscrambling the words below!

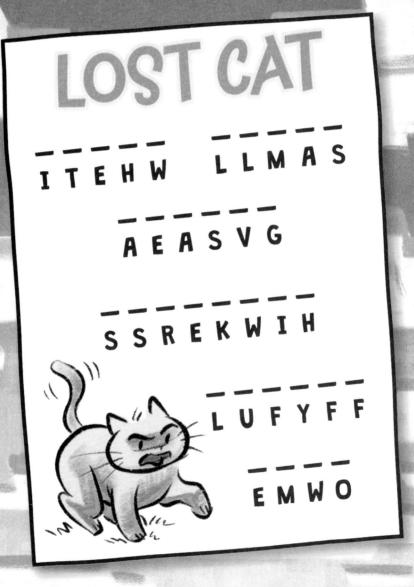

# LOST CAT

_ _ _ _ _   _ _ _ _ _

I T E H W   L L M A S

_ _ _ _ _ _

A E A S V G

_ _ _ _ _ _ _ _

S S R E K W I H

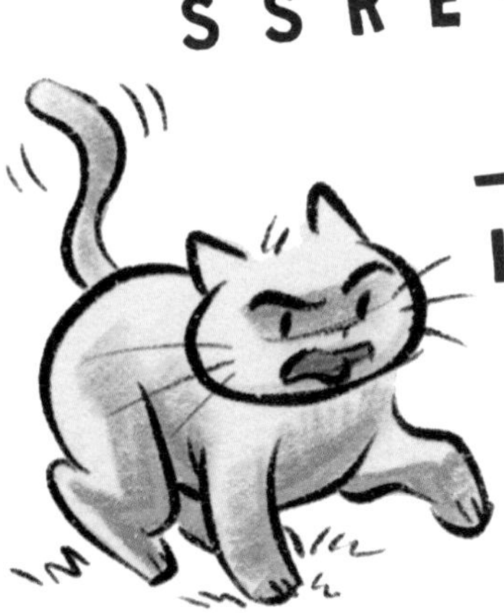

_ _ _ _ _ _

L U F Y F F

_ _ _ _

E M W O

A pet is very special to a family. Tell us a little bit about YOUR pet—or the kind of pet you WISH to have—and what makes them special.

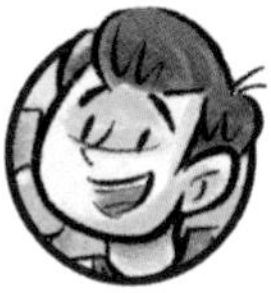

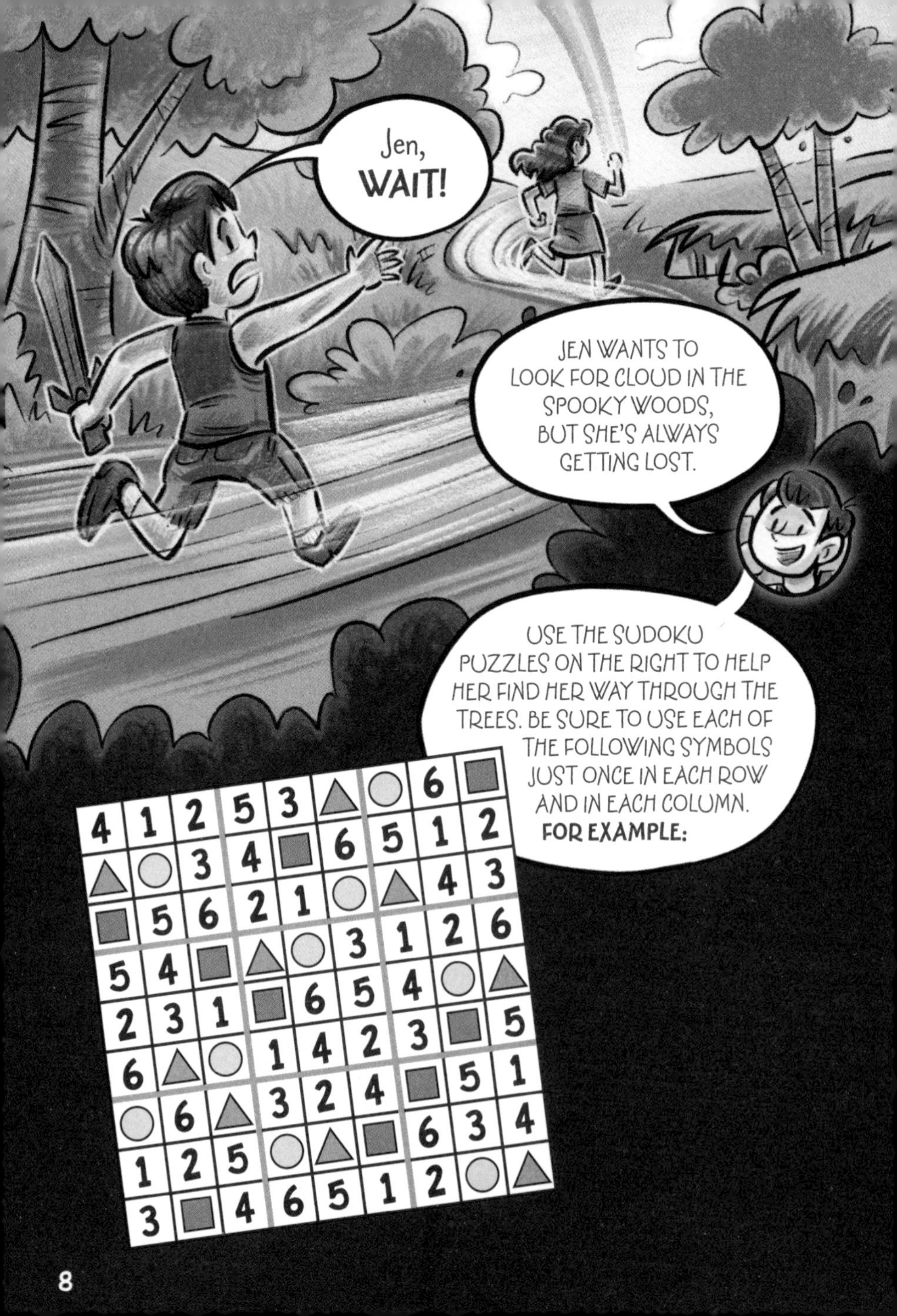
Jen, WAIT!
JEN WANTS TO LOOK FOR CLOUD IN THE SPOOKY WOODS, BUT SHE'S ALWAYS GETTING LOST.
USE THE SUDOKU PUZZLES ON THE RIGHT TO HELP HER FIND HER WAY THROUGH THE TREES. BE SURE TO USE EACH OF THE FOLLOWING SYMBOLS JUST ONCE IN EACH ROW AND IN EACH COLUMN.
**FOR EXAMPLE:**

| | | | | | | | | |
|---|---|---|---|---|---|---|---|---|
| 4 | 1 | 2 | 5 | 3 | △ | ○ | 6 | □ |
| △ | ○ | 3 | 4 | □ | 6 | 5 | 1 | 2 |
| □ | 5 | 6 | 2 | 1 | ○ | △ | 4 | 3 |
| 5 | 4 | □ | △ | ○ | 3 | 1 | 2 | 6 |
| 2 | 3 | 1 | □ | 6 | 5 | 4 | ○ | △ |
| 6 | △ | ○ | 1 | 4 | 2 | 3 | □ | 5 |
| ○ | 6 | △ | 3 | 2 | 4 | □ | 5 | 1 |
| 1 | 2 | 5 | ○ | △ | □ | 6 | 3 | 4 |
| 3 | □ | 4 | 6 | 5 | 1 | 2 | ○ | △ |

9

I CAN'T FIND **CLOUD** ANYWHERE, BUT A MYSTERIOUS FIGURE IS APPROACHING FROM THE DARKNESS!

CAN YOU GUESS WHICH POPULAR MMOS CHARACTER IT IS BASED ON THE ANSWERS IN THIS CROSSWORD PUZZLE?

## ACROSS

2. The color of the sky.
5. When you want what others have, you are_____ of them.
6. What you use to cover a wound.
7. A long blade with a handle.

## DOWN

1. A small cucumber kept in a jar of vinegar and other liquid.
2. Your favorite friend of them all.
3. Information that you keep from other people.
4. A person who comes back from the dead as a walking monster that eats other people.

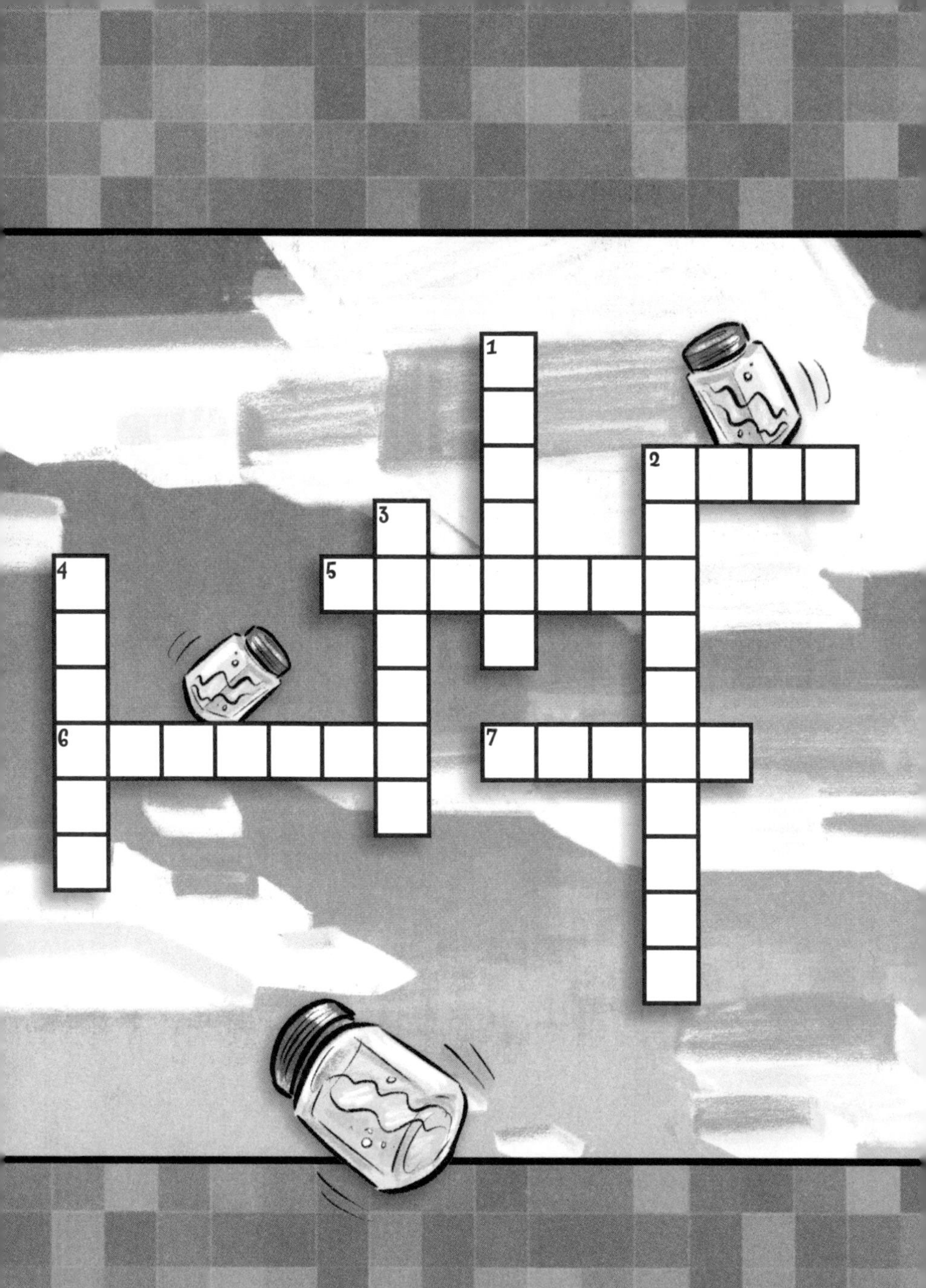
1
2
3
4
5
6
7

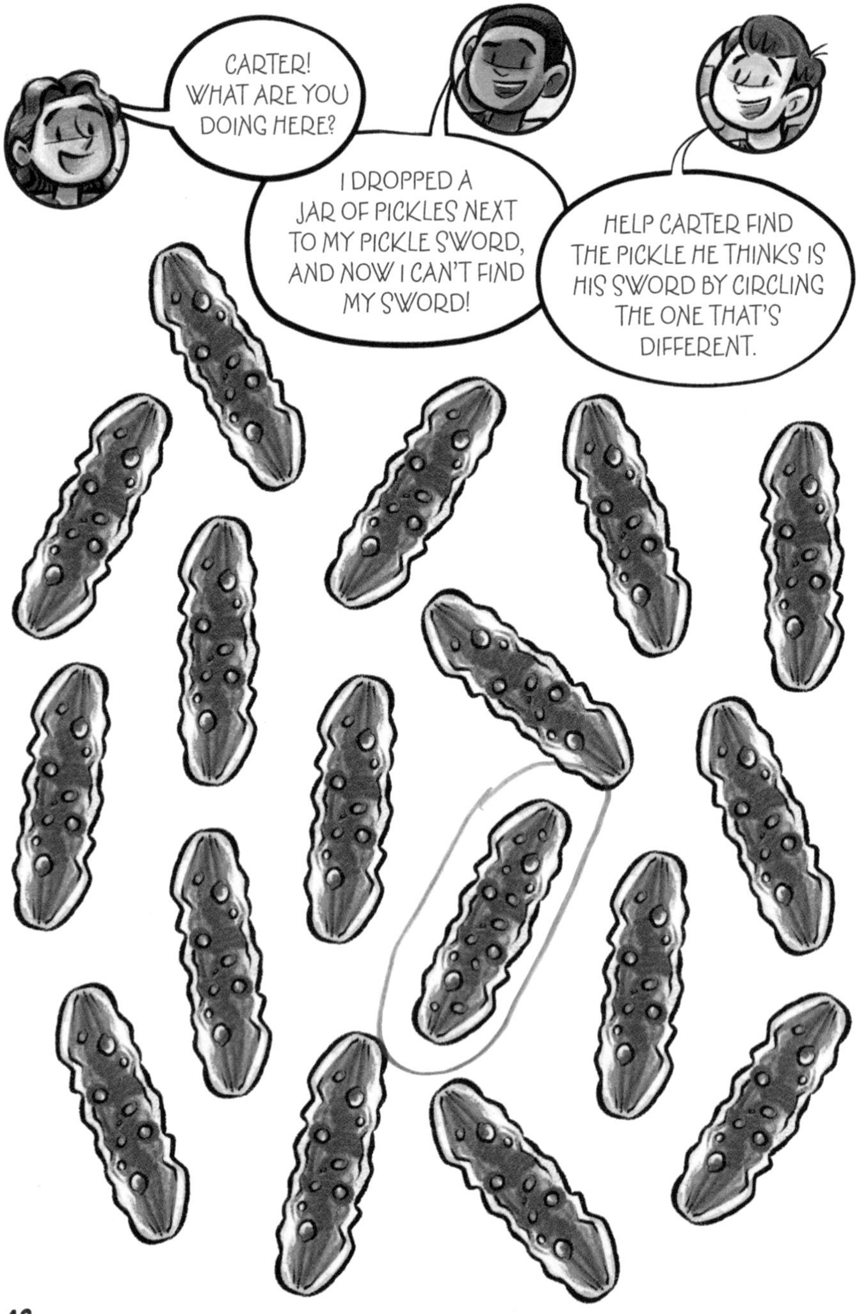
CARTER! WHAT ARE YOU DOING HERE?
I DROPPED A JAR OF PICKLES NEXT TO MY PICKLE SWORD, AND NOW I CAN'T FIND MY SWORD!
HELP CARTER FIND THE PICKLE HE THINKS IS HIS SWORD BY CIRCLING THE ONE THAT'S DIFFERENT.

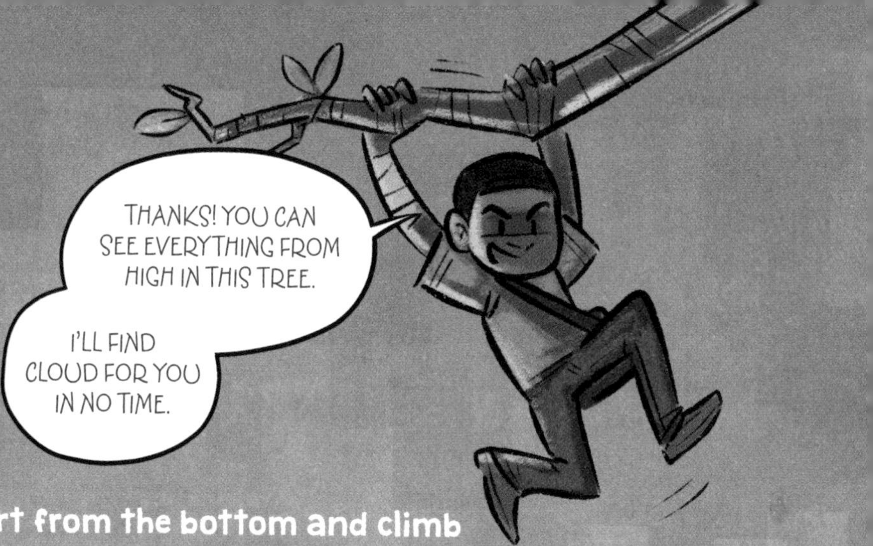
THANKS! YOU CAN SEE EVERYTHING FROM HIGH IN THIS TREE.
I'LL FIND CLOUD FOR YOU IN NO TIME.

**Start from the bottom and climb the branches by filling in the missing numbers that complete the math problems.**

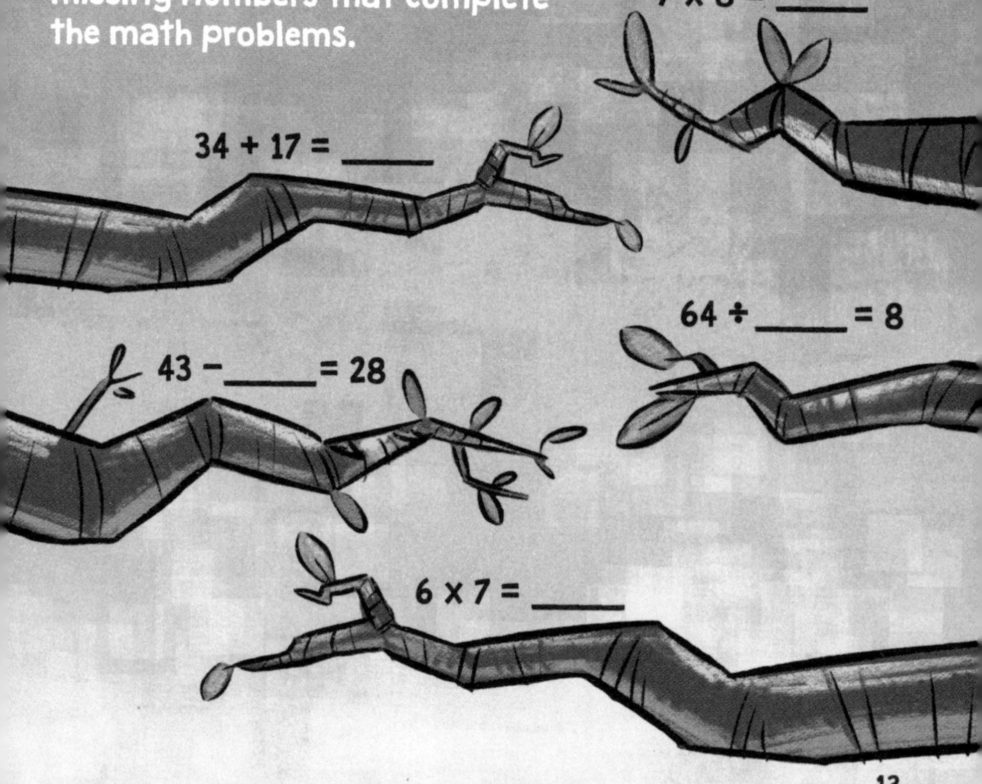

7 x 8 = ____

34 + 17 = ____

64 ÷ ____ = 8

43 − ____ = 28

6 x 7 = ____

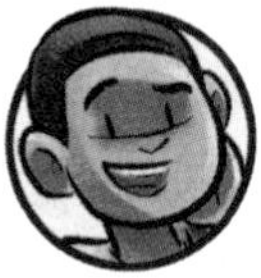

I don't see Cloud, but I do see SOMETHING!

Connect the dots and see what I see!

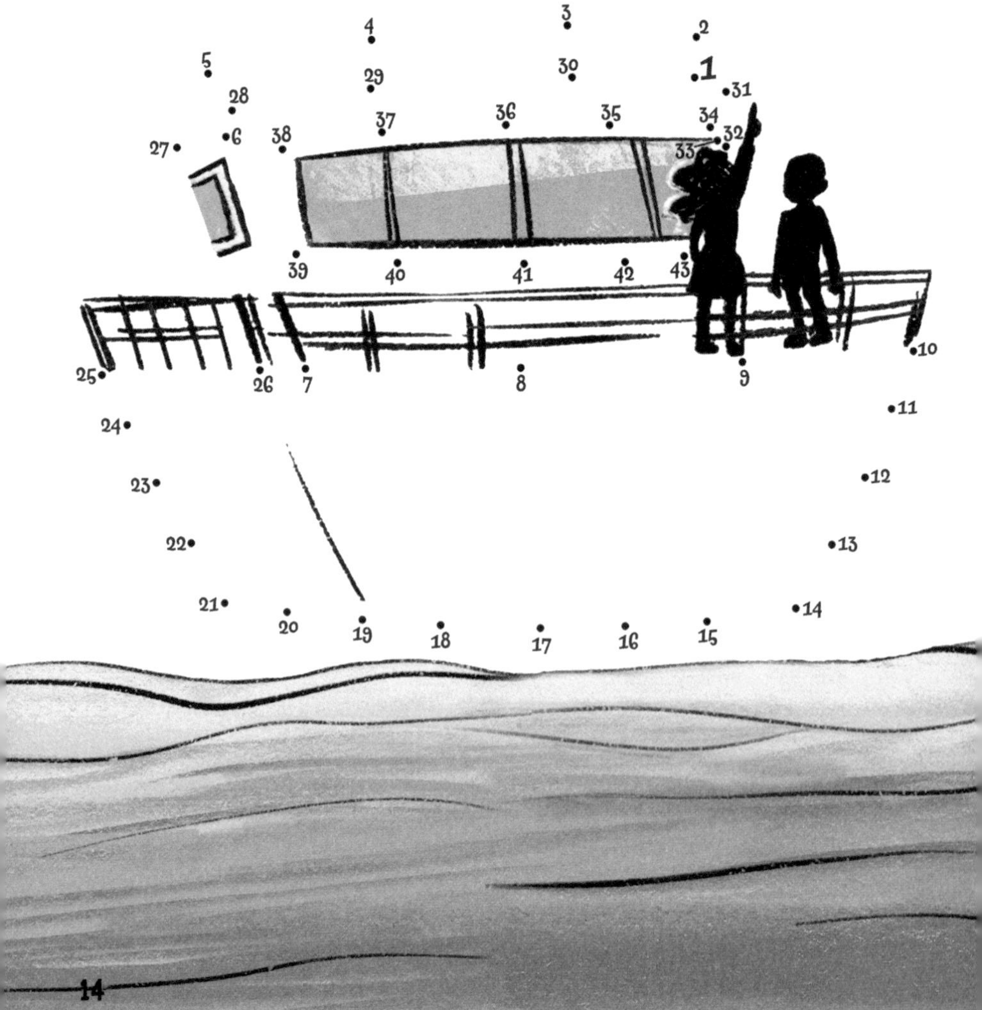

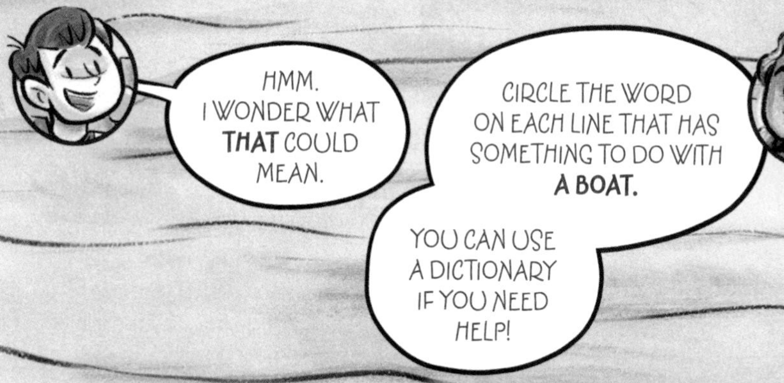
HMM. I WONDER WHAT **THAT** COULD MEAN.
CIRCLE THE WORD ON EACH LINE THAT HAS SOMETHING TO DO WITH **A BOAT.**
YOU CAN USE A DICTIONARY IF YOU NEED HELP!

**TAPESTRY – PROPELLER – BAGGAGE**

---

**ANCHOR – ORCHARD – ARENA**

---

**COAX – KAYAK – PRACTICE**

---

**OAR – ARENA – PEER**

---

**BOMBY – JEN – CAPTAIN COOKIE**

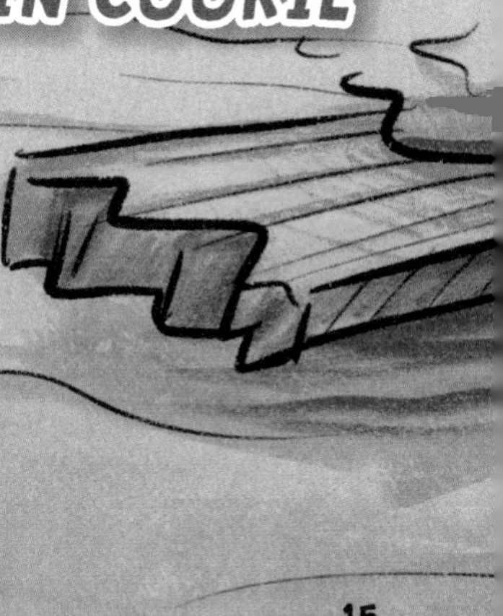

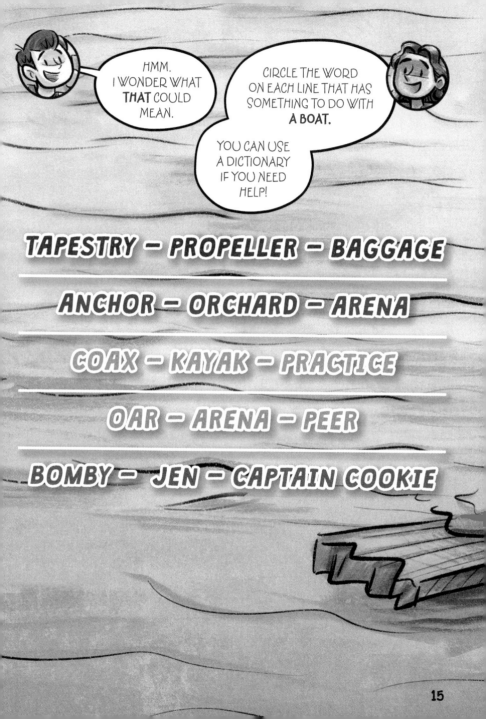

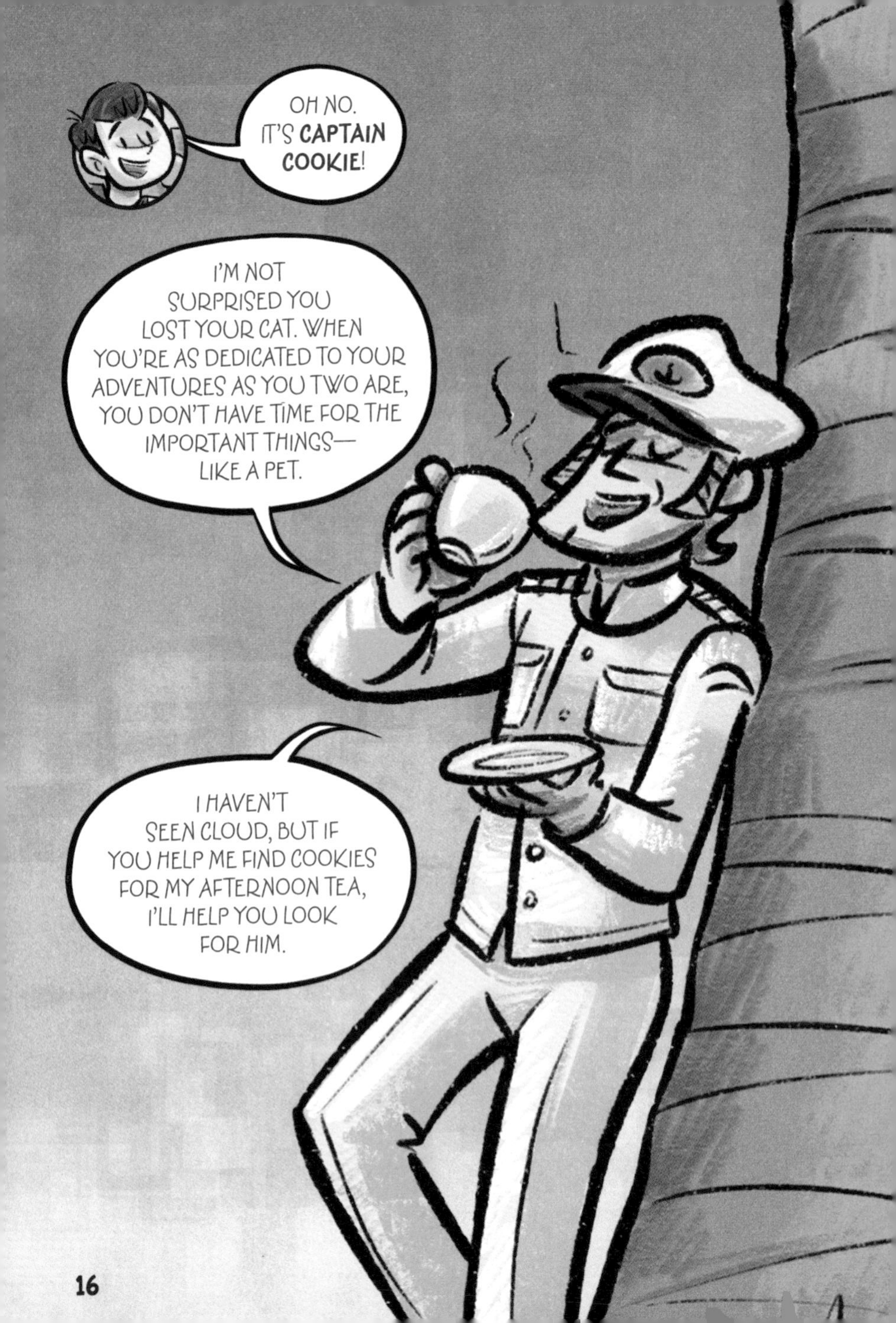
OH NO. IT'S **CAPTAIN COOKIE**!
I'M NOT SURPRISED YOU LOST YOUR CAT. WHEN YOU'RE AS DEDICATED TO YOUR ADVENTURES AS YOU TWO ARE, YOU DON'T HAVE TIME FOR THE IMPORTANT THINGS—LIKE A PET.
I HAVEN'T SEEN CLOUD, BUT IF YOU HELP ME FIND COOKIES FOR MY AFTERNOON TEA, I'LL HELP YOU LOOK FOR HIM.

# Find these words in the puzzle below!

BISCOTTI      SANDWICH
CHOCOLATE CHIP      SHORTBREAD
GINGERBREAD      SNICKERDOODLE
GINGER SNAP      SUGAR
MACADAMIA      WAFER
MACAROON

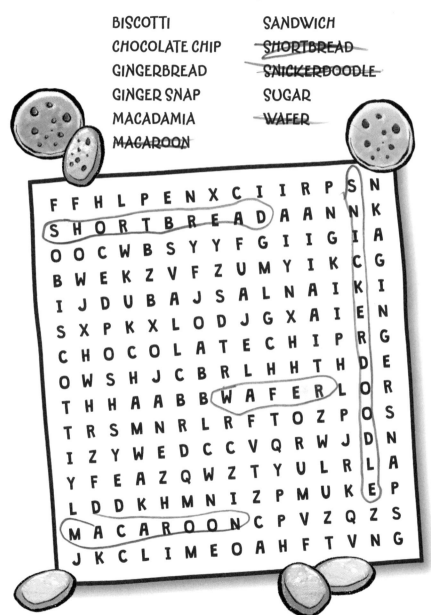

```
F F H L P E N X C I I R P S N
S H O R T B R E A D A A N N K
O O C W B S Y Y F G I I G I A
B W E K Z V F Z U M Y I K C G
I J D U B A J S A L N A I K I
S X P K X L O D J G X A I E N
C H O C O L A T E C H I P R G
O W S H J C B R L H H T H D E
T H H A A B B W A F E R L O R
T R S M N R L R F T O Z P O S
I Z Y W E D C C V Q R W J D N
Y F E A Z Q W Z T Y U L R L A
L D D K H M N I Z P M U K E P
M A C A R O O N C P V Z Q Z S
J K C L I M E O A H F T V N G
```

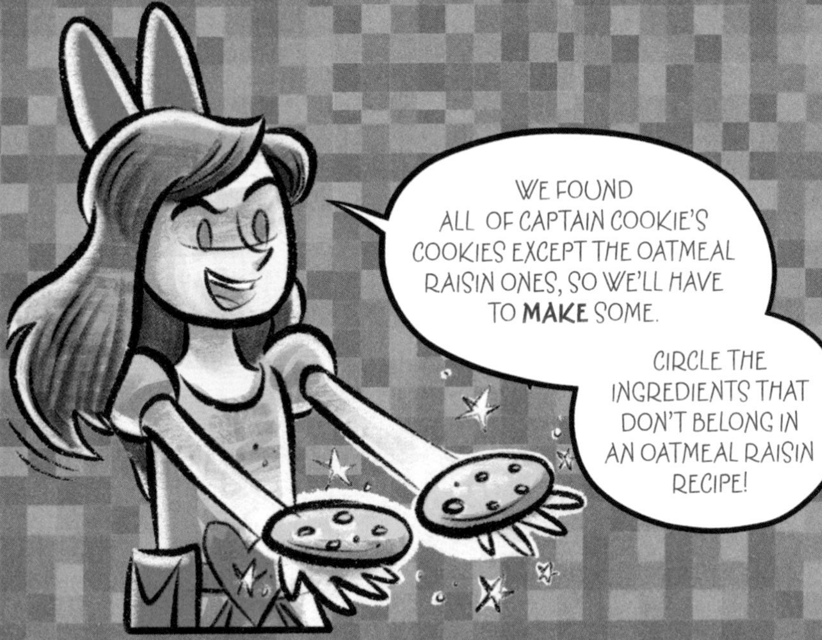
WE FOUND ALL OF CAPTAIN COOKIE'S COOKIES EXCEPT THE OATMEAL RAISIN ONES, SO WE'LL HAVE TO **MAKE** SOME.
CIRCLE THE INGREDIENTS THAT DON'T BELONG IN AN OATMEAL RAISIN RECIPE!

HOT SAUCE

FROG LEGS

FINGER CHEESE

FLOUR

MUSHROOM SYRUP

RAISINS

SUGAR

ALMONDS

BACON

SALT

BUTTER

OATMEAL

Eat through the captain's oatmeal raisin cookie by drawing ONE line that passes through all the raisins without crossing over that line! There's more than one possible answer.

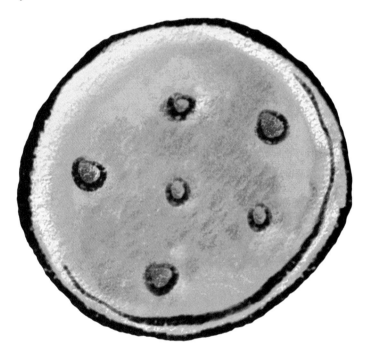

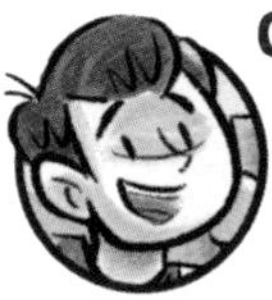

**Captain Cookie means well, but no matter what he says to compliment us, it doesn't come out right.**

**Using the clues on the right, insert words into the blank spaces in the word balloons to complete Captain Cookie's comments.**

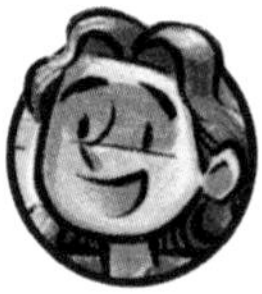

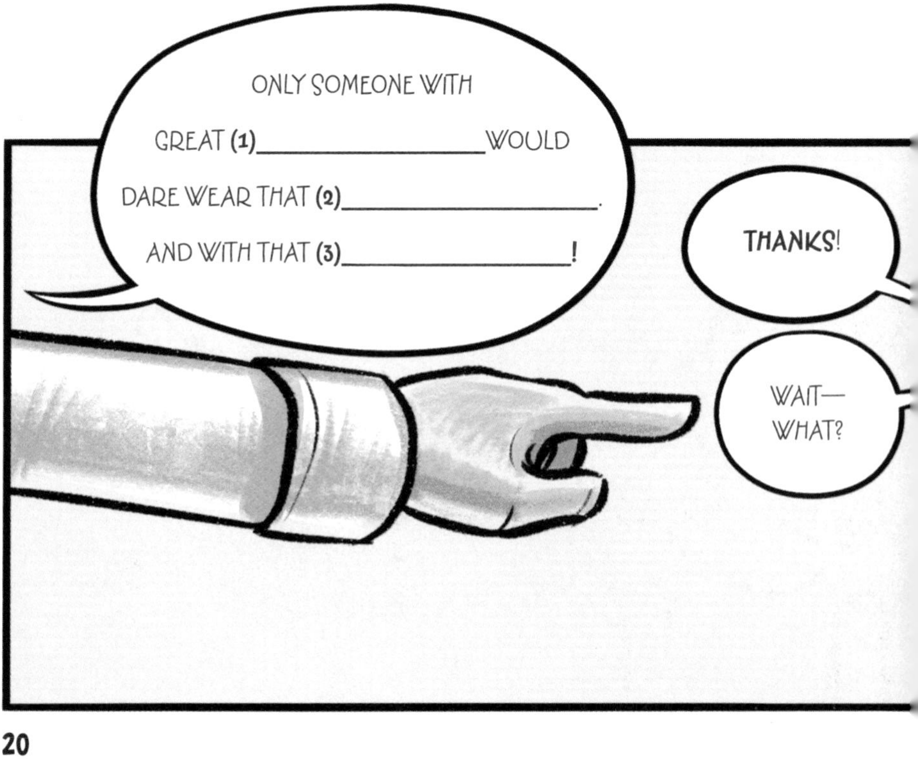

ONLY SOMEONE WITH GREAT (1)________________ WOULD DARE WEAR THAT (2)________________. AND WITH THAT (3)________________!
THANKS!
WAIT— WHAT?

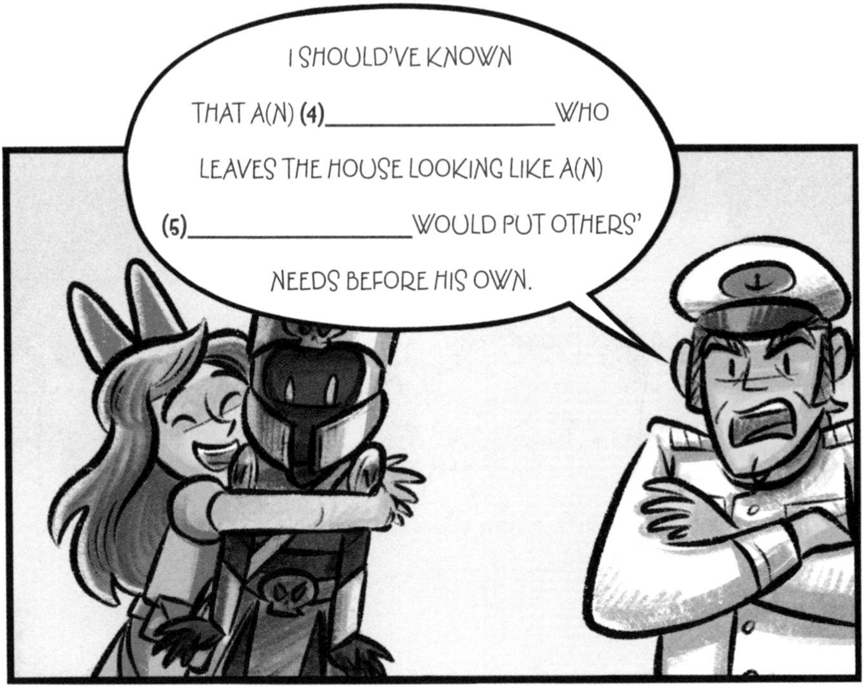
I SHOULD'VE KNOWN
THAT A(N) (4)__________________ WHO
LEAVES THE HOUSE LOOKING LIKE A(N)
(5)__________________ WOULD PUT OTHERS'
NEEDS BEFORE HIS OWN.

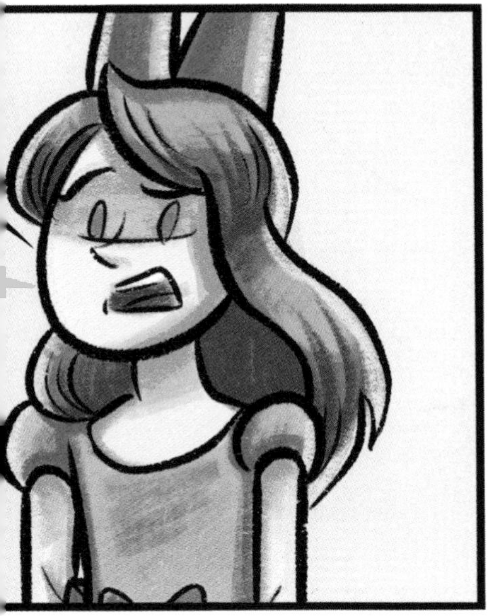

## CLUES:

1. A quality you admire in someone (ex. courage, sense of humor)
2. Something you wear
3. A type of makeup
4. A job (ex. firefighter)
5. An animal

Show Captain Cookie the real way to compliment someone. What are some of your favorite things about your best friends.

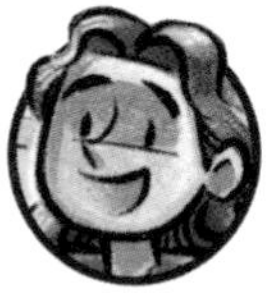

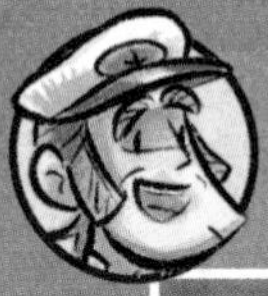

**Now let's find that cat!**

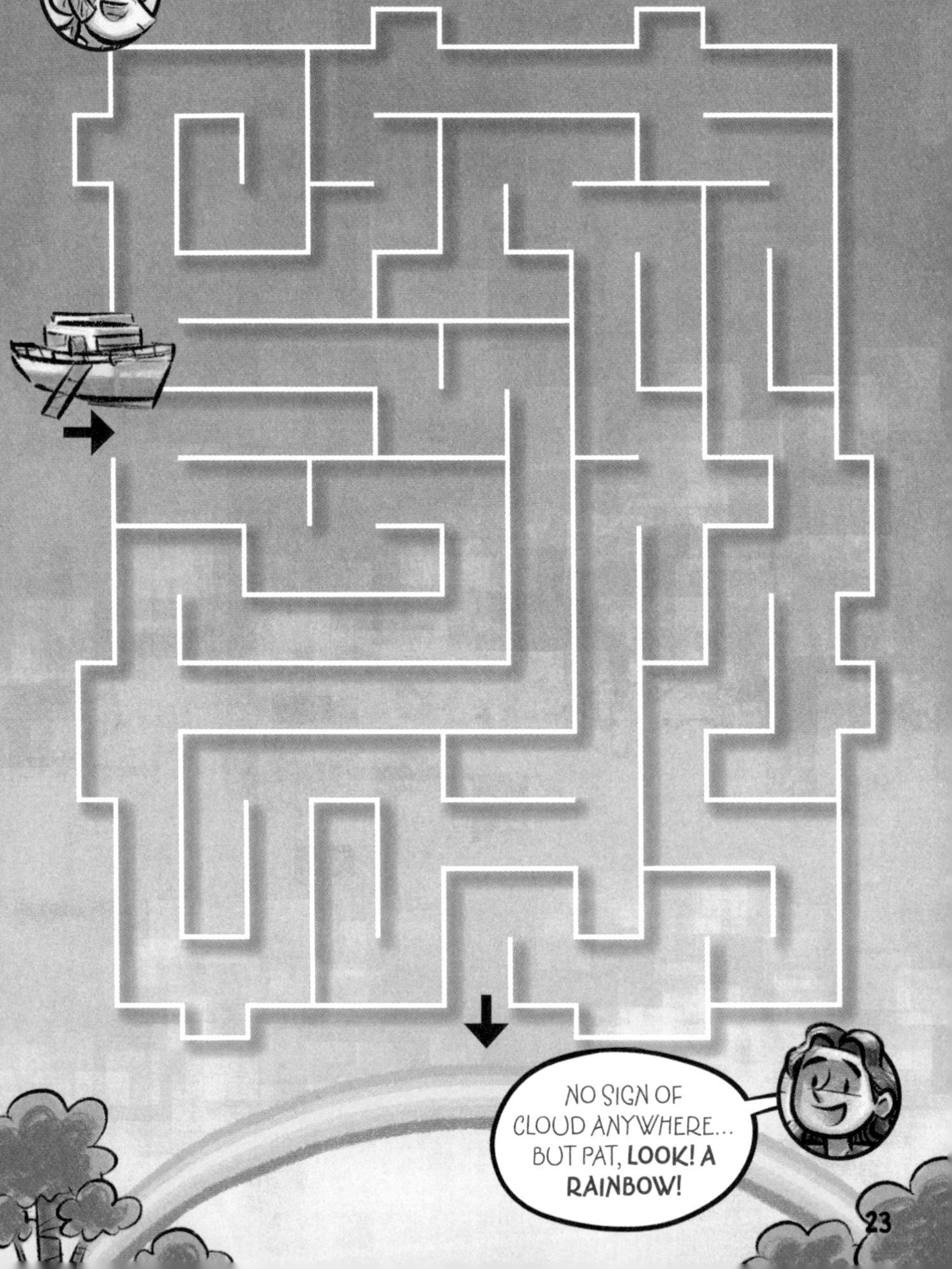
NO SIGN OF CLOUD ANYWHERE... BUT PAT, **LOOK! A RAINBOW!**

THAT'S NO RAINBOW—IT'S GIZMO!

**Use the code below to name the colors in Gizmo's rainbow!**

| | | | |
|---|---|---|---|
| | E=V | L=O | |
| | F=U | M=N | |
| | G=T | N=M | S=H |
| A=Z | H=S | O=L | T=G | X=C |
| B=Y | I=R | P=K | U=F | Y=B |
| C=X | J=Q | Q=J | V=E | Z=A |
| D=W | K=P | R=I | W=D |

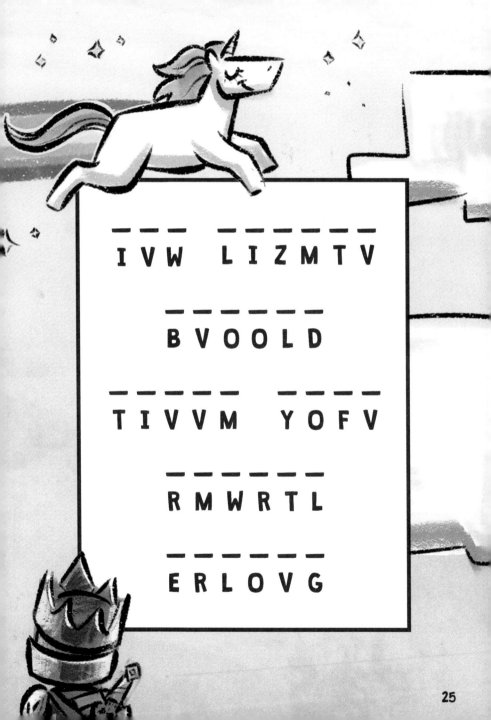

\_\_\_ _____
I V W   L I Z M T V

_____
B V O O L D

\_\_\_\_\_ \_\_\_\_
T I V V M   Y O F V

_____
R M W R T L

_____
E R L O V G

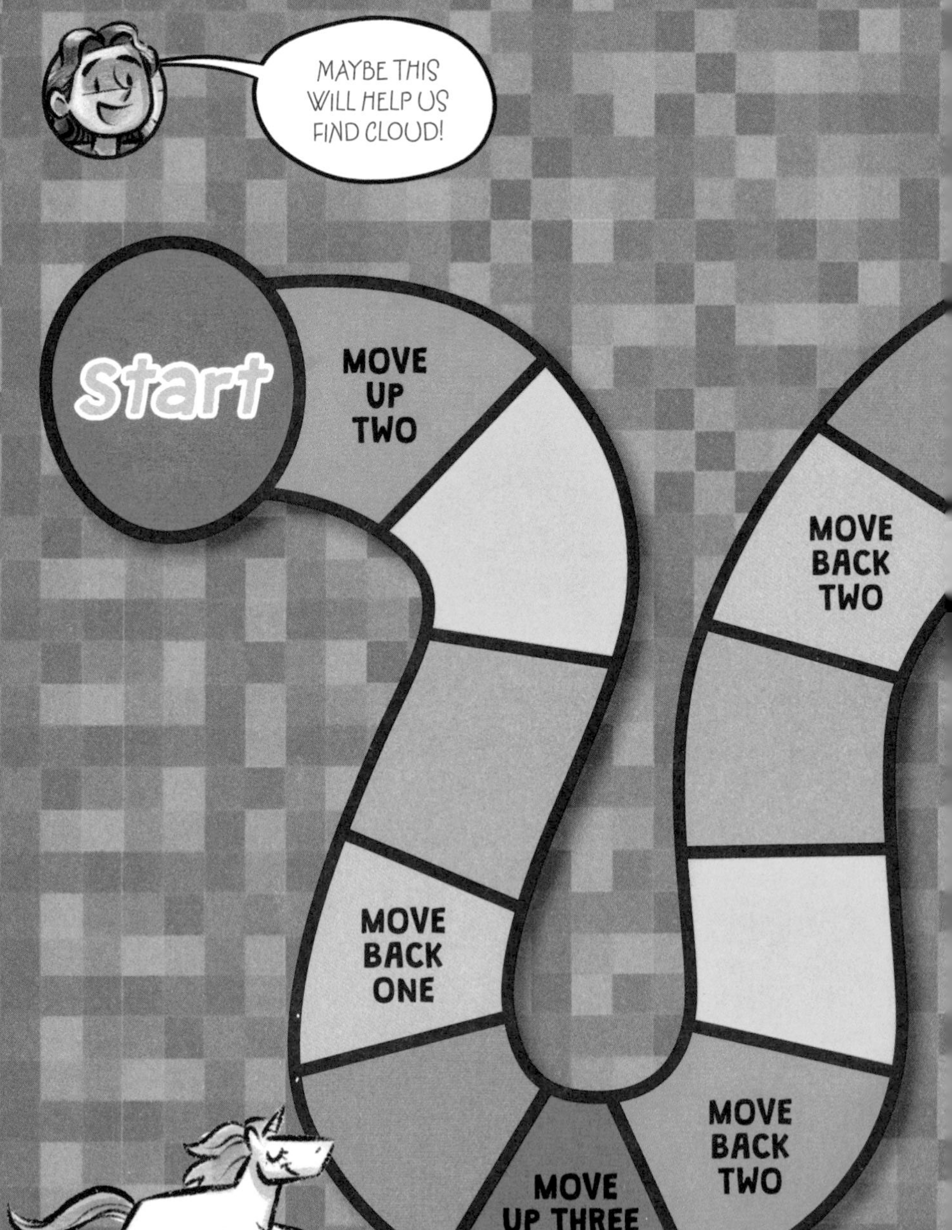
MAYBE THIS WILL HELP US FIND CLOUD!
Start
MOVE UP TWO
MOVE BACK TWO
MOVE BACK ONE
MOVE BACK TWO
MOVE UP THREE

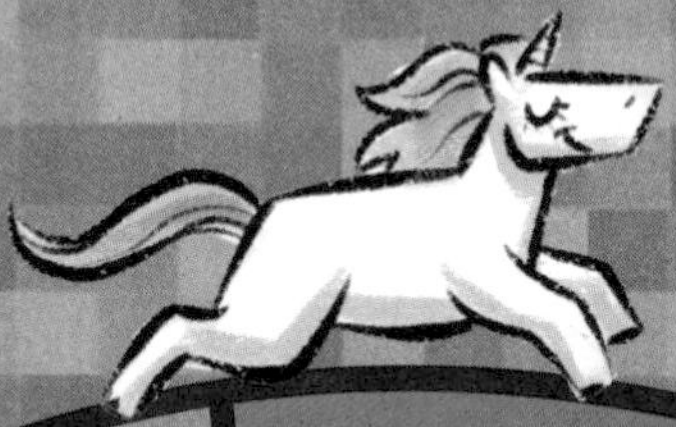

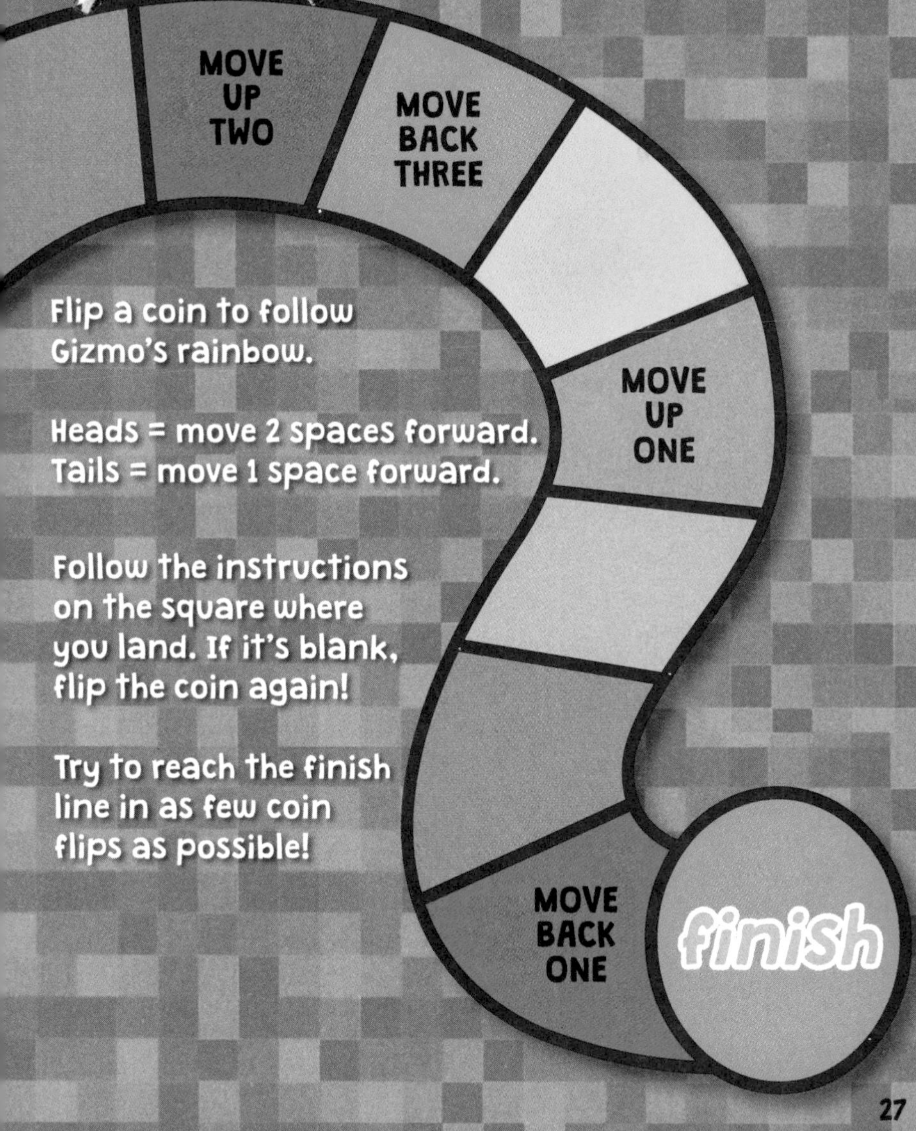
MOVE UP TWO
MOVE BACK THREE
MOVE UP ONE
MOVE BACK ONE
finish

Flip a coin to follow Gizmo's rainbow.

Heads = move 2 spaces forward.
Tails = move 1 space forward.

Follow the instructions on the square where you land. If it's blank, flip the coin again!

Try to reach the finish line in as few coin flips as possible!

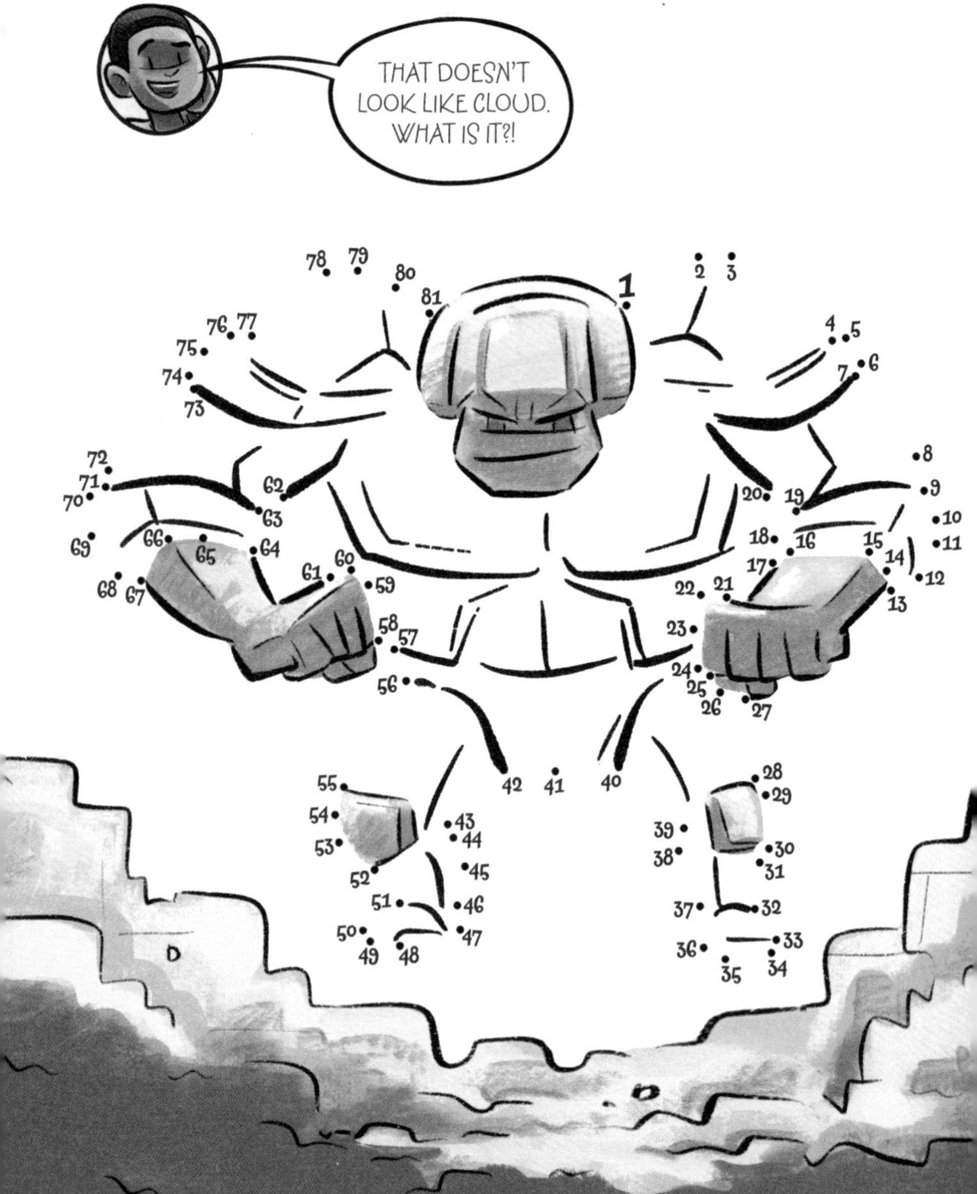
THAT DOESN'T LOOK LIKE CLOUD. WHAT IS IT?!

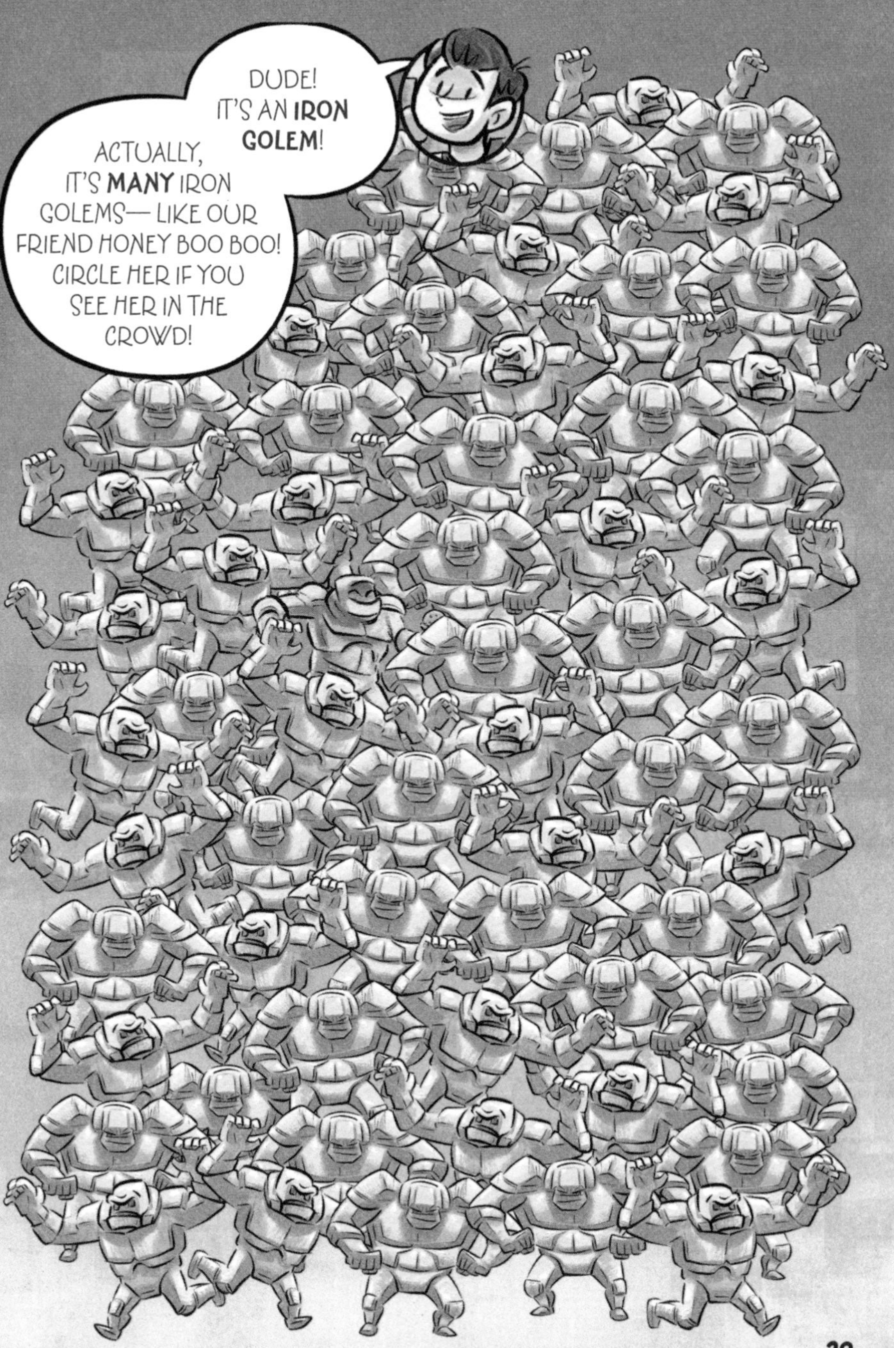
DUDE! IT'S AN **IRON GOLEM**!
ACTUALLY, IT'S **MANY** IRON GOLEMS— LIKE OUR FRIEND HONEY BOO BOO! CIRCLE HER IF YOU SEE HER IN THE CROWD!

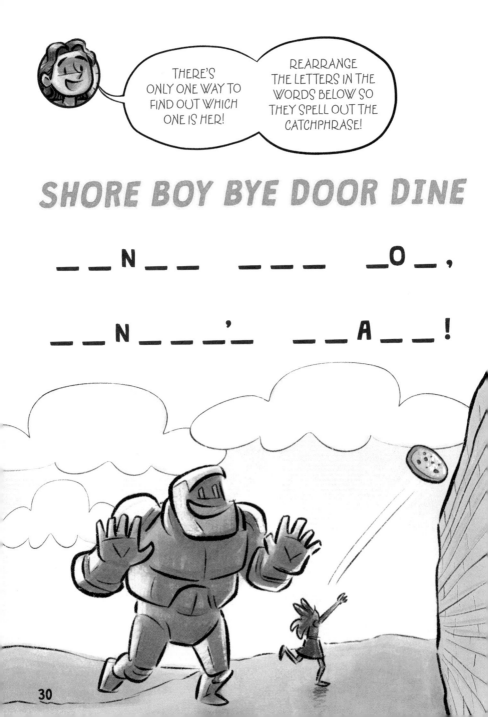

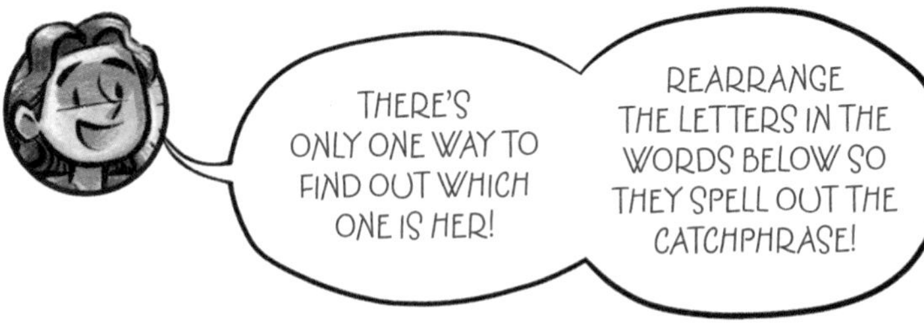
THERE'S ONLY ONE WAY TO FIND OUT WHICH ONE IS HER!
REARRANGE THE LETTERS IN THE WORDS BELOW SO THEY SPELL OUT THE CATCHPHRASE!

## SHORE BOY BYE DOOR DINE

_ _ N _ _   _ _ _   _ O _ ,

_ _ N _ _ _ ’ _   _ _ A _ _ !

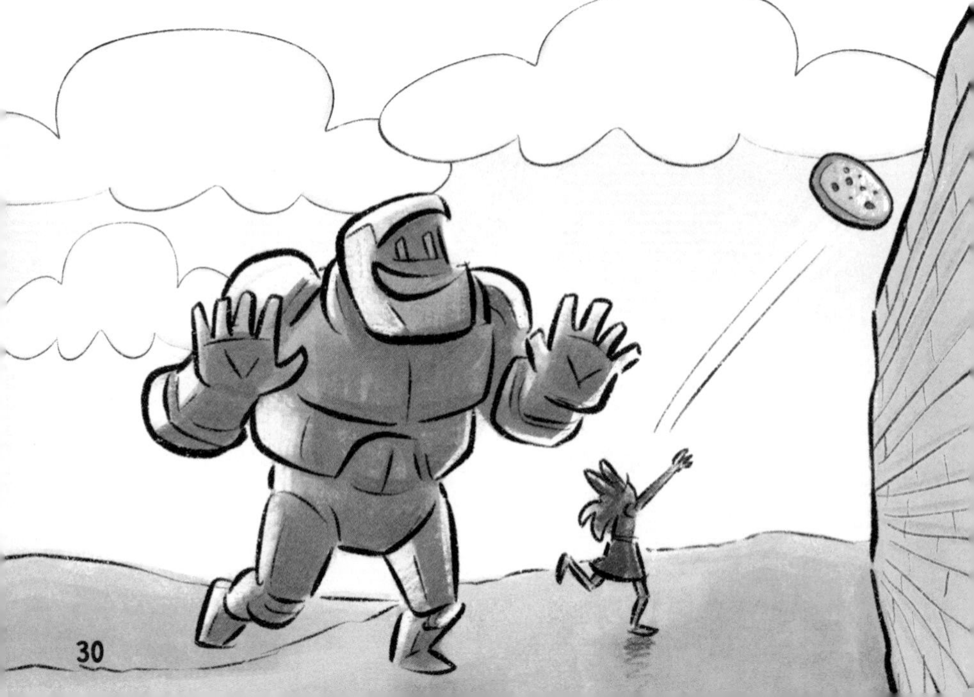

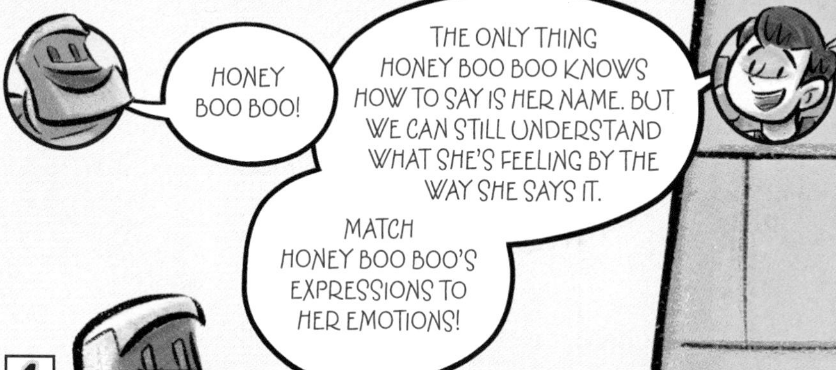
HONEY BOO BOO!
THE ONLY THING HONEY BOO BOO KNOWS HOW TO SAY IS HER NAME. BUT WE CAN STILL UNDERSTAND WHAT SHE'S FEELING BY THE WAY SHE SAYS IT.
MATCH HONEY BOO BOO'S EXPRESSIONS TO HER EMOTIONS!

1
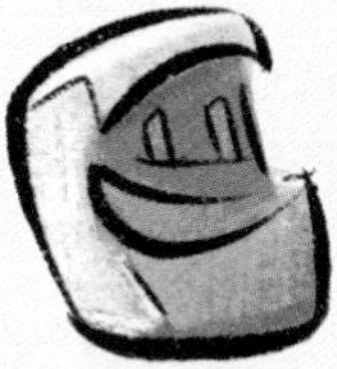

2
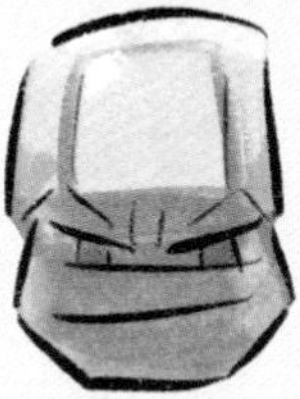

3
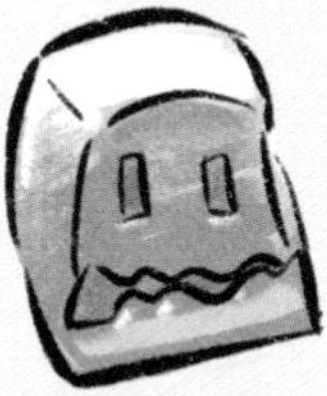

4
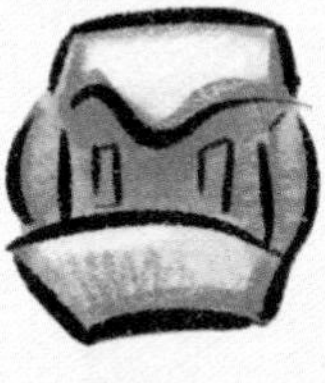

5
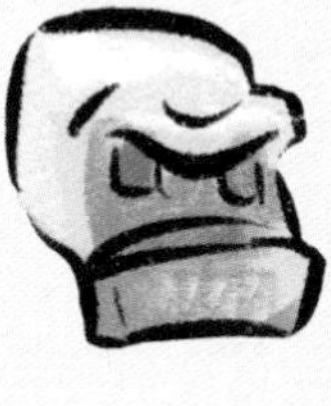

**CLUES:**

- ☐ Angry
- ☐ Excited
- ☐ Disappointed
- ☐ Sad
- ☐ Worried

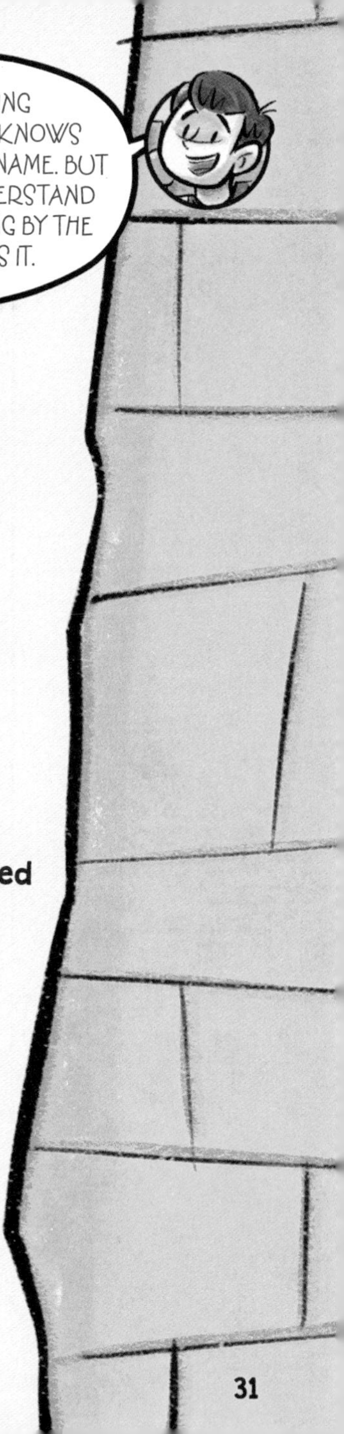

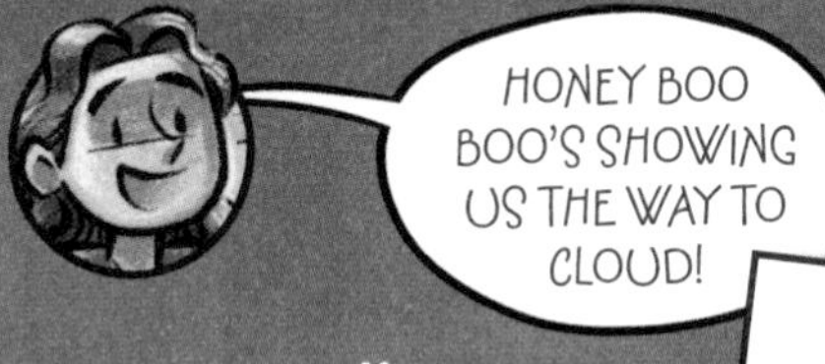
HONEY BOO BOO'S SHOWING US THE WAY TO CLOUD!

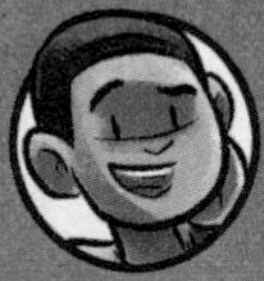

Follow those cookie crumbs in the puzzles by filling in the empty squares with the numbers and icons. But be sure to use each of them just once in each row and in each column.

| | | | | | | | | |
|---|---|---|---|---|---|---|---|---|
| | 3 | 2 | | | 5 | 1 | 6 | |
| | 5 | | | | 6 | | | |
| | | △ | | 3 | | ○ | | 5 |
| | △ | | 6 | | 1 | | 3 | ○ |
| | | | 2 | | | | | ■ |
| | | | ○ | | | | | 1 |
| ■ | 4 | | 5 | | | | | 3 |
| △ | 2 | 5 | | | ○ | | | |
| ○ | | | | | | △ | | 6 |

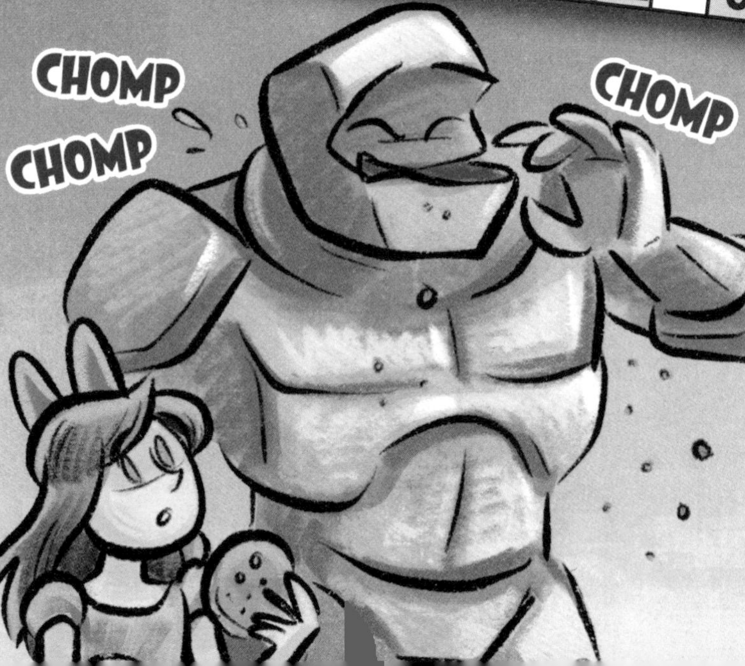
CHOMP
CHOMP
CHOMP

| | | | | | | | | |
|---|---|---|---|---|---|---|---|---|
| | 1 | | | 4 | ○ | | | |
| △ | | | | | | | | ○ |
| 3 | 2 | | | | 1 | △ | | ■ |
| | | | | | | | ○ | |
| | △ | 6 | | | | ■ | | |
| ■ | | 5 | 2 | 6 | | | | |
| | | | 5 | | 3 | | 6 | |
| | | 2 | | | △ | | | |
| | | | 4 | | | | 1 | 3 |

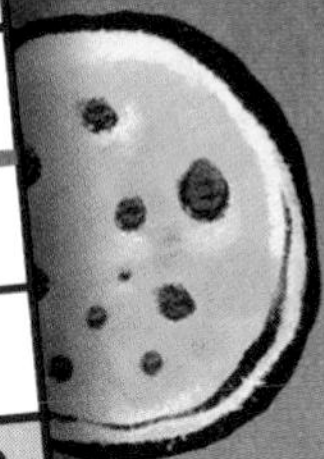

| | | | | | | | | |
|---|---|---|---|---|---|---|---|---|
| | | | 2 | | 5 | | | |
| | | ○ | | 4 | | | | |
| | | 2 | | | △ | | 3 | |
| 2 | | | | 6 | | ○ | 1 | |
| | | | | | | | 6 | |
| | | ■ | | | | 4 | | 5 |
| 3 | | 5 | | ○ | | | 2 | |
| | | | | | | 6 | ■ | |
| 1 | 4 | | 3 | | | | | |

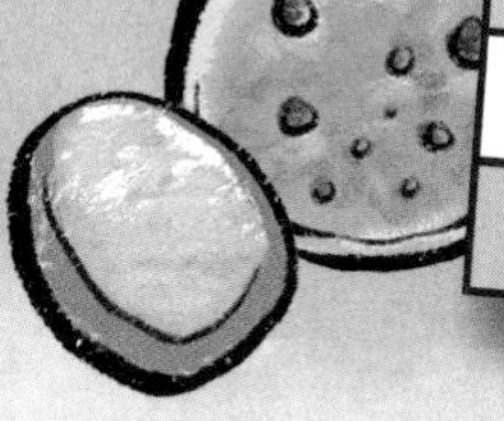

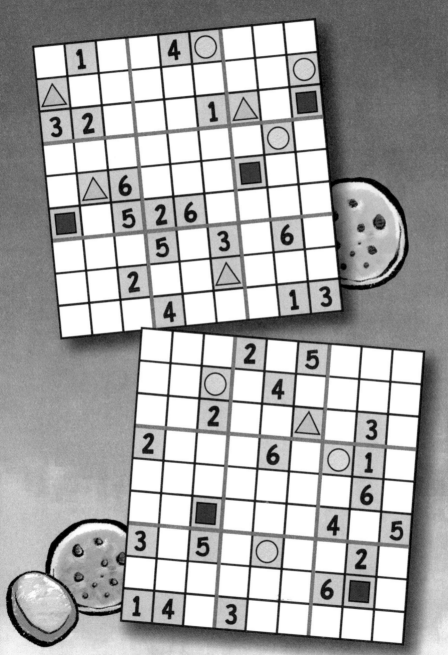

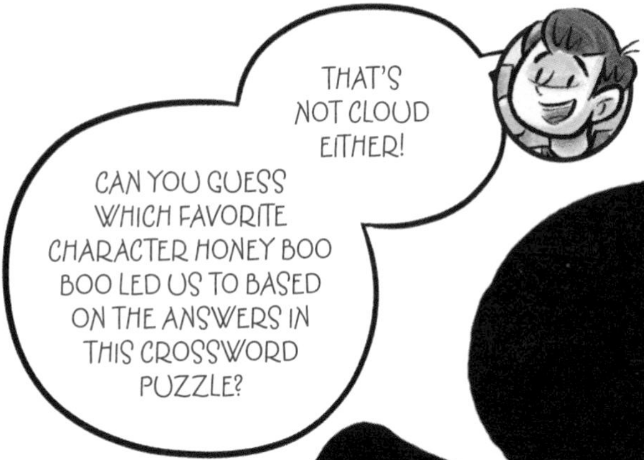
THAT'S NOT CLOUD EITHER!
CAN YOU GUESS WHICH FAVORITE CHARACTER HONEY BOO BOO LED US TO BASED ON THE ANSWERS IN THIS CROSSWORD PUZZLE?

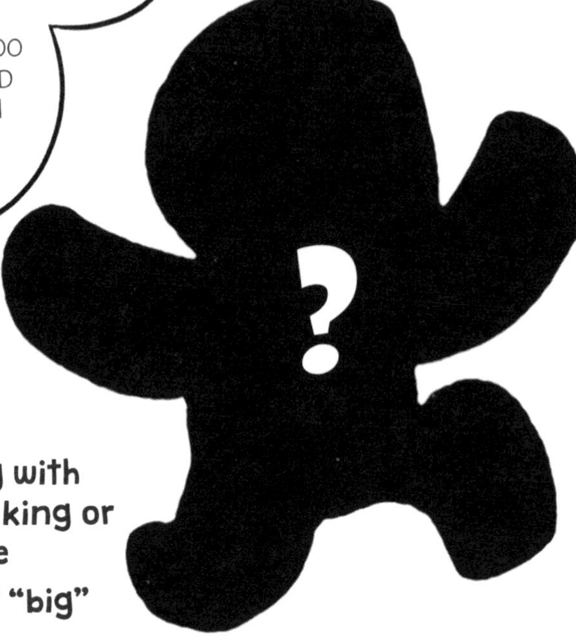
?

## ACROSS

2. A large building with towers where a king or queen often live
4. The opposite of "big"
5. TNT
6. Your best _______ is the person you love to spend time with.

## DOWN

1. The color you get when you mix yellow and blue.
3. What you call a piece of meat between two pieces of bread.
4. An eight-legged bug

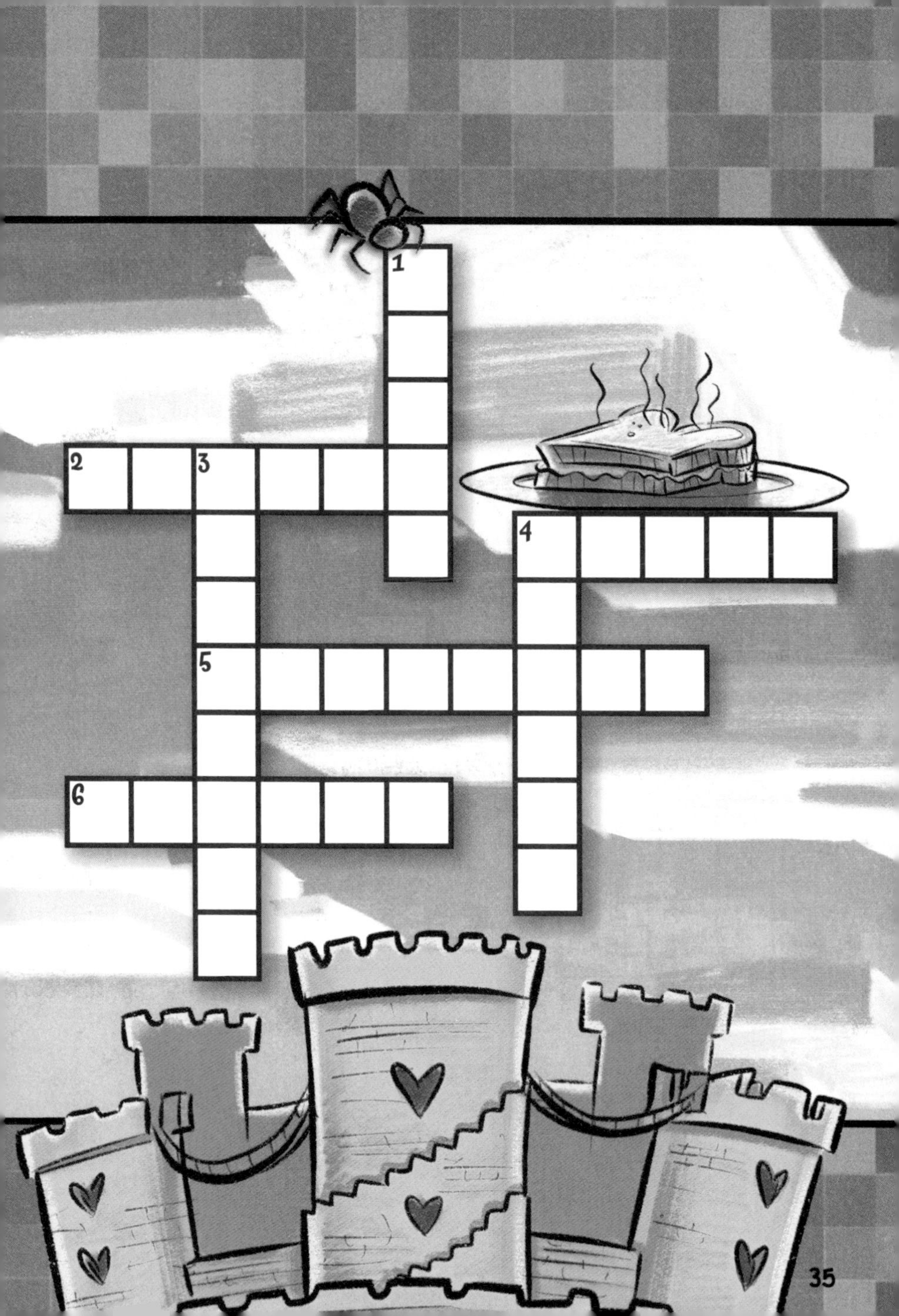
1
2
3
4
5
6

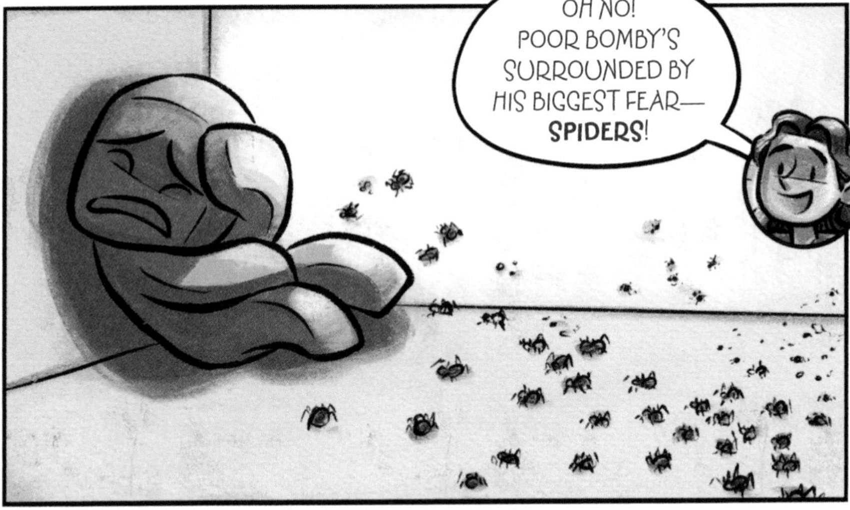
OH NO!
POOR BOMBY'S
SURROUNDED BY
HIS BIGGEST FEAR—
SPIDERS!

Clear a path for him by crossing out the matching pairs of spiders below as you find them! Find the one that doesn't have a match!

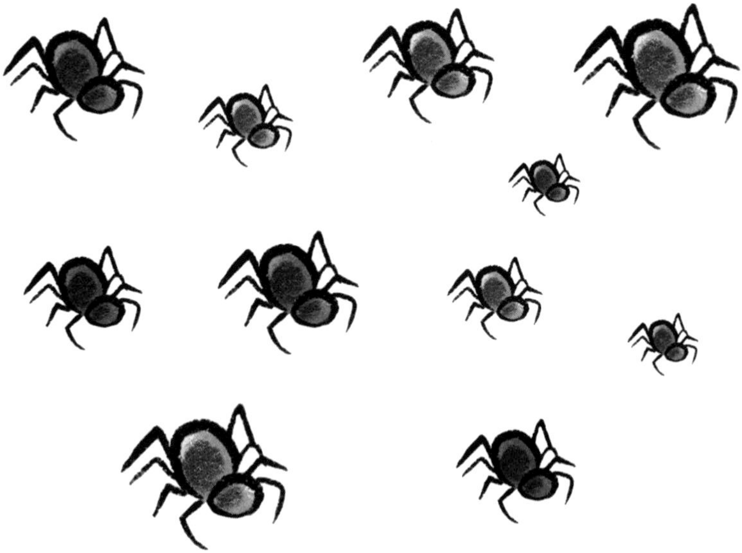

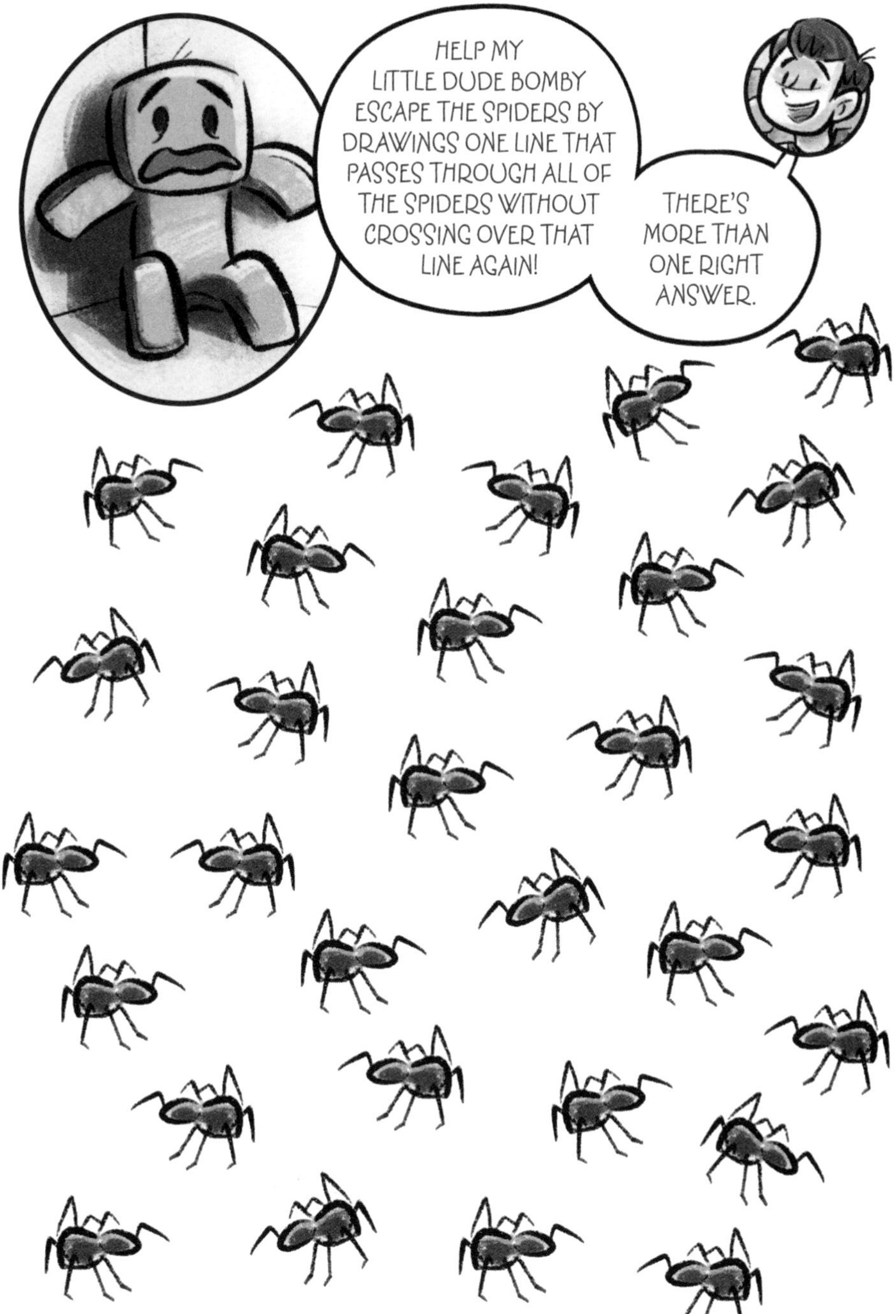
HELP MY LITTLE DUDE BOMBY ESCAPE THE SPIDERS BY DRAWINGS ONE LINE THAT PASSES THROUGH ALL OF THE SPIDERS WITHOUT CROSSING OVER THAT LINE AGAIN!
THERE'S MORE THAN ONE RIGHT ANSWER.

**Poor little Bomby is soooo scared of spiders.
Are you afraid of anything? What is it?
Tell us about a time you faced your fears!**

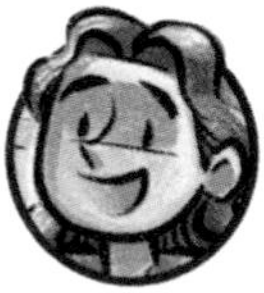

Make your way through the maze and avoid Bomby's bomb holes!

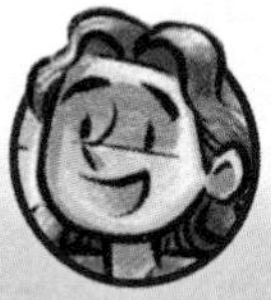

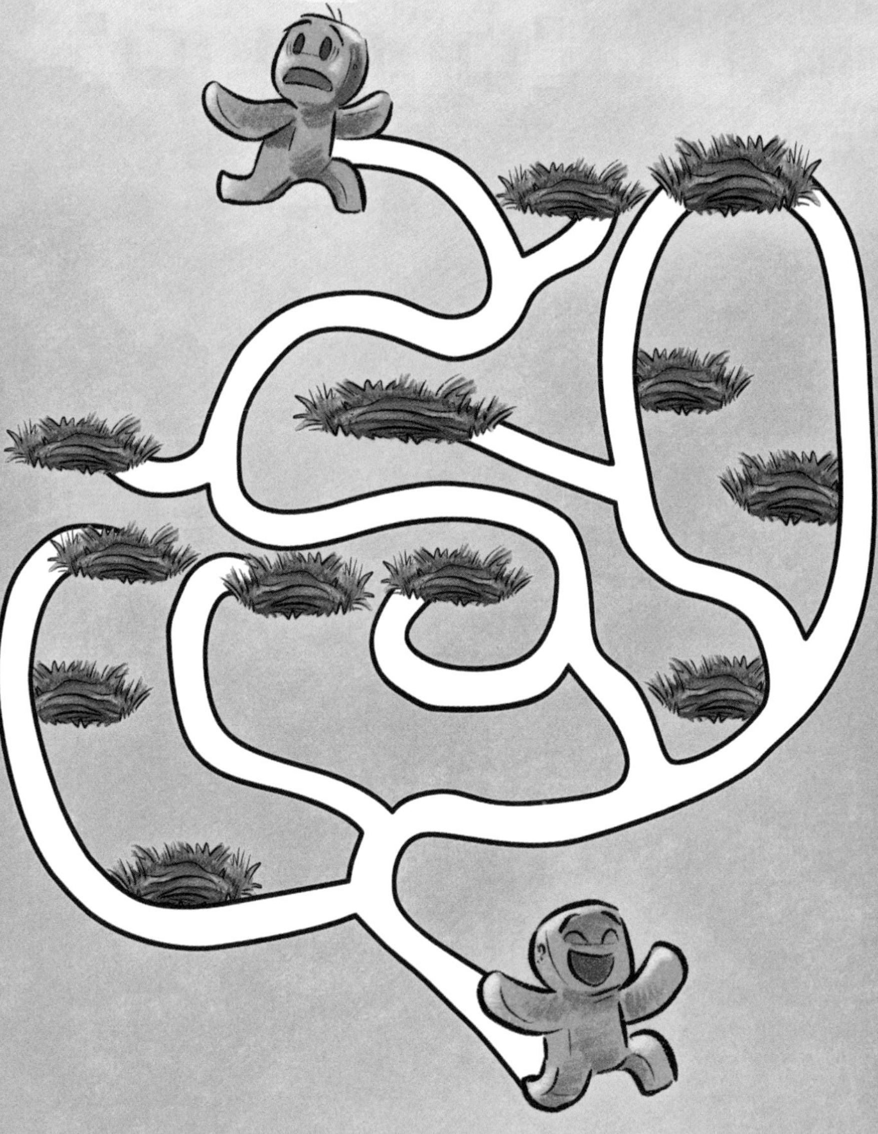

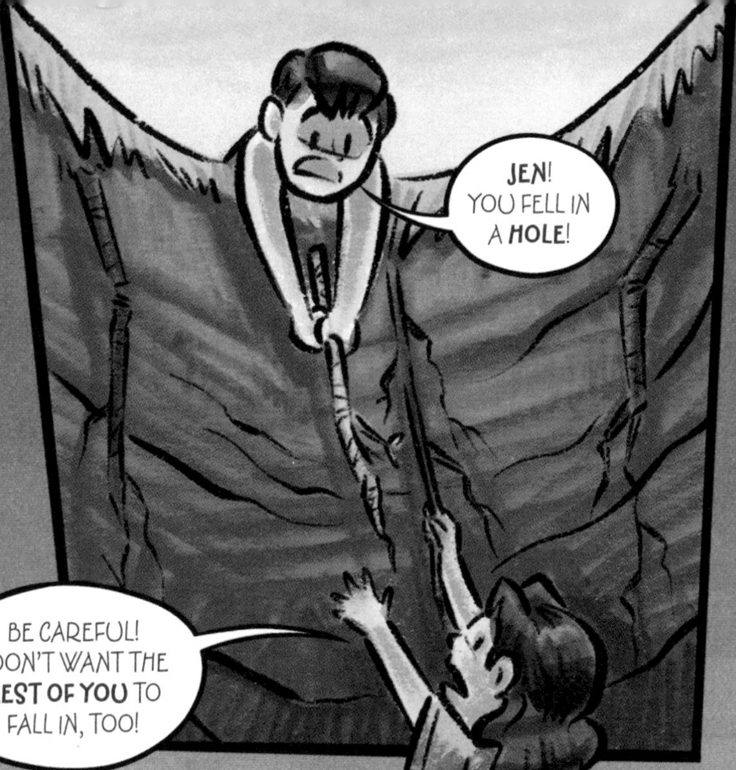
JEN! YOU FELL IN A HOLE!
BE CAREFUL! I DON'T WANT THE REST OF YOU TO FALL IN, TOO!

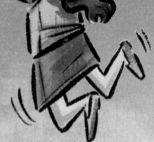

Find the answer to each problem on the right. Then look at the key below to find the letter that corresponds to each answer and fill in the boxes to make sound effects!

## LETTER KEY:

D = 214 H = 287 P = 268

T = 305 U = 255 W = 220

124 + 181 = _

132 + 155 = _

179 + 76 = _

150 + 118 = _

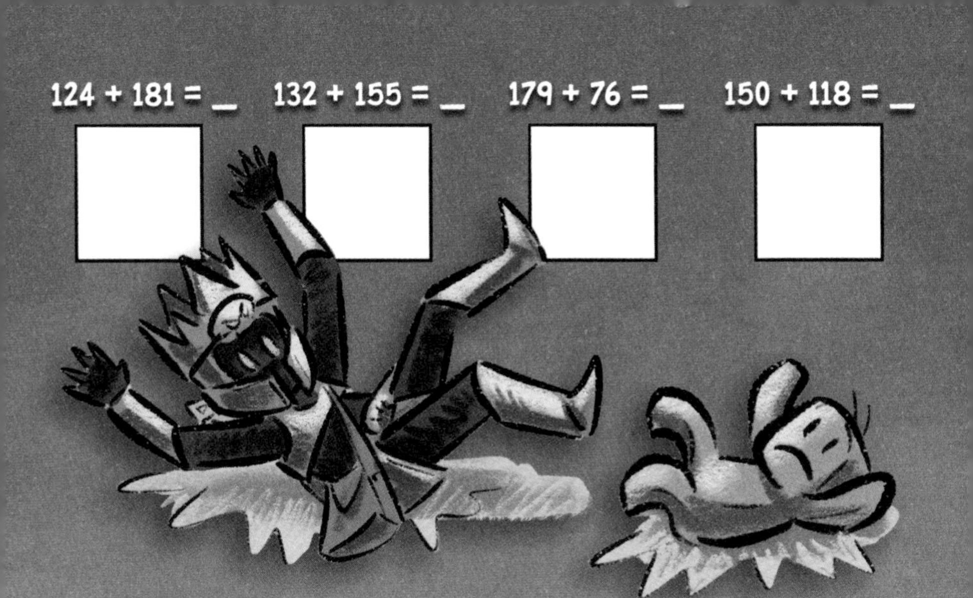

432 − 127 = _

389 − 102 = _

442 − 187 = _

344 − 130 = _

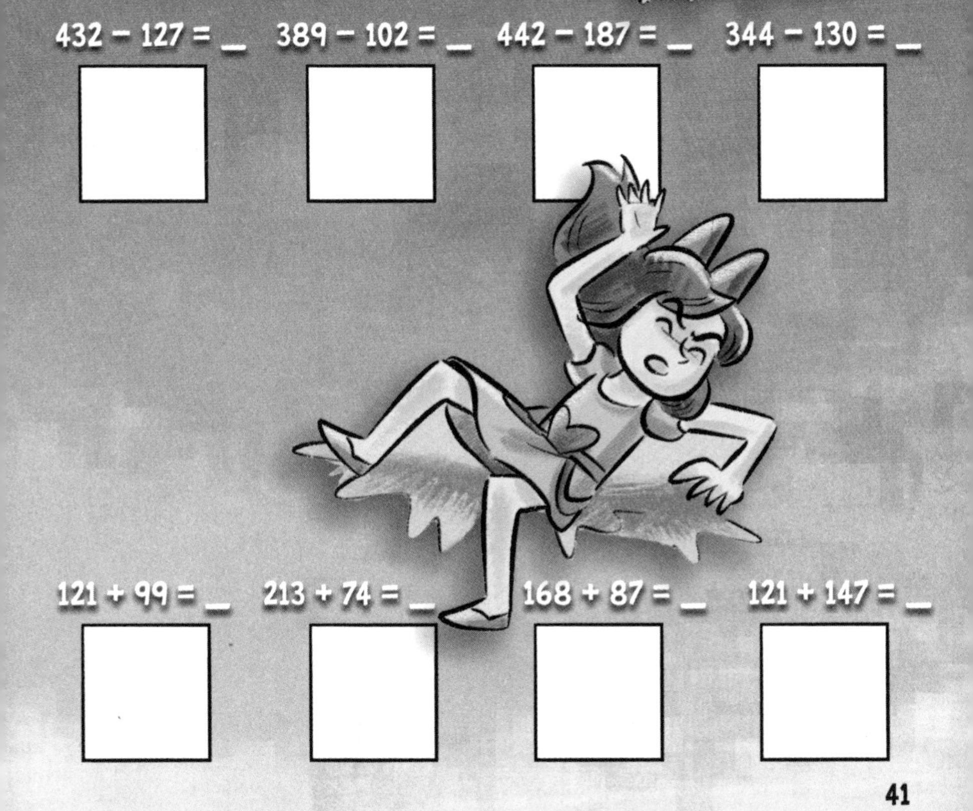

121 + 99 = _

213 + 74 = _

168 + 87 = _

121 + 147 = _

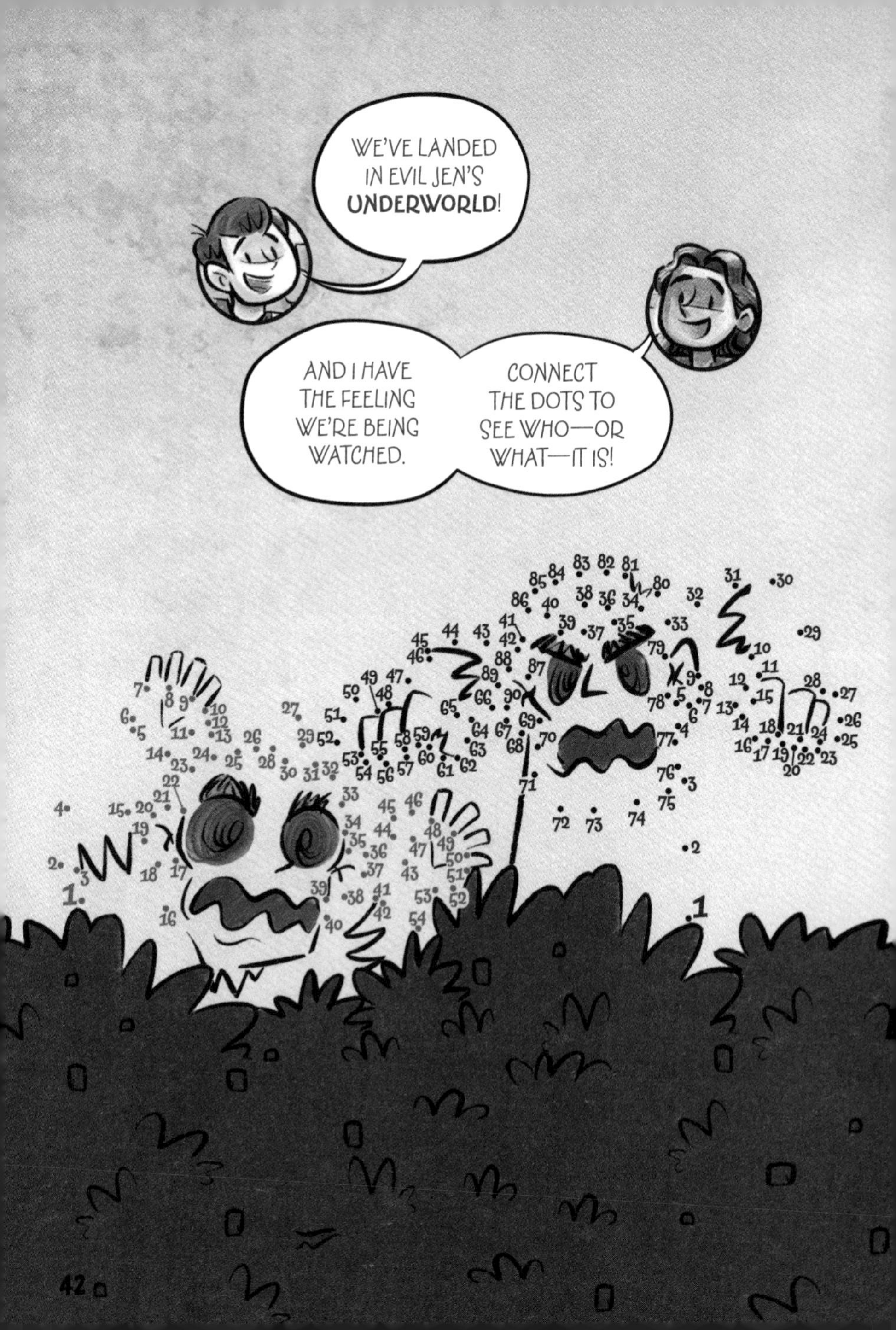
WE'VE LANDED IN EVIL JEN'S **UNDERWORLD**!
AND I HAVE THE FEELING WE'RE BEING WATCHED.
CONNECT THE DOTS TO SEE WHO—OR WHAT—IT IS!

I **HATE** ZOMBIES! BE CAREFUL—SOME ZOMBIE BITES CAN TURN YOU INTO A ZOMBIE TOO! **I KNOW. I WAS ONE** ONCE!

LET'S SEE HOW YOU THINK **YOU'D** LOOK AS A ZOMBIE!

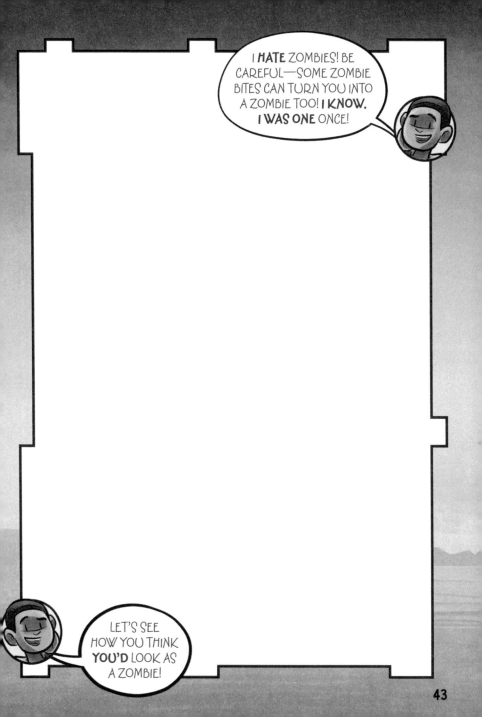

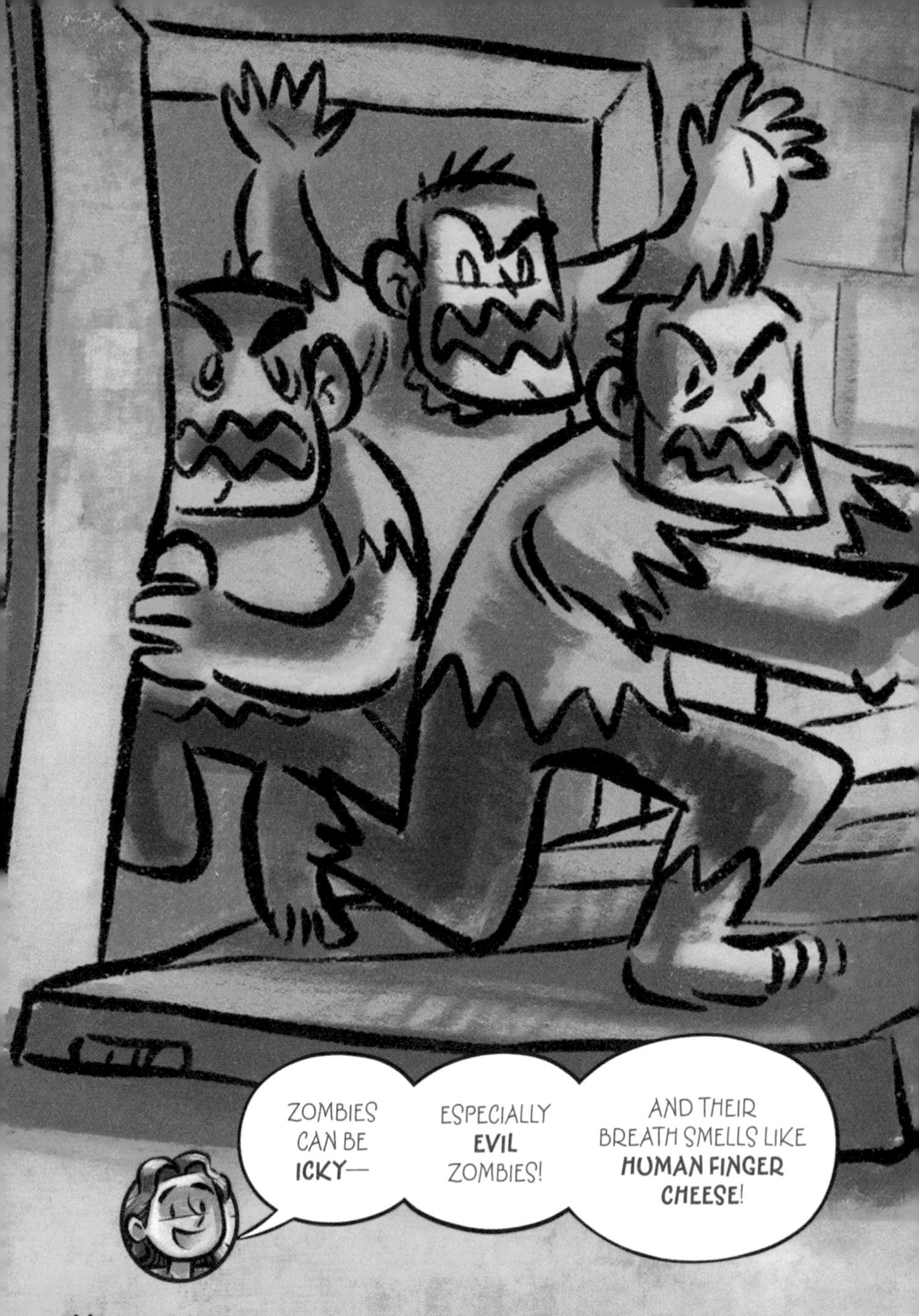
ZOMBIES CAN BE **ICKY**—
ESPECIALLY **EVIL** ZOMBIES!
AND THEIR BREATH SMELLS LIKE **HUMAN FINGER CHEESE**!

# Find these words in the puzzle below that describe Evil Jen's Evil Zombies!

BITE          GREEN         SPAWNER
BRAINS        HORDE         STINKY
CREEPY        SLOW          UNDEAD
                            UNDERWORLD

```
F D K L R U B J V F D W N C W
T N A K E J N A Q A J E G R K
S U K Y N F T D E B E M A E E
P L G F X J Z D E R R L W E A
I Q O S A J N B G R S A S P F
L I Z W P U H C B C W H I Y E
X G Z B S T I N K Y B O Q N P
H O R D E S R Q B Y I I R T S
S O I Q R Z Z X M B T W I L D
M P F B H R D U U D E X F N D
G U A U X X T W Z Y Y I P G A
Q G S W W M P N Y I Y S V T T
H E O A N D D G L L B D Y T G
P S D D X E C E D V M T V S T
Z D D V D U R R C S D L E O L
```

45

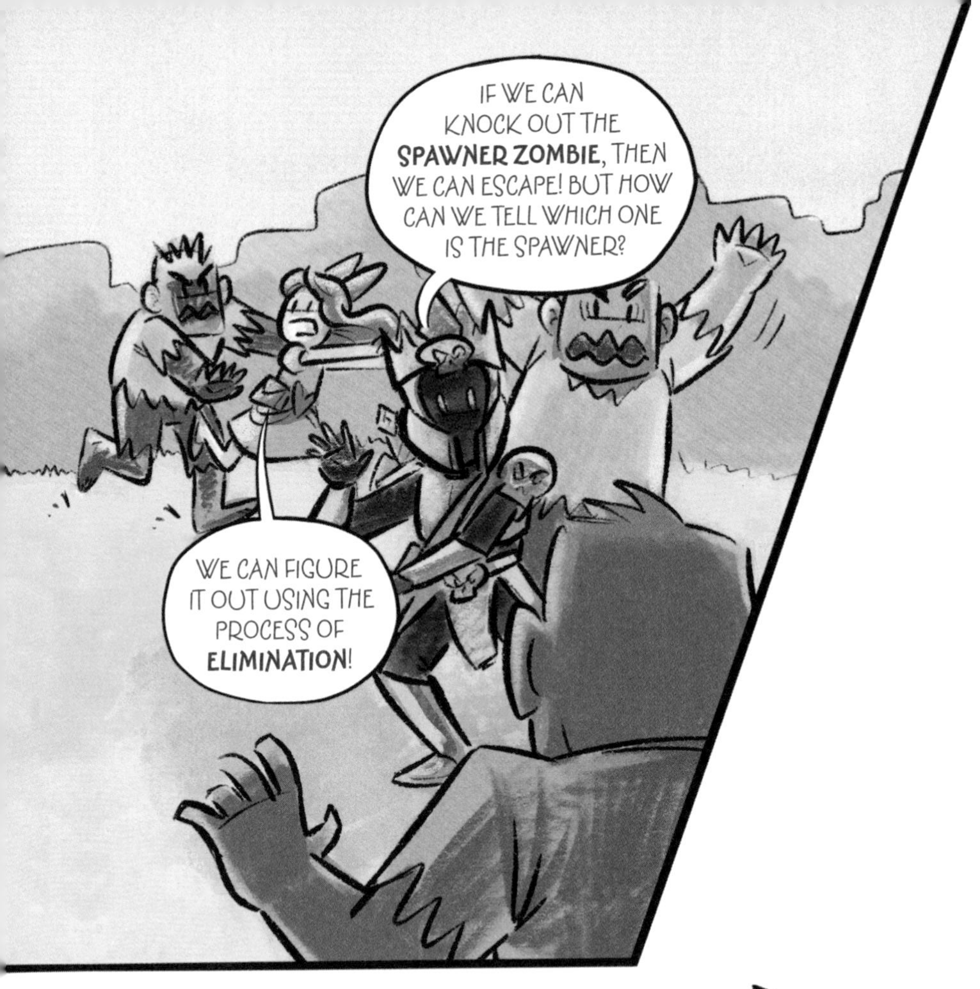
IF WE CAN KNOCK OUT THE SPAWNER ZOMBIE, THEN WE CAN ESCAPE! BUT HOW CAN WE TELL WHICH ONE IS THE SPAWNER?
WE CAN FIGURE IT OUT USING THE PROCESS OF ELIMINATION!

## Cross out all zombies that:

- Don't have two eyes
- Have no hair
- Have blue eyes
- Have only one ear
- Have no ears

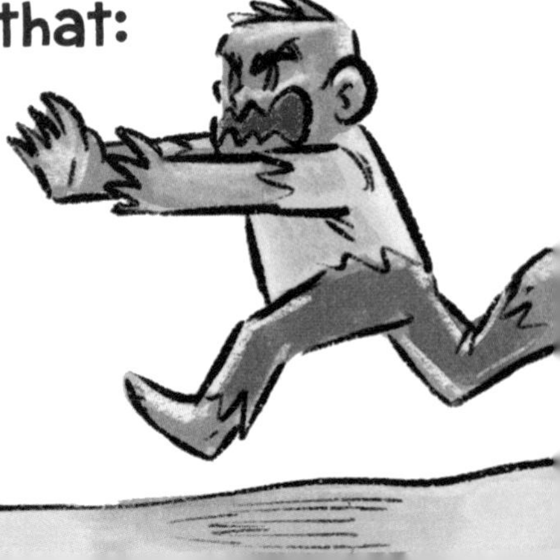

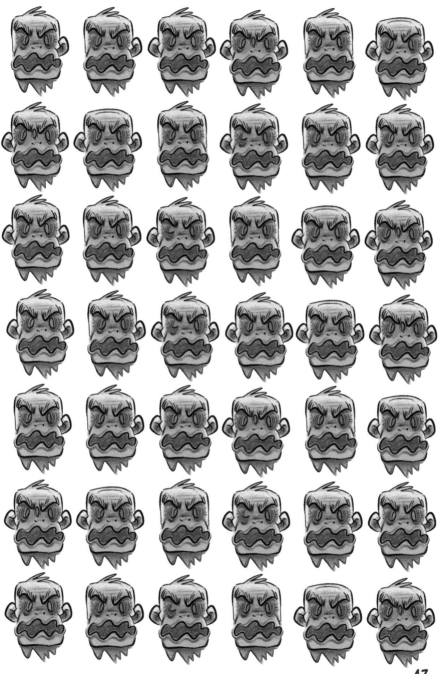

**Draw what you think will happen next!**

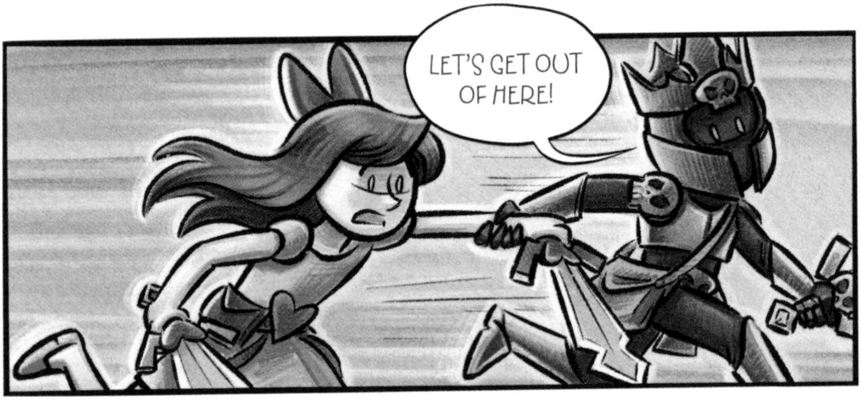
LET'S GET OUT OF HERE!

# Draw what you think will happen next!

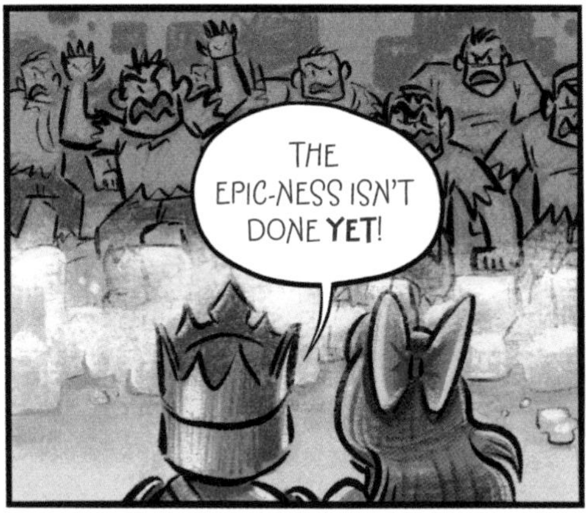
THE EPIC-NESS ISN'T DONE **YET**!

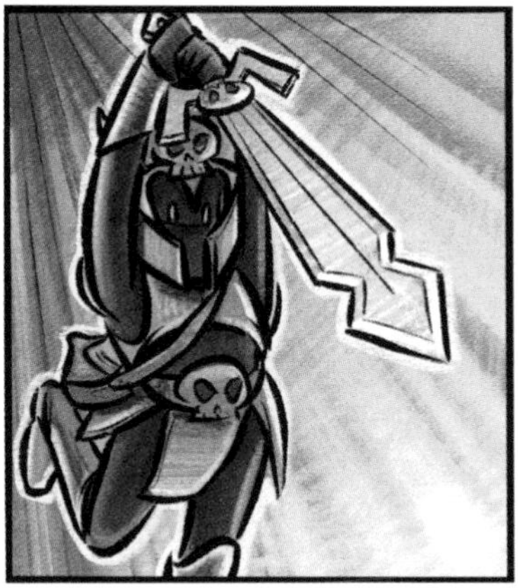

Zombies have a unique way of talking. What's your zombie catchphrase?

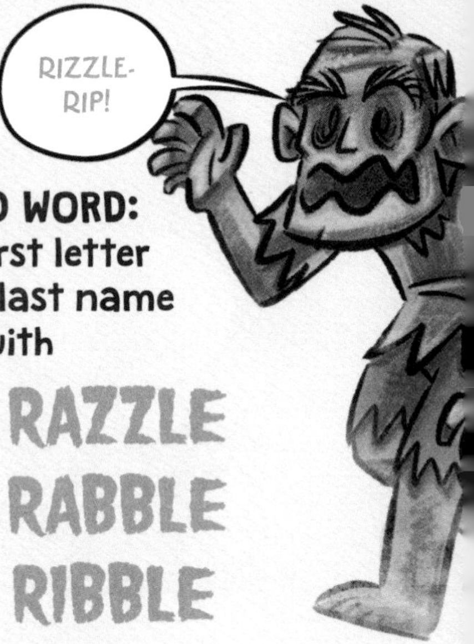
RIZZLE-RIP!

**FIRST WORD:**
If the first letter of your first name starts with

A – E = RIG

F – J = RIZ

K – N = RIB

O – S = RIGGLE

T – Z = RIZZLE

**SECOND WORD:**
If the first letter of your last name starts with

A – E = RAZZLE

F – J = RABBLE

K – N = RIBBLE

O – S = RAZ

T – Z = RIP

____________________ ____________________

**Now SAY IT OUT LOUD!**

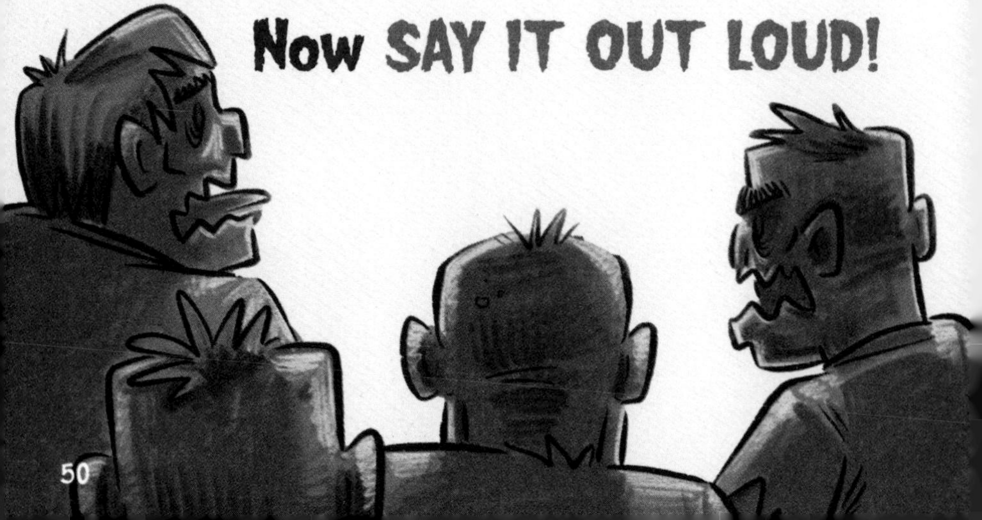

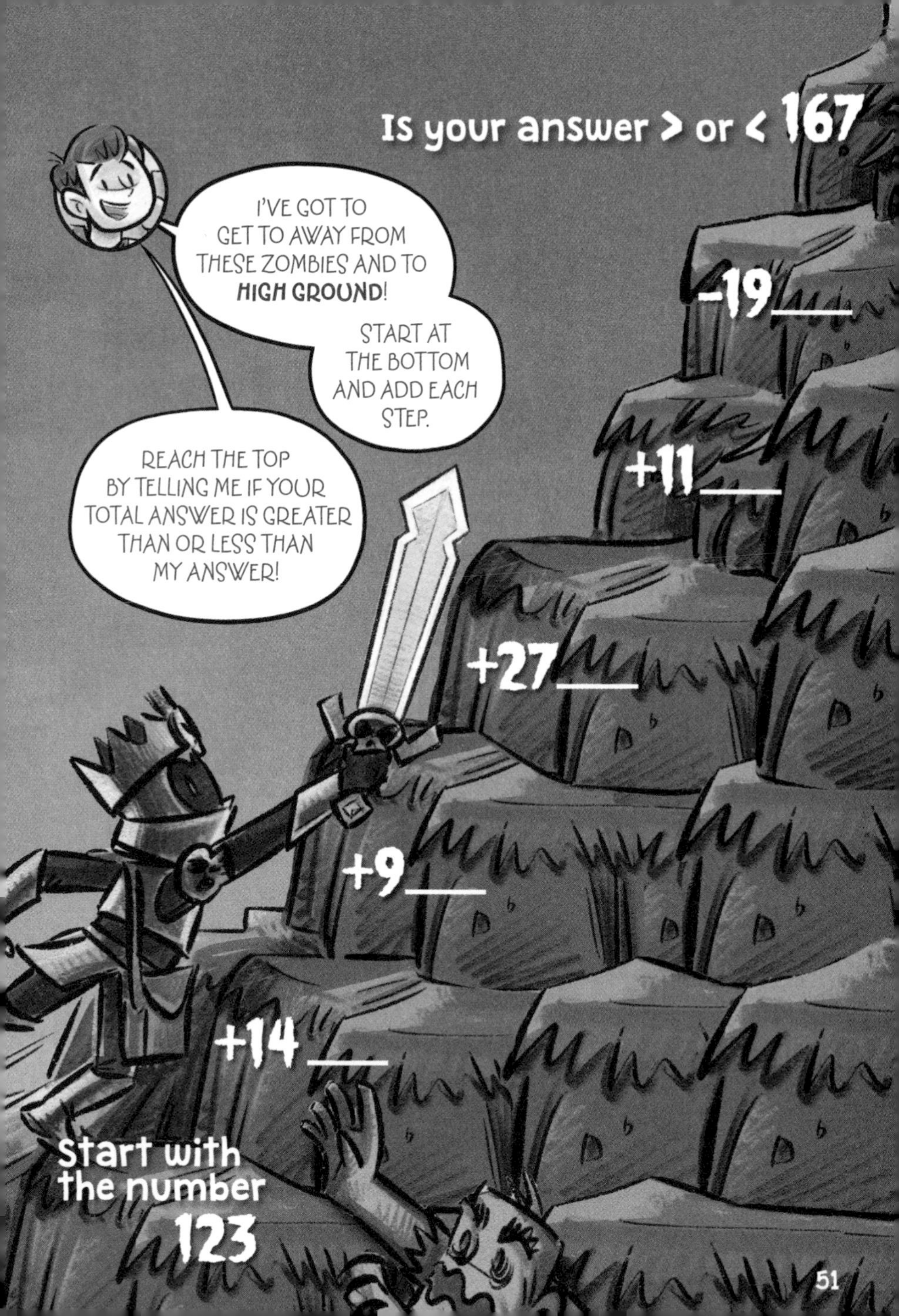

Is your answer > or < 167
I'VE GOT TO GET TO AWAY FROM THESE ZOMBIES AND TO **HIGH GROUND**!
START AT THE BOTTOM AND ADD EACH STEP.
REACH THE TOP BY TELLING ME IF YOUR TOTAL ANSWER IS GREATER THAN OR LESS THAN MY ANSWER!
-19 ____
+11 ____
+27 ____
+9 ____
+14 ____
Start with the number 123

# ESCAPE THE ZOMBIES!

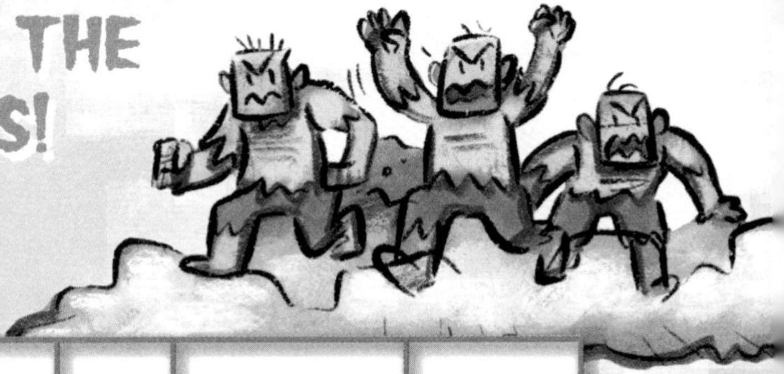

Start

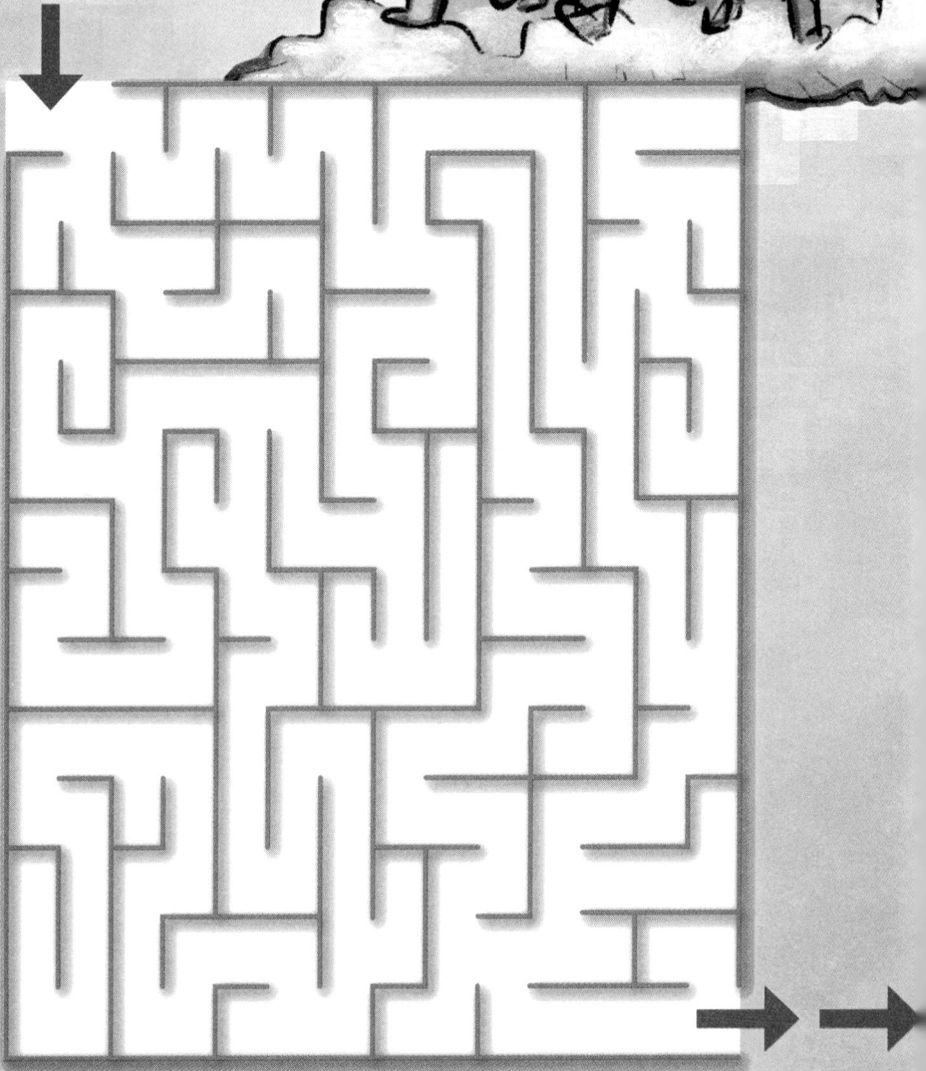

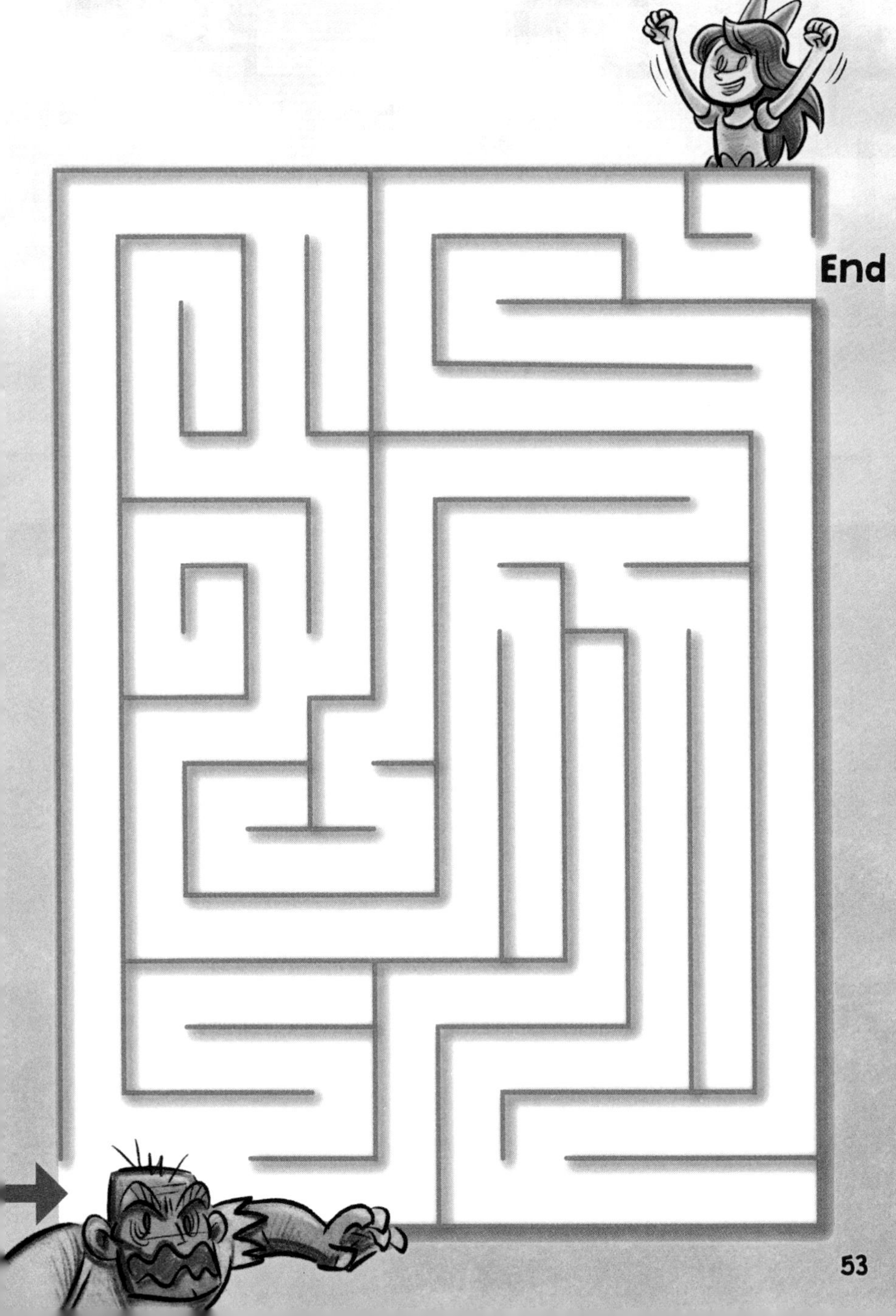
End

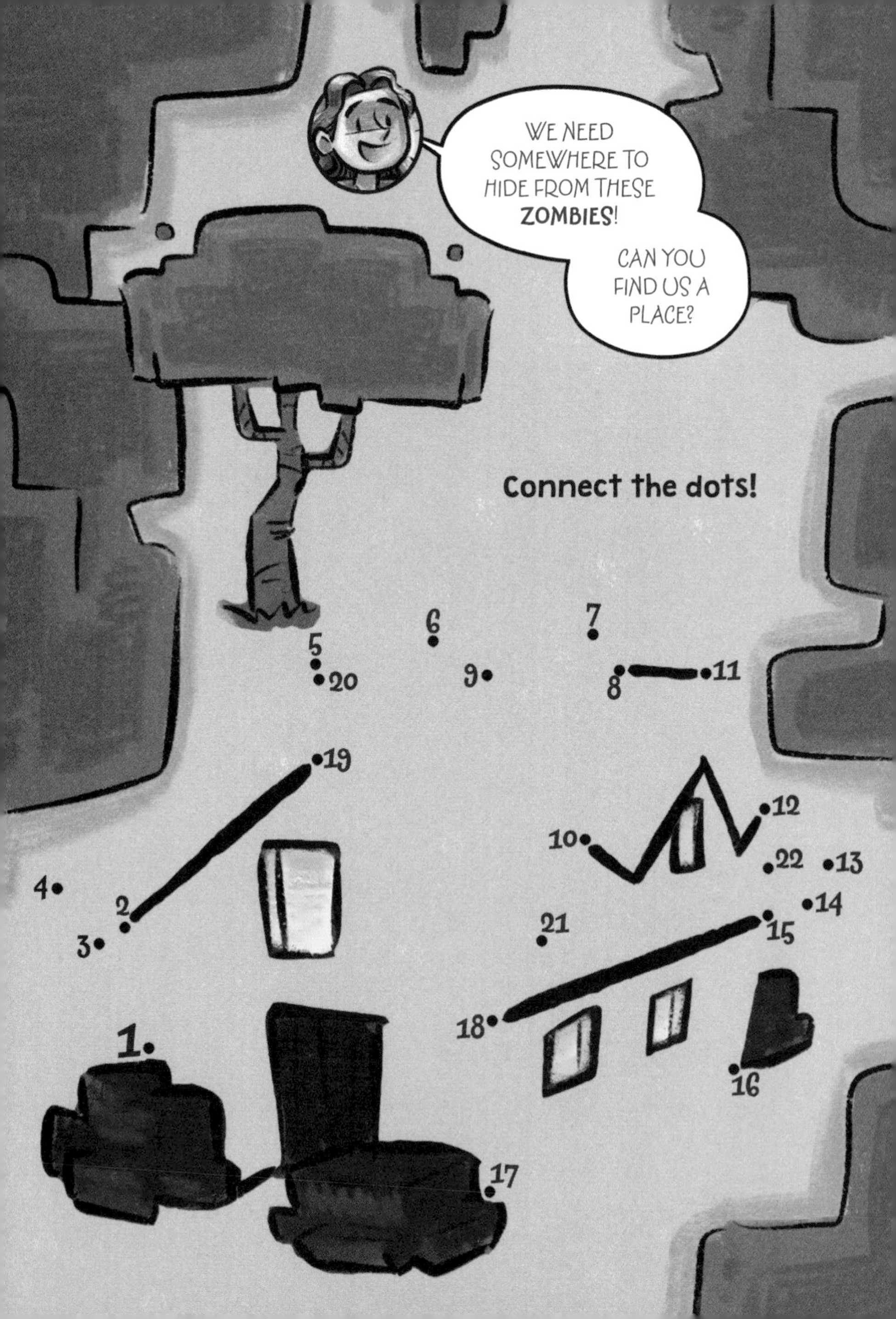
WE NEED SOMEWHERE TO HIDE FROM THESE **ZOMBIES**!
CAN YOU FIND US A PLACE?
Connect the dots!

## YOU BE THE WRITER!

Fill in the word balloons with your characters' funniest lines!

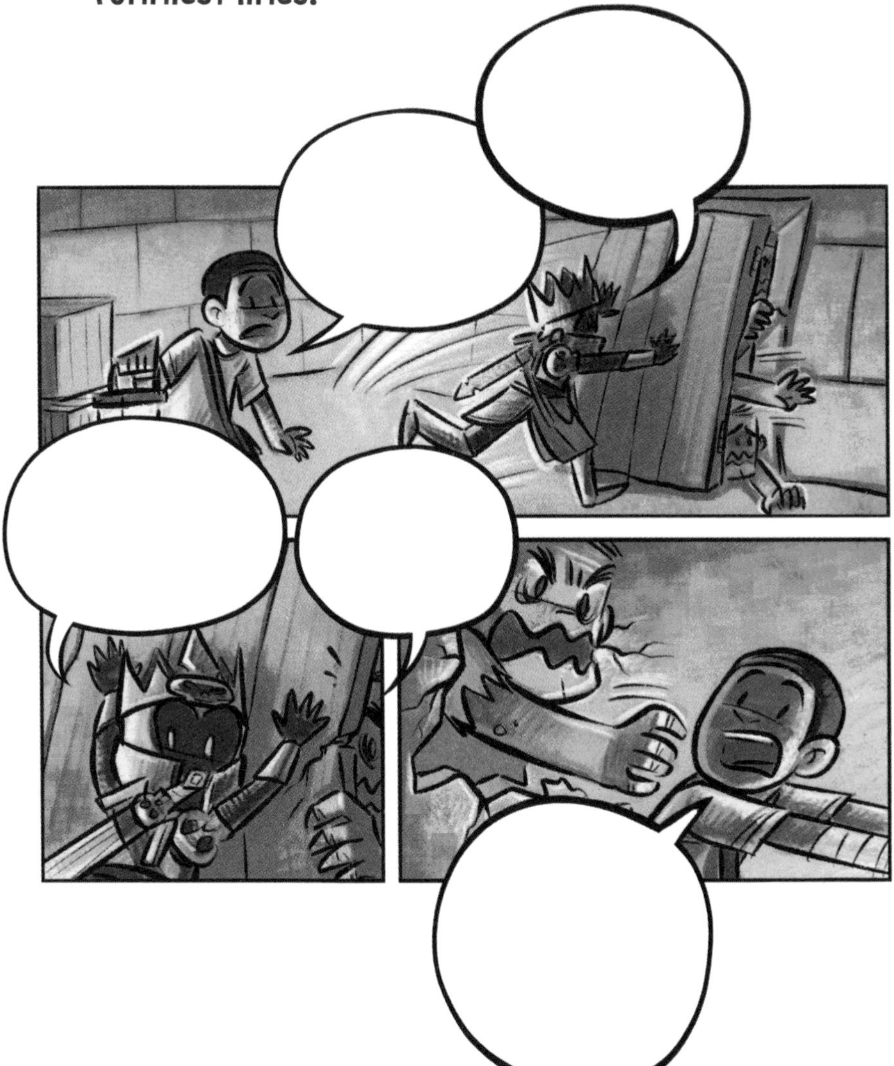

# YOU BE THE WRITER!

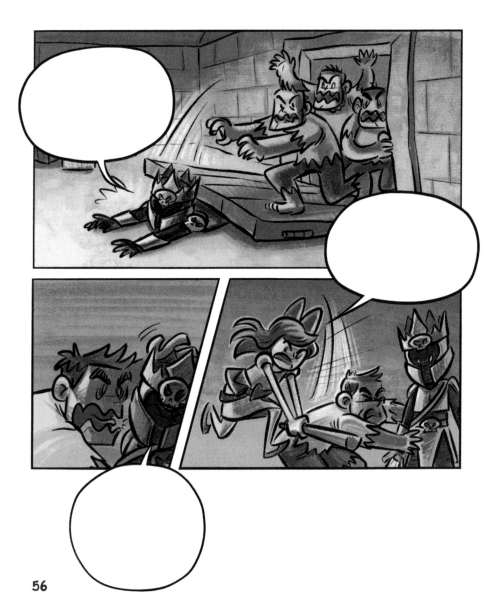

Fill in the word balloons with your characters' funniest lines!

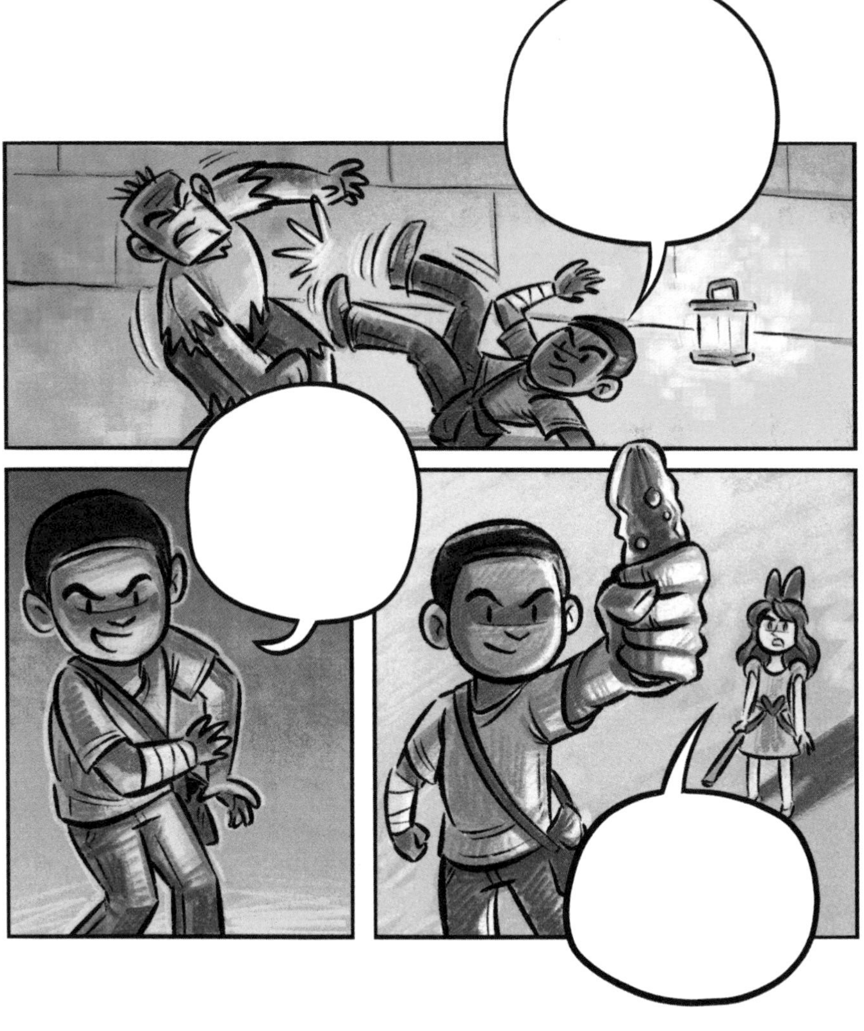

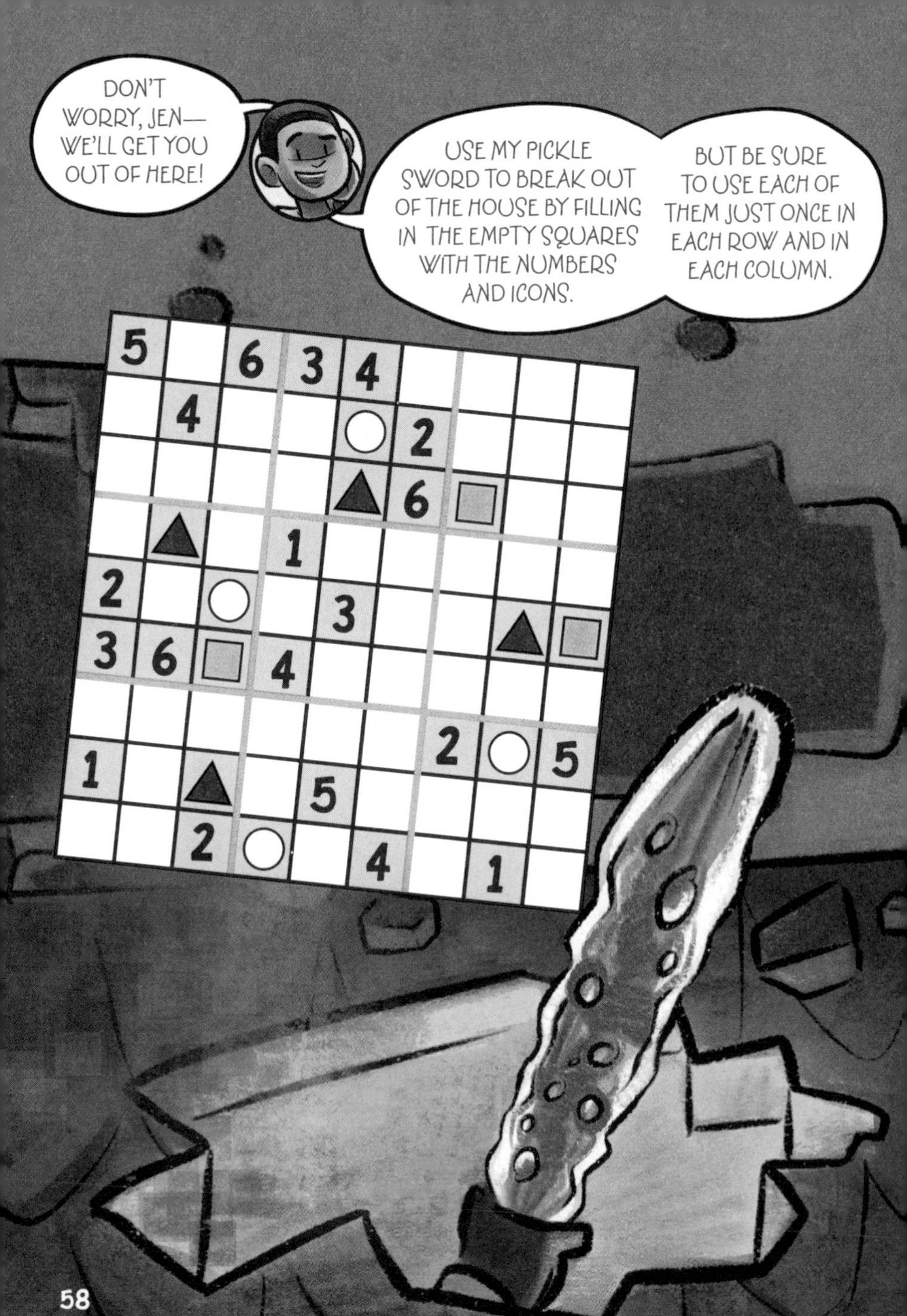
DON'T WORRY, JEN— WE'LL GET YOU OUT OF HERE!
USE MY PICKLE SWORD TO BREAK OUT OF THE HOUSE BY FILLING IN THE EMPTY SQUARES WITH THE NUMBERS AND ICONS.
BUT BE SURE TO USE EACH OF THEM JUST ONCE IN EACH ROW AND IN EACH COLUMN.

| | | | | | | | | |
|---|---|---|---|---|---|---|---|---|
| 5 | | 6 | 3 | 4 | | | | |
| | 4 | | | ○ | 2 | | | |
| | | | | ▲ | 6 | ■ | | |
| | ▲ | | 1 | | | | | |
| 2 | | ○ | | 3 | | | ▲ | ■ |
| 3 | 6 | ■ | 4 | | | | | |
| | | | | | | 2 | ○ | 5 |
| 1 | | ▲ | | 5 | | | | |
| | | 2 | ○ | | 4 | | 1 | |

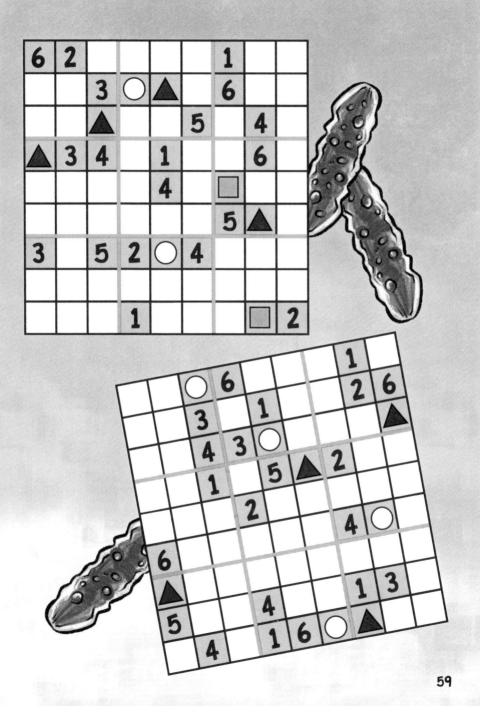

59

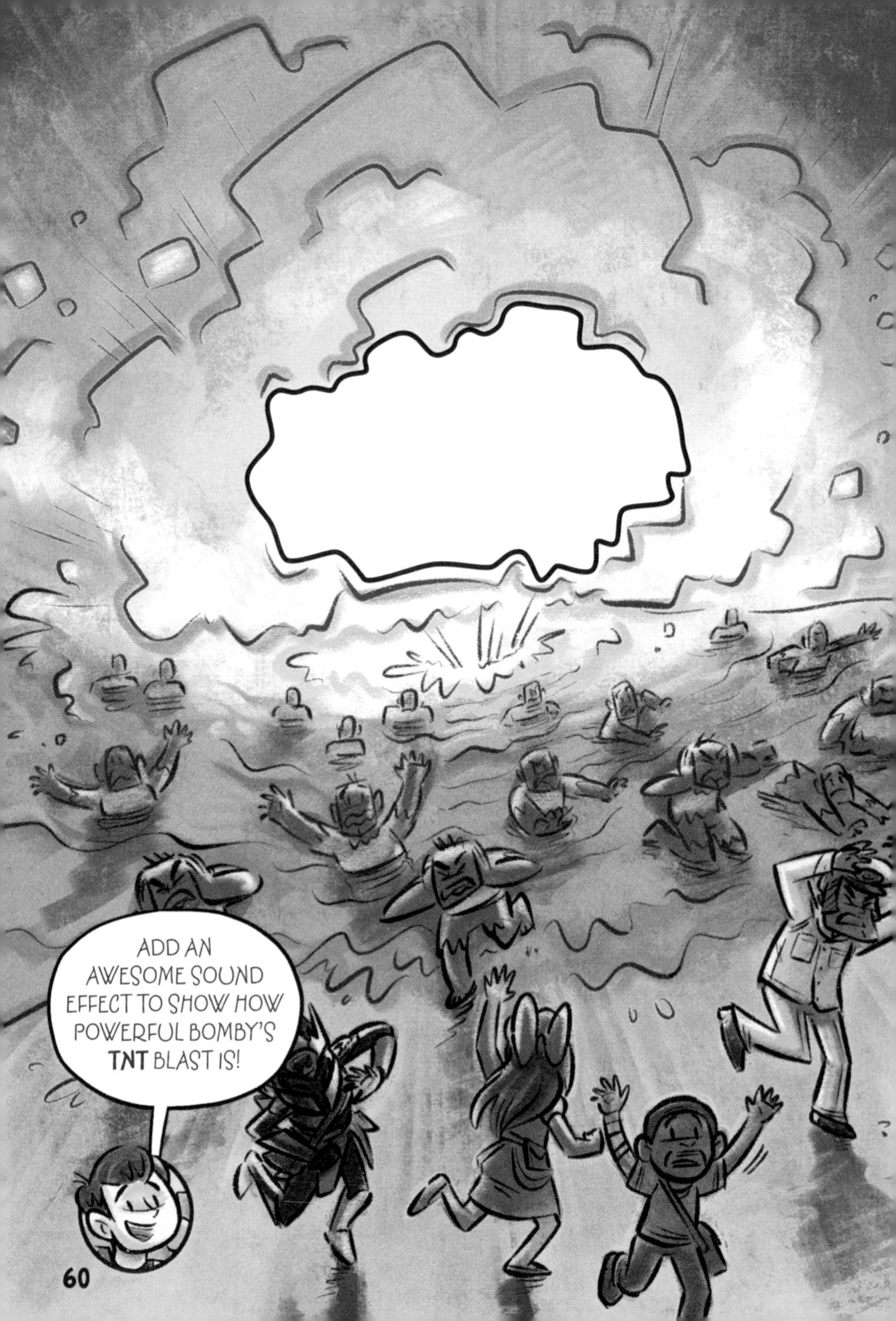
ADD AN AWESOME SOUND EFFECT TO SHOW HOW POWERFUL BOMBY'S **TNT** BLAST IS!

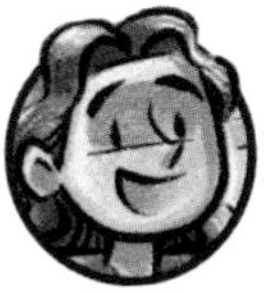

Every one of our friends has special talent and skill. Bomby's the best at blowing stuff up! Carter really knows how to use his pickle sword and help us find our way. Captain Cookie knows all about boats...kinda.

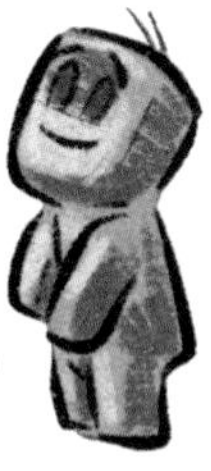

What is your special talent or skill?
Tell us about a time you had to use it.

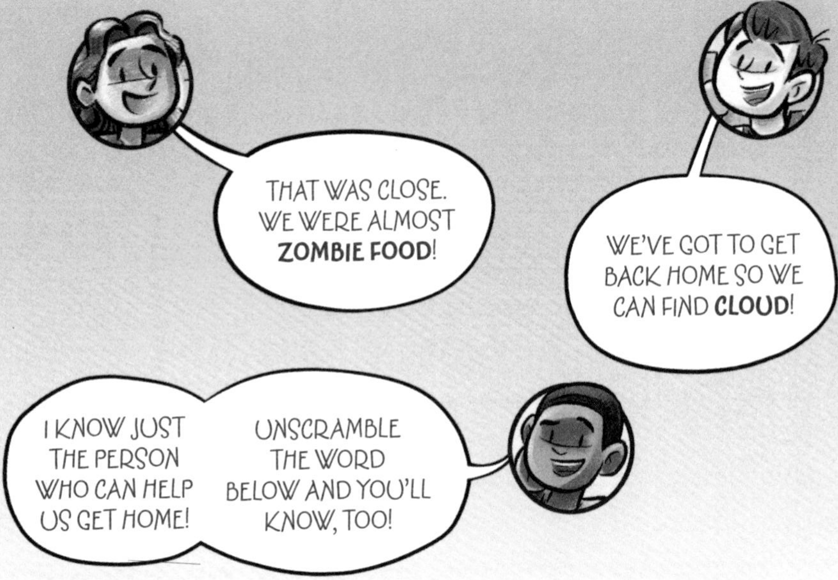
THAT WAS CLOSE. WE WERE ALMOST **ZOMBIE FOOD**!
WE'VE GOT TO GET BACK HOME SO WE CAN FIND **CLOUD**!
I KNOW JUST THE PERSON WHO CAN HELP US GET HOME!
UNSCRAMBLE THE WORD BELOW AND YOU'LL KNOW, TOO!

# RM AIWBONR

__ __. __ __ __ __ __ __ __

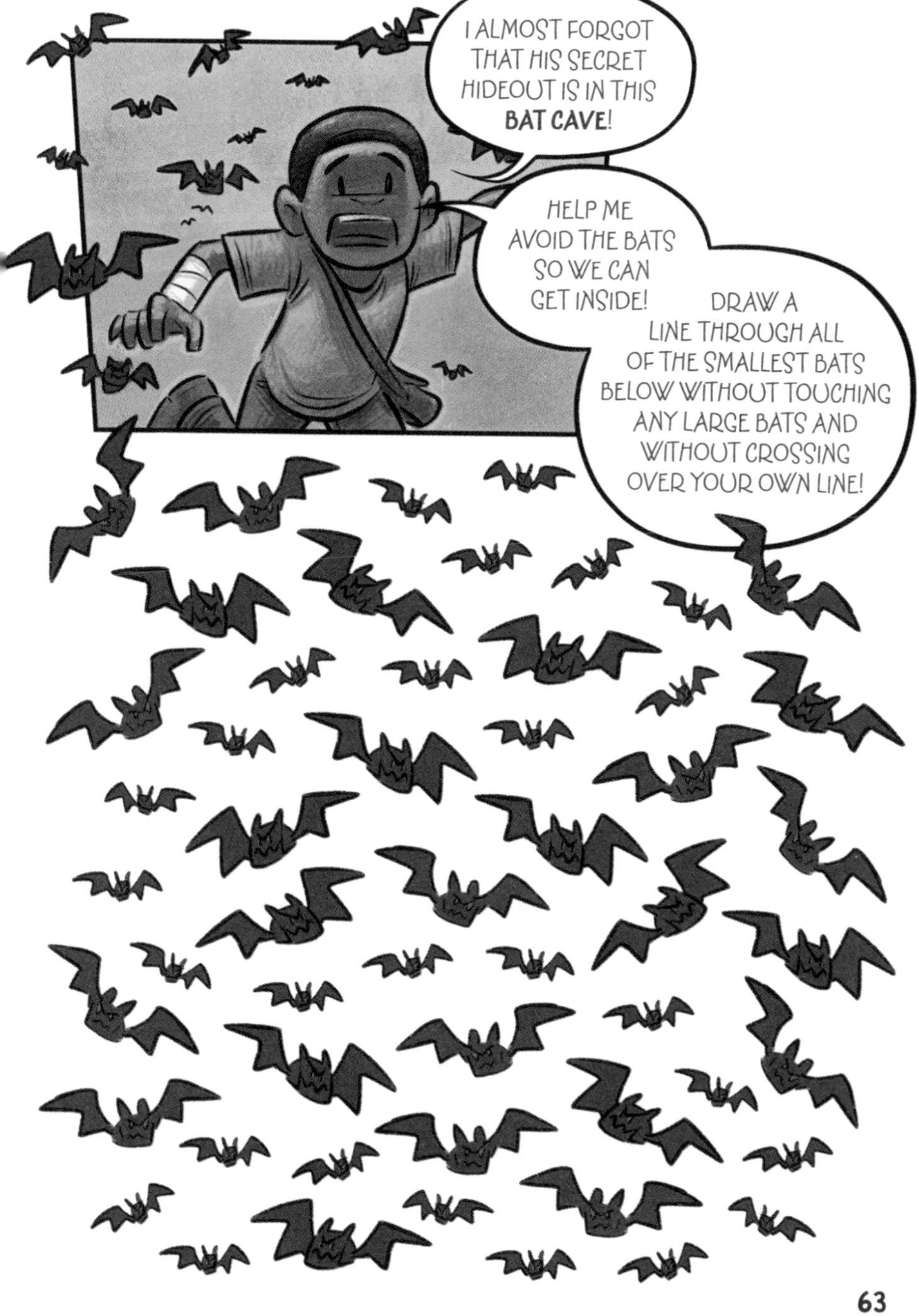
I ALMOST FORGOT THAT HIS SECRET HIDEOUT IS IN THIS **BAT CAVE**!
HELP ME AVOID THE BATS SO WE CAN GET INSIDE! DRAW A LINE THROUGH ALL OF THE SMALLEST BATS BELOW WITHOUT TOUCHING ANY LARGE BATS AND WITHOUT CROSSING OVER YOUR OWN LINE!

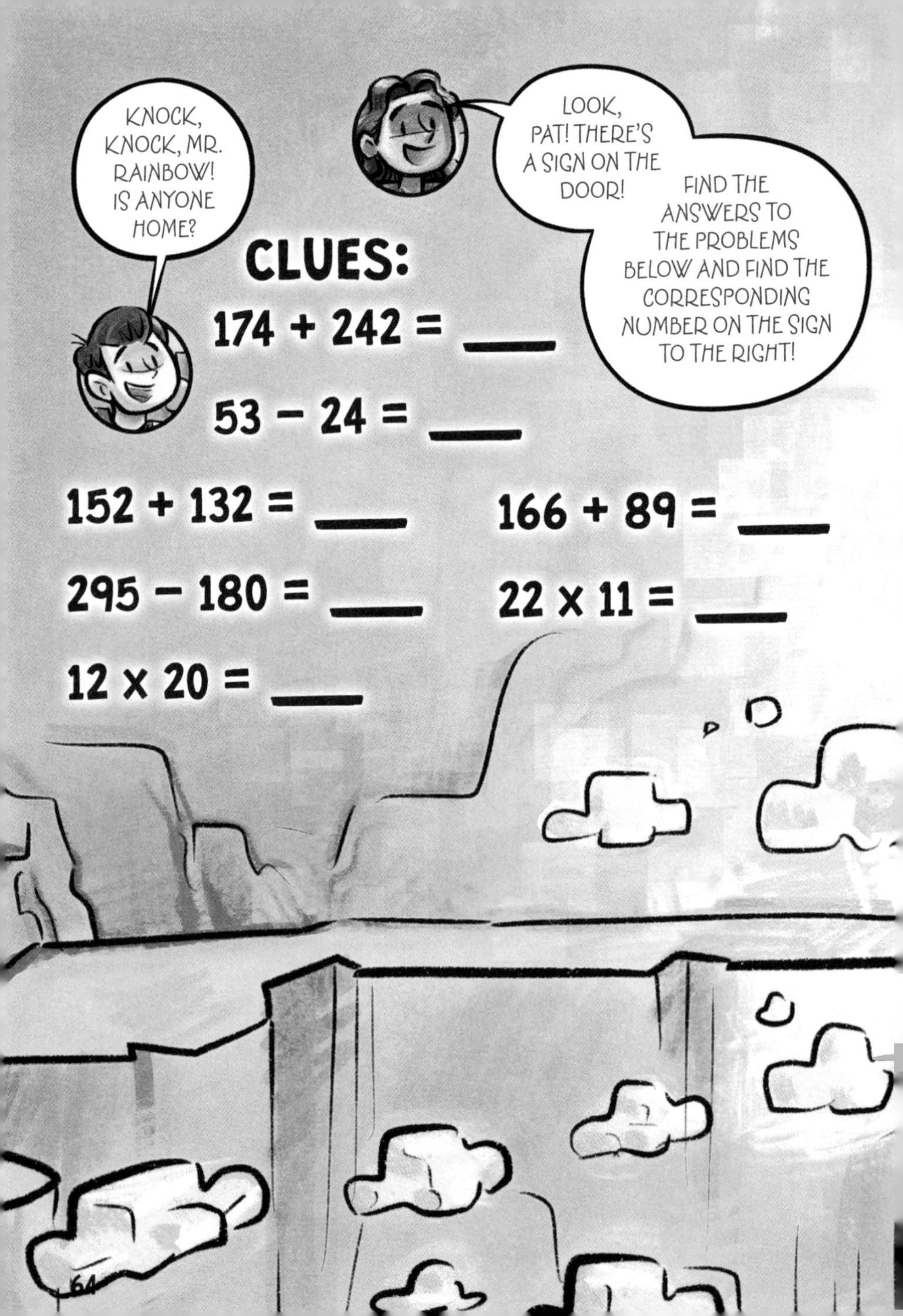
KNOCK, KNOCK, MR. RAINBOW! IS ANYONE HOME?
LOOK, PAT! THERE'S A SIGN ON THE DOOR!
FIND THE ANSWERS TO THE PROBLEMS BELOW AND FIND THE CORRESPONDING NUMBER ON THE SIGN TO THE RIGHT!

# CLUES:

174 + 242 = ____

53 − 24 = ____

152 + 132 = ____

166 + 89 = ____

295 − 180 = ____

22 x 11 = ____

12 x 20 = ____

Color in the letters that match the answers on the left. Unscramble the letters and fill in your answer below.

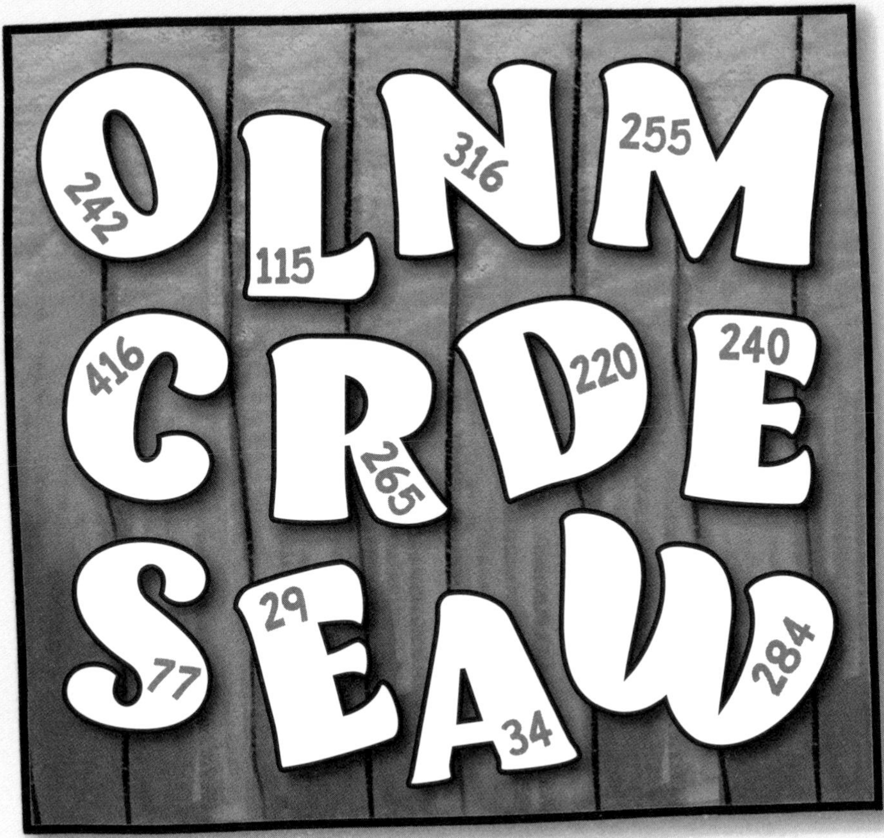
O 242
L 115
N 316
M 255
C 416
R 265
D 220
E 240
S 77
E 29
A 34
W 284

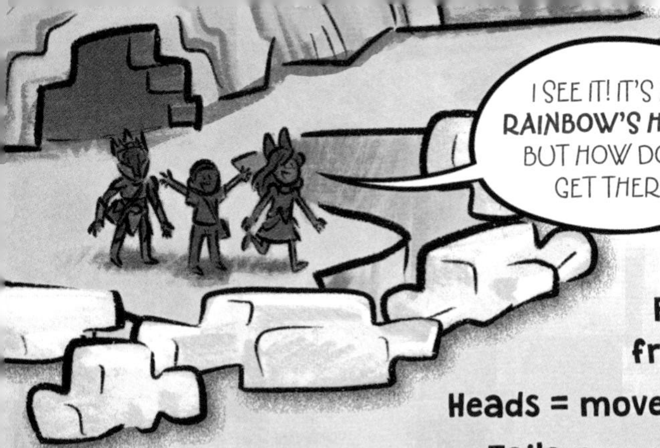
I SEE IT! IT'S **MR. RAINBOW'S HOUSE!** BUT HOW DO WE GET THERE?

Flip a coin to jump from cloud to cloud.

Heads = move 2 spaces forward.

Tails = move 1 space forward.

Follow the instructions on the square where you land.

If the square is blank, flip the coin again!

Try to reach the castle in as few coin flips as possible!

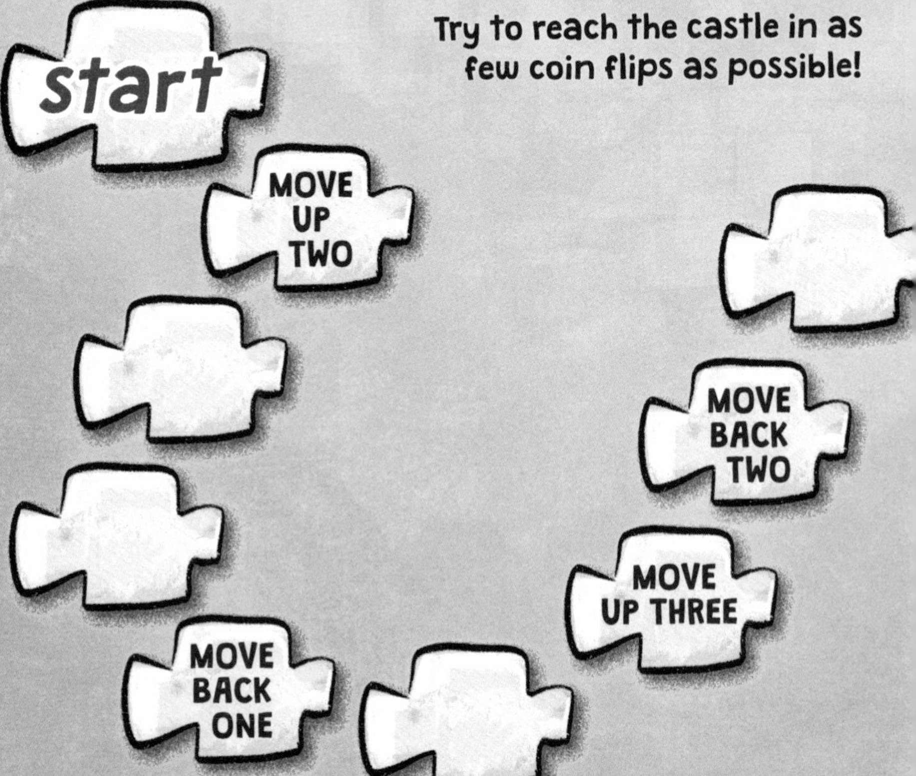
start
MOVE UP TWO
MOVE BACK ONE
MOVE UP THREE
MOVE BACK TWO

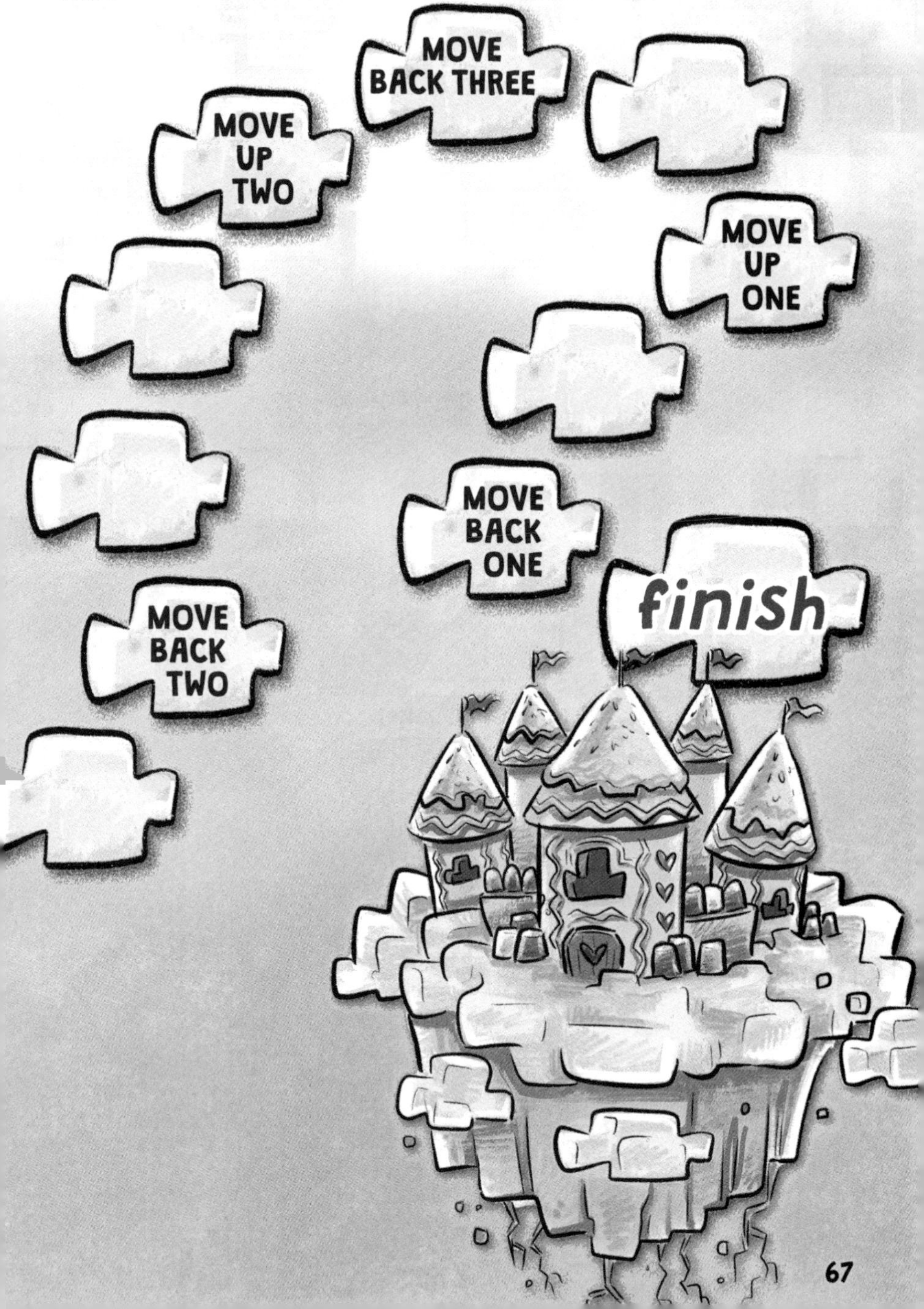
MOVE BACK THREE
MOVE UP TWO
MOVE UP ONE
MOVE BACK ONE
MOVE BACK TWO
finish

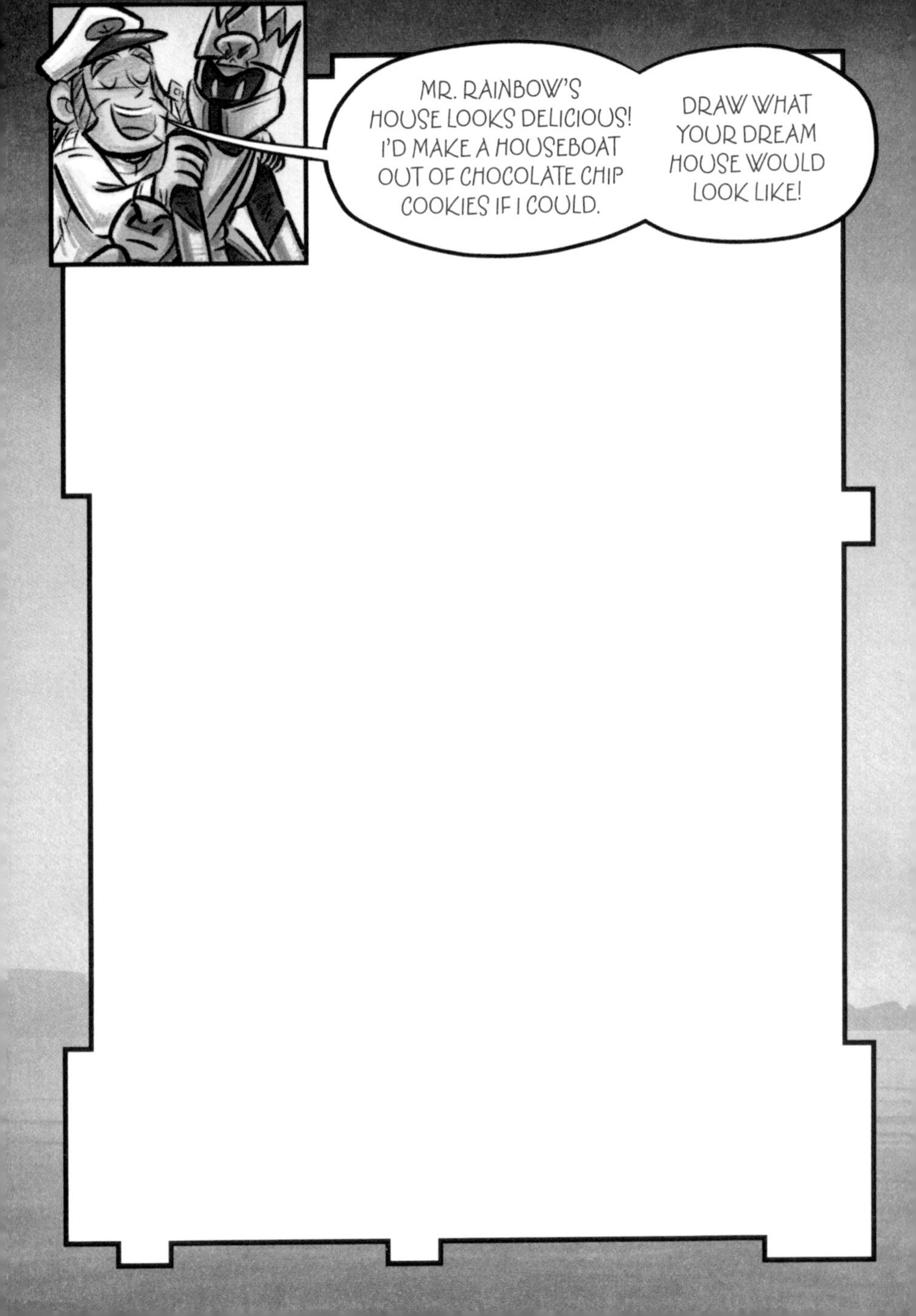
MR. RAINBOW'S HOUSE LOOKS DELICIOUS! I'D MAKE A HOUSEBOAT OUT OF CHOCOLATE CHIP COOKIES IF I COULD.
DRAW WHAT YOUR DREAM HOUSE WOULD LOOK LIKE!

CARTER! WHAT BRINGS YOU TO MR. RAINBOW'S SECRET LAIR?

WELL, MY FRIENDS HERE LOST THEIR CAT, AND— WAIT A MINUTE! WHICH ONE OF YOU SAID THAT?

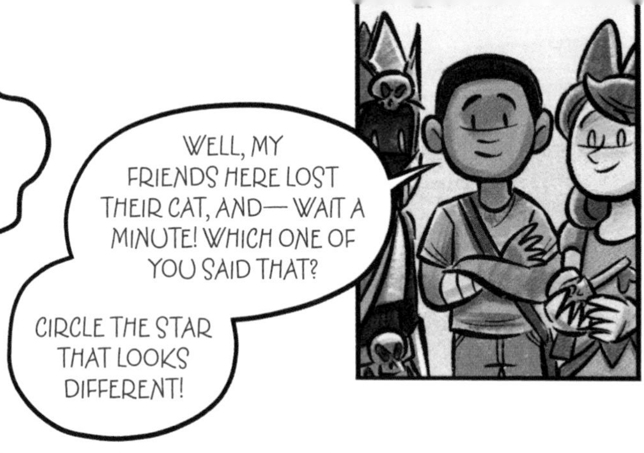

CIRCLE THE STAR THAT LOOKS DIFFERENT!

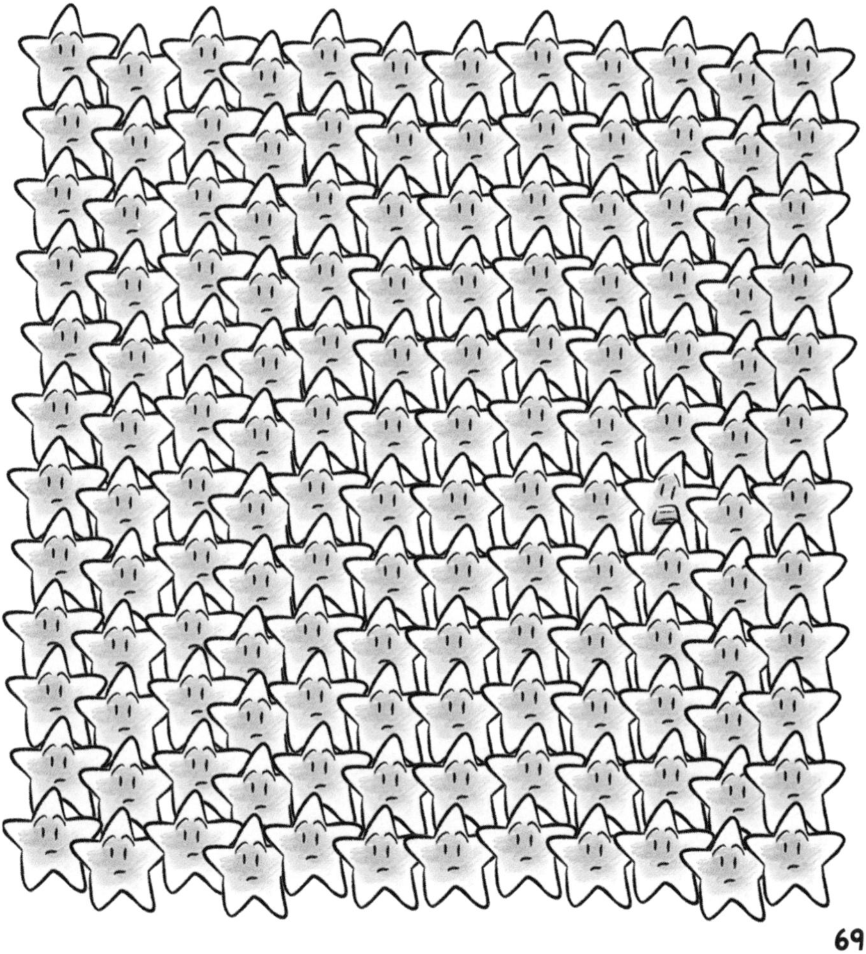

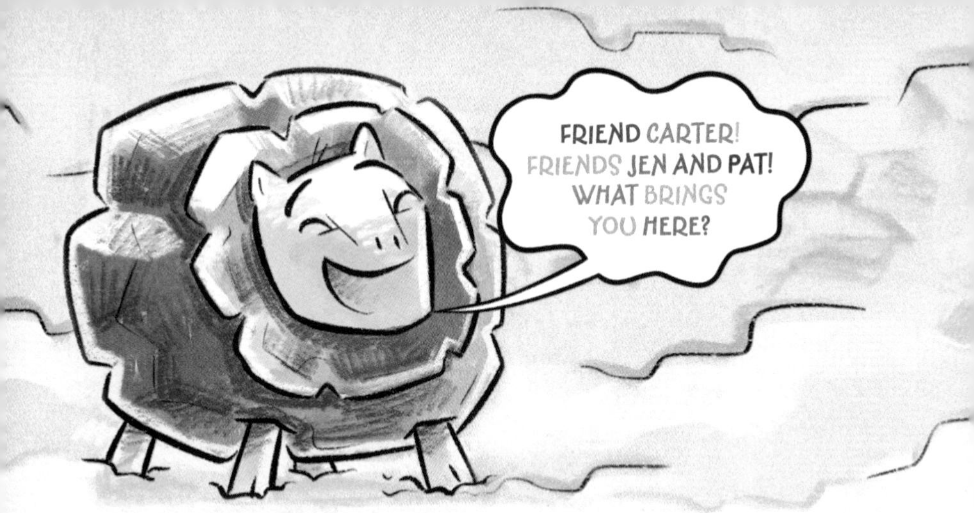
FRIEND CARTER! FRIENDS JEN AND PAT! WHAT BRINGS YOU HERE?

**MR. RAINBOW** is so friendly that he enjoys welcoming visitors in different languages!

Find all of the different ways to say "hello" in the puzzle to the right!

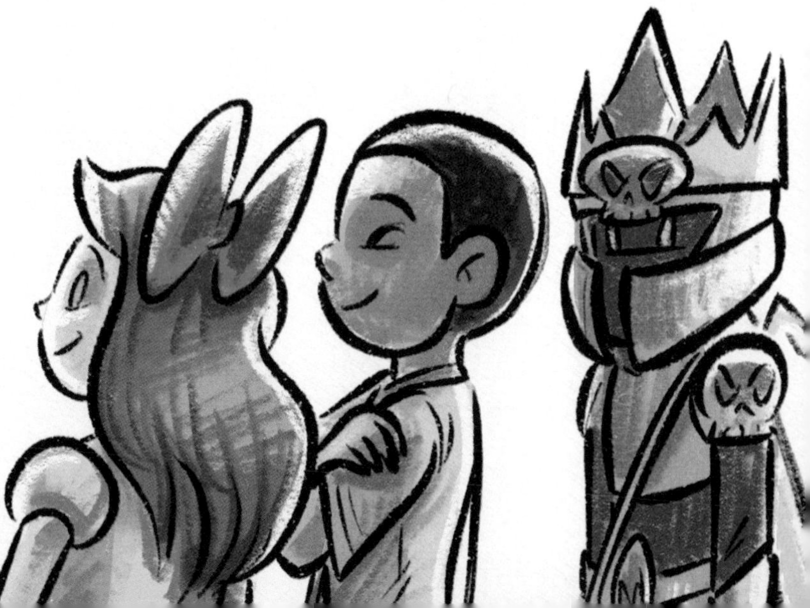

```
N N Y C W O W E A G Z J L P R
F X A N U L L B R K D G J L H
H U X Y T T A F O X R T V N E
Z N V F H H J N A H A Q O X L
Q O J A R O N N X H V N G W L
O B R A J I H B U J S A H V O
W B M E C O A C R A T M R C P
U S G H S A L A A M V A P X L
F P I L I K L X O B U S V H N
D W F T T B A G U O Y T G I U
A G U T E N T A G A T E X W Q
P F N I H A U K L W E A K R O
N N H B O N J O U R U Y S A Q
U F K M L R H W S M A P I N Z
S N M B A R S T C R R C O H Y
```

BONJOUR      HOLA      NAY HOH
CIAO         JAMBO    NI HAU
GUTEN TAG   KONNICHI WA  SALAAM
HALLA       MARHABA  ZDRAVSTVUYTE
HELLO       NAMASTE

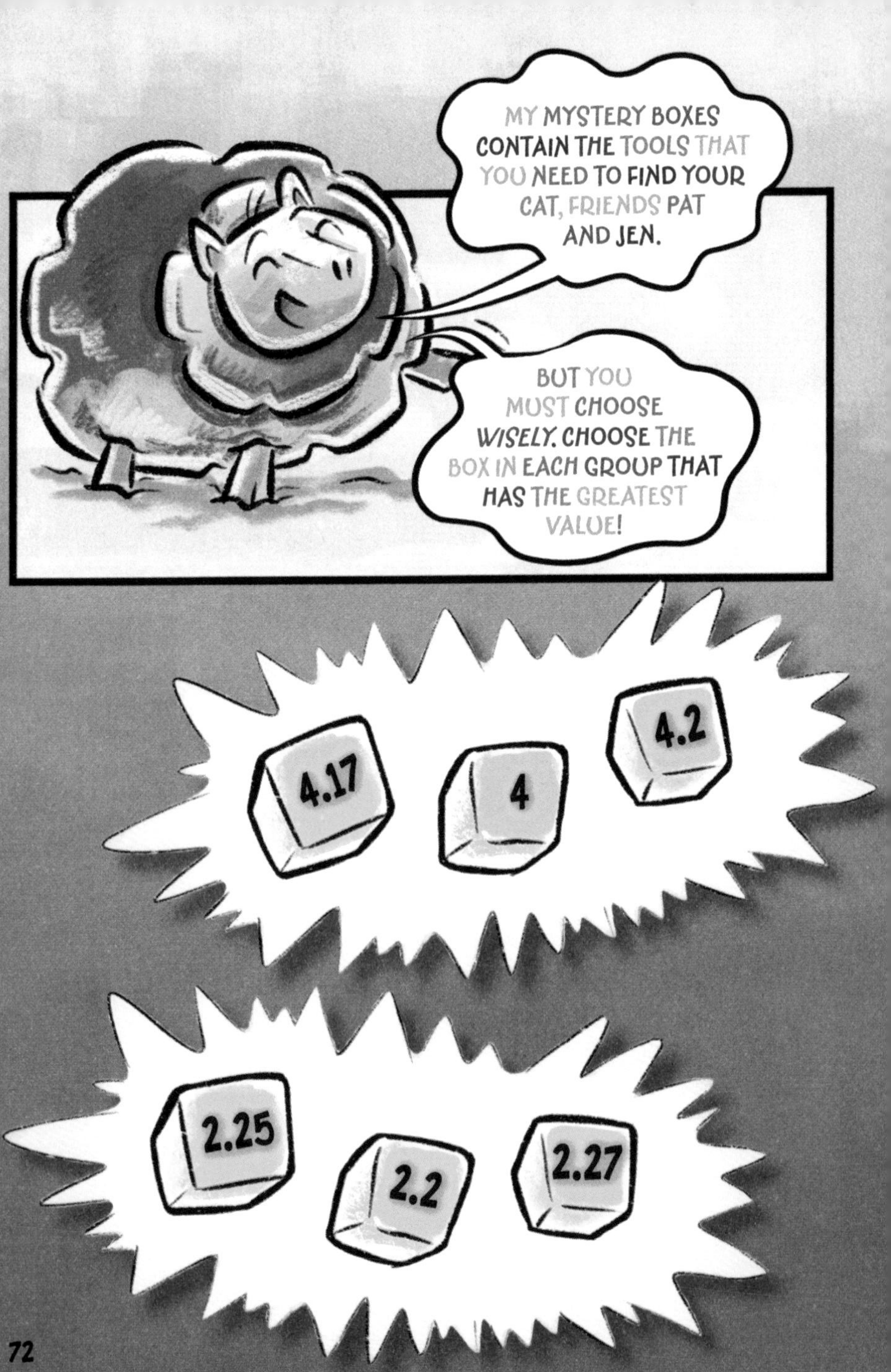
MY MYSTERY BOXES CONTAIN THE TOOLS THAT YOU NEED TO FIND YOUR CAT, FRIENDS PAT AND JEN.
BUT YOU MUST CHOOSE *WISELY*. CHOOSE THE BOX IN EACH GROUP THAT HAS THE GREATEST VALUE!
4.17
4
4.2
2.25
2.2
2.27

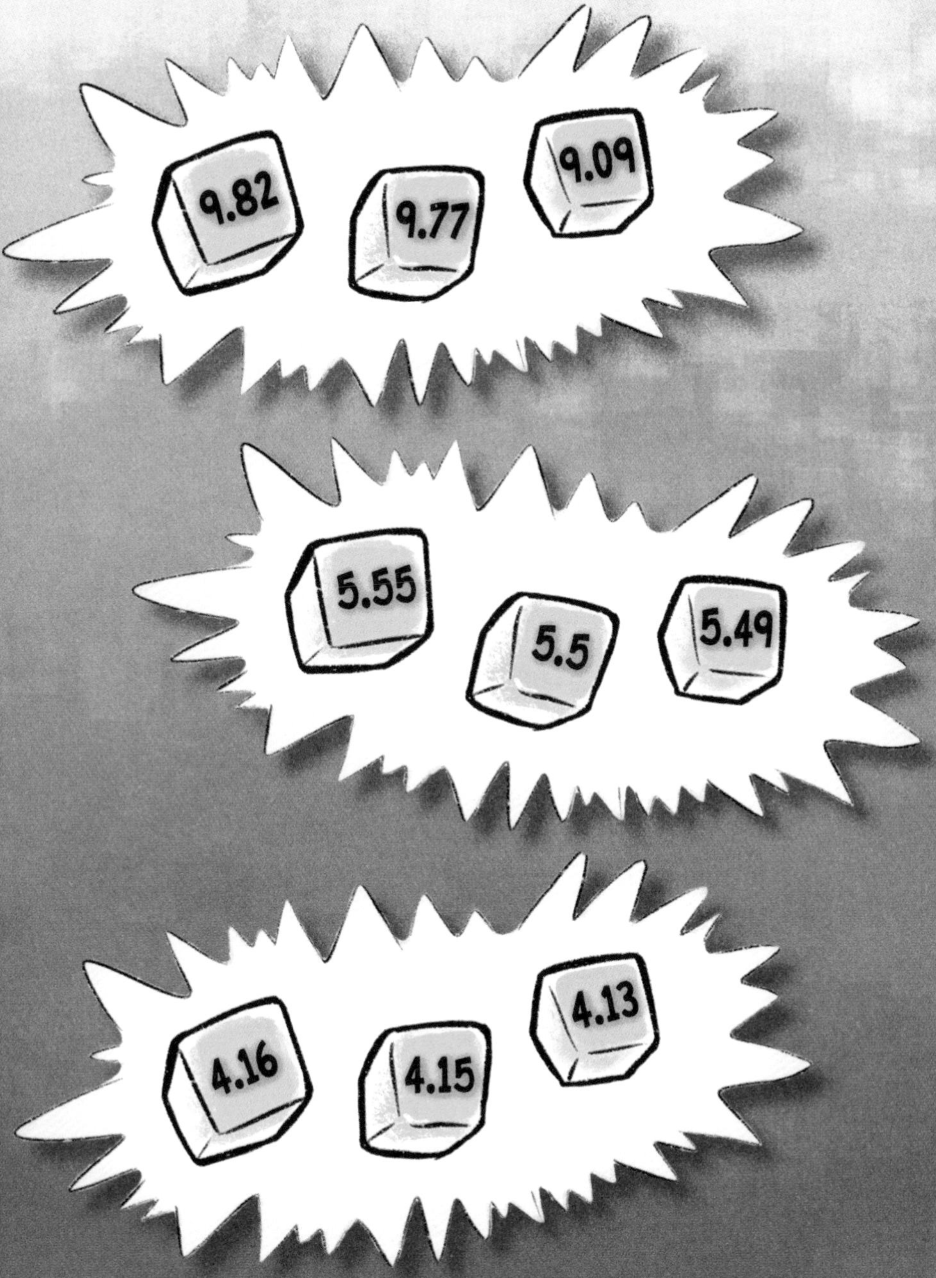
9.82
9.77
9.09
5.55
5.5
5.49
4.16
4.15
4.13

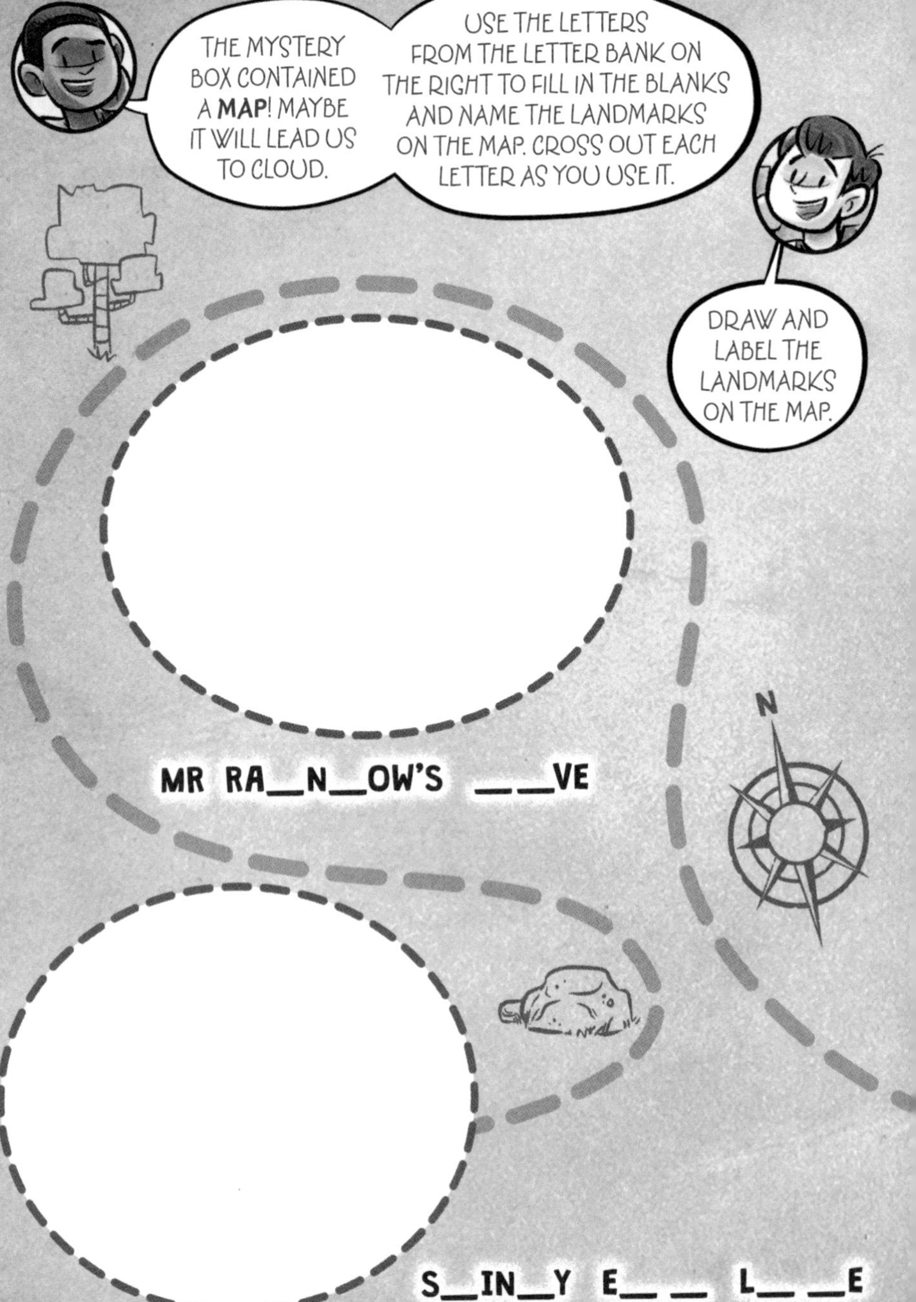
THE MYSTERY BOX CONTAINED A **MAP**! MAYBE IT WILL LEAD US TO CLOUD.
USE THE LETTERS FROM THE LETTER BANK ON THE RIGHT TO FILL IN THE BLANKS AND NAME THE LANDMARKS ON THE MAP. CROSS OUT EACH LETTER AS YOU USE IT.
DRAW AND LABEL THE LANDMARKS ON THE MAP.
MR RA__N__OW'S ___VE
N
S__IN__Y E__ __ L__ __E

THIS MAP LEADS TO EVIL JEN'S CASTLE!
DID EVIL JEN TAKE CLOUD?

CR__ __TY T__E CA__ __ON

**LETTER BANK**

| | | | | |
|---|---|---|---|---|
| I | B | C | A | M |
| B | W | O | T | K |
| Y | E | A | K | U |
| S | O | N | Y | V |
| L | J | N | S | E |

ZO__ __IE __ __ODS

E__I__ __E__'S CA__TL__

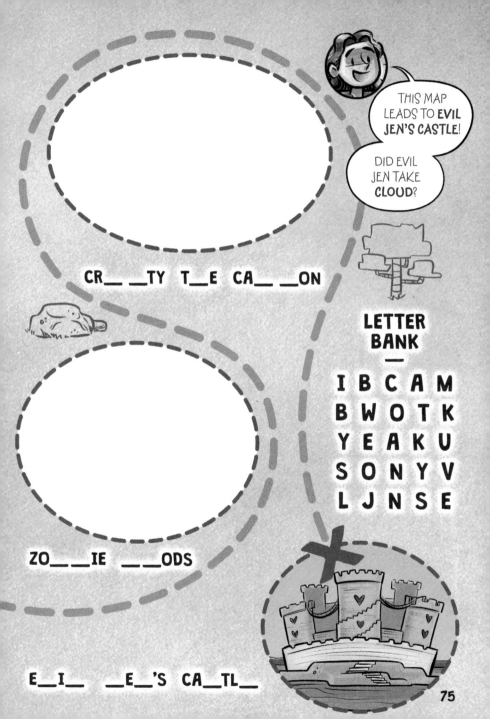

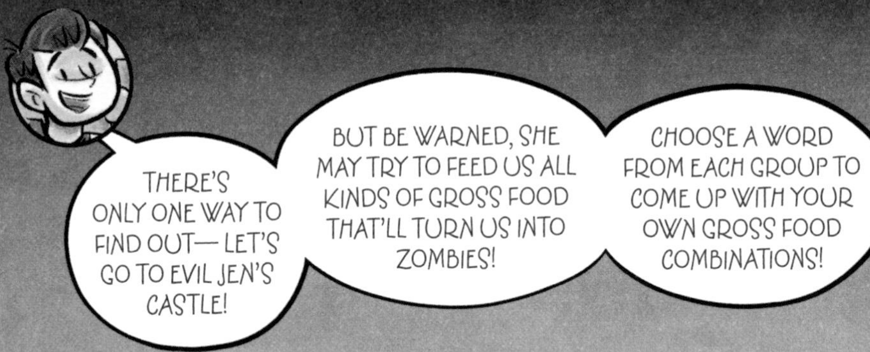
THERE'S ONLY ONE WAY TO FIND OUT— LET'S GO TO EVIL JEN'S CASTLE!
BUT BE WARNED, SHE MAY TRY TO FEED US ALL KINDS OF GROSS FOOD THAT'LL TURN US INTO ZOMBIES!
CHOOSE A WORD FROM EACH GROUP TO COME UP WITH YOUR OWN GROSS FOOD COMBINATIONS!

| | |
|---|---|
| Muddy Frog | Stew |
| Spider Butt | Sandwich |
| Monkey Eye | Soup |
| Finger Cheese | Burrito |

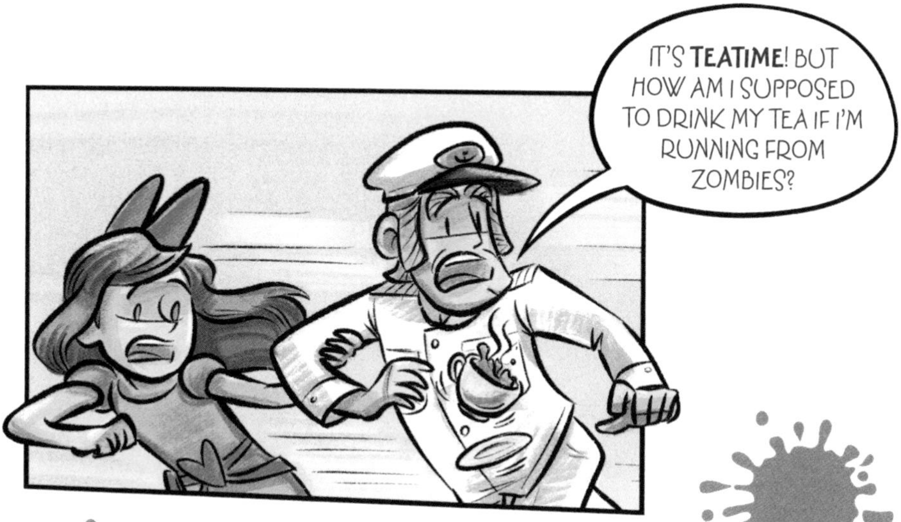
IT'S **TEATIME**! BUT HOW AM I SUPPOSED TO DRINK MY TEA IF I'M RUNNING FROM ZOMBIES?

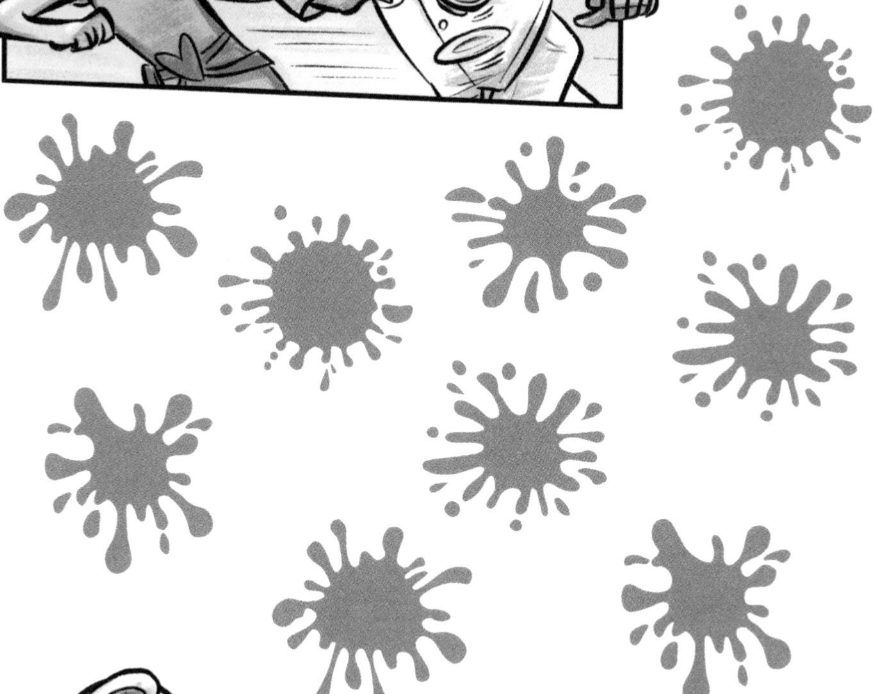

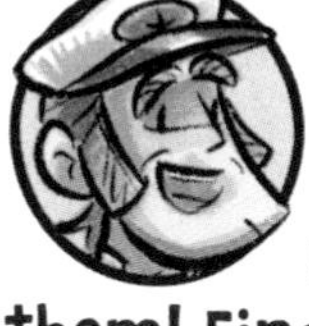

Clean up my spills by crossing out the matching pairs of tea stains as you find them! Find the one that doesn't have a match!

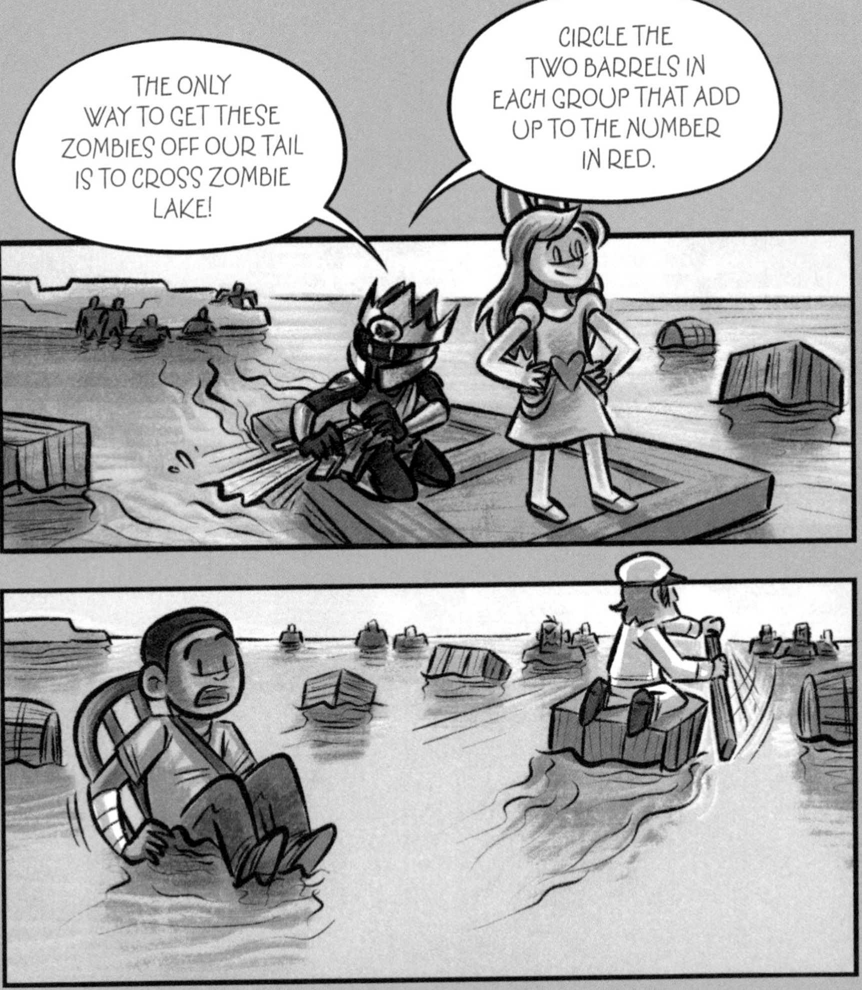
THE ONLY WAY TO GET THESE ZOMBIES OFF OUR TAIL IS TO CROSS ZOMBIE LAKE!
CIRCLE THE TWO BARRELS IN EACH GROUP THAT ADD UP TO THE NUMBER IN RED.

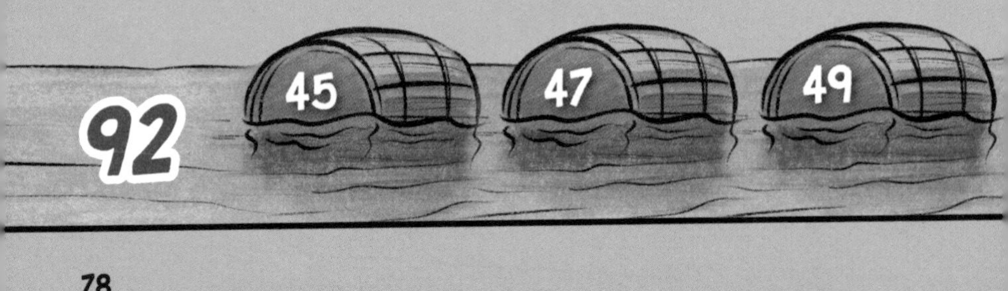
92
45
47
49

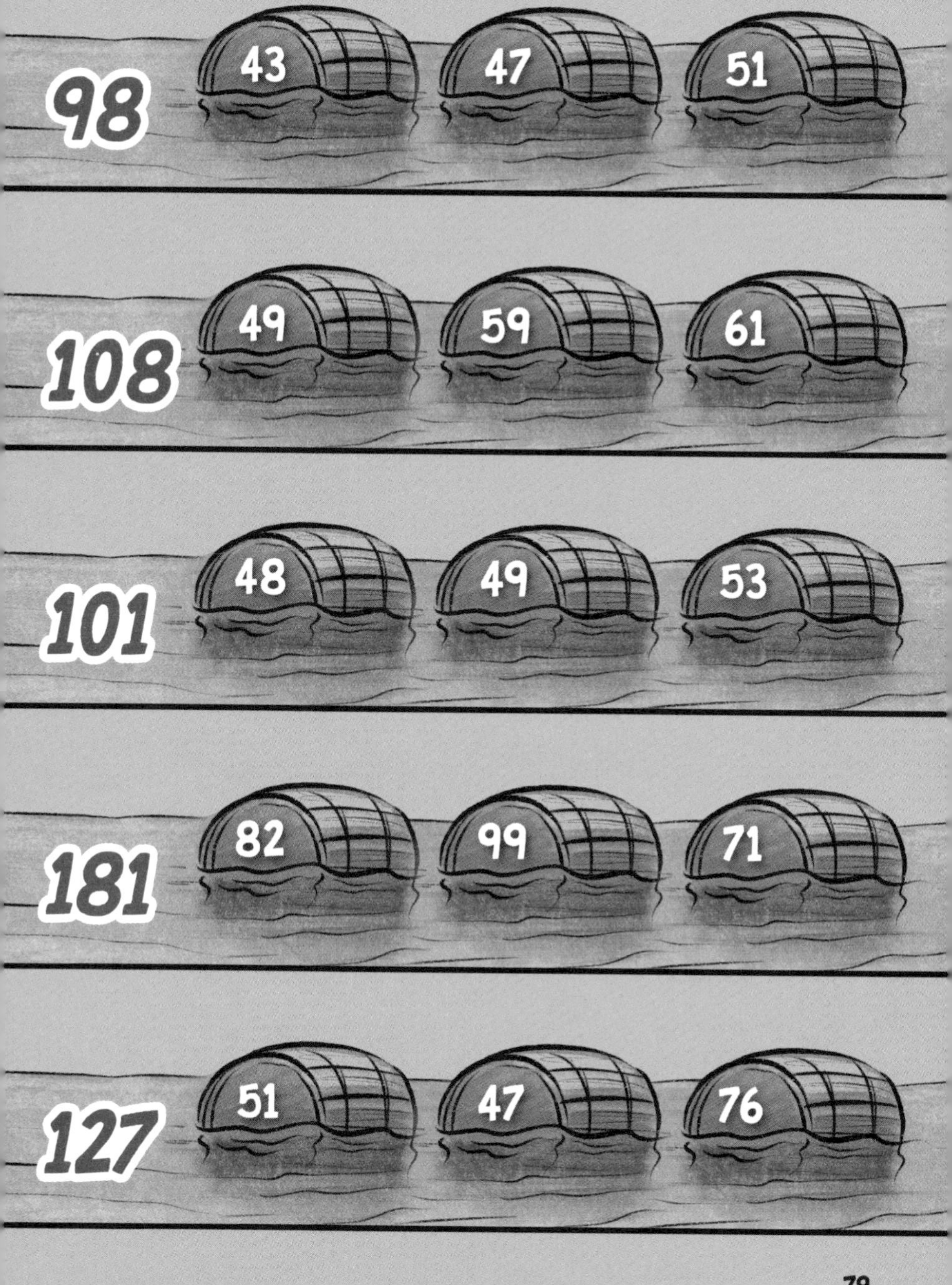
98
43
47
51
108
49
59
61
101
48
49
53
181
82
99
71
127
51
47
76

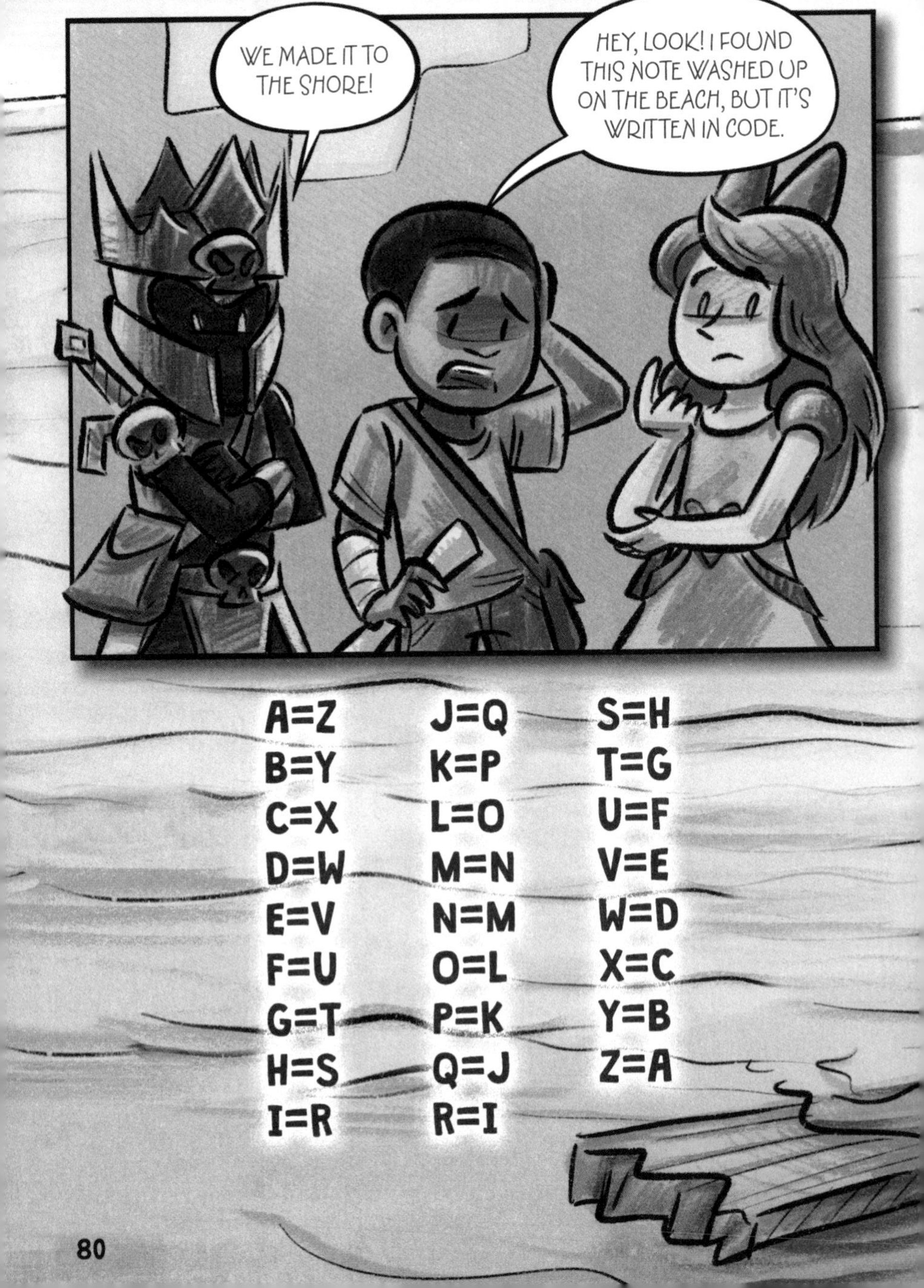
WE MADE IT TO THE SHORE!
HEY, LOOK! I FOUND THIS NOTE WASHED UP ON THE BEACH, BUT IT'S WRITTEN IN CODE.

| | | |
|---|---|---|
| A=Z | J=Q | S=H |
| B=Y | K=P | T=G |
| C=X | L=O | U=F |
| D=W | M=N | V=E |
| E=V | N=M | W=D |
| F=U | O=L | X=C |
| G=T | P=K | Y=B |
| H=S | Q=J | Z=A |
| I=R | R=I | |

**Use the key on the left to figure out what it says!**

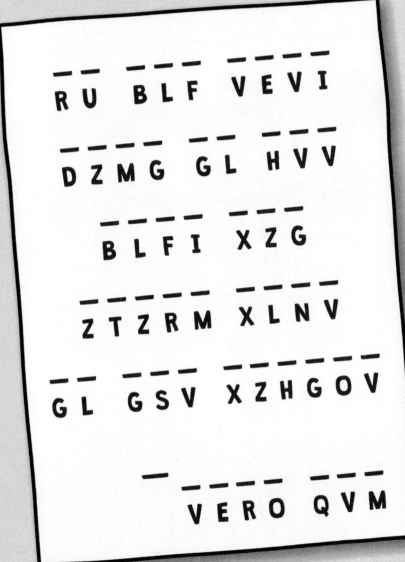

RU BLF VEVI

DZMG GL HVV

BLFI XZG

ZTZRM XLNV

GL GSV XZHGOV

VERO QVM

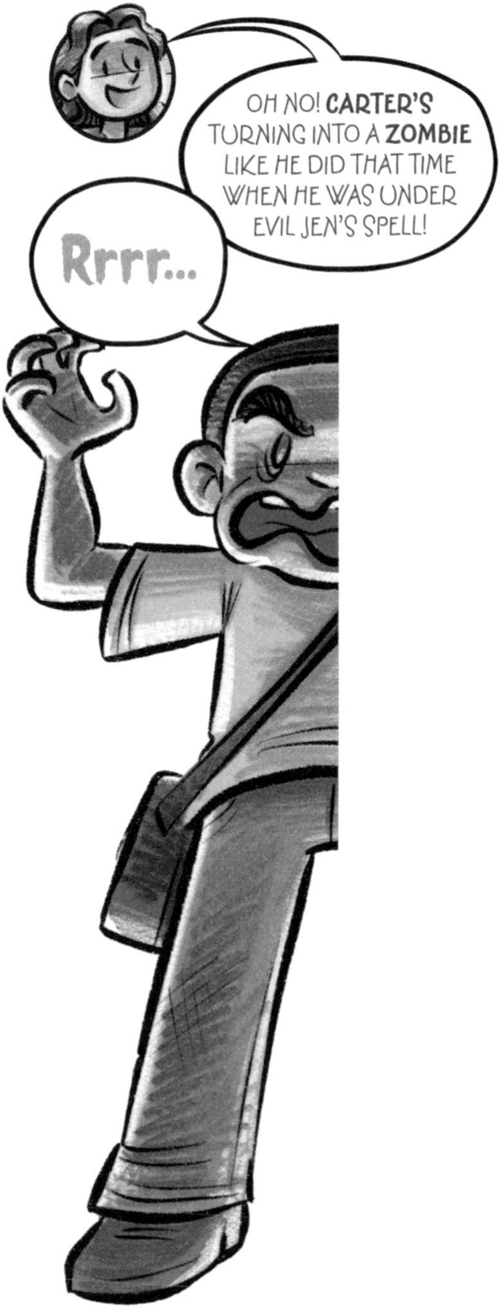
OH NO! CARTER'S TURNING INTO A ZOMBIE LIKE HE DID THAT TIME WHEN HE WAS UNDER EVIL JEN'S SPELL!
Rrrr...

**Draw Carter's zombie half to complete his transformation!**

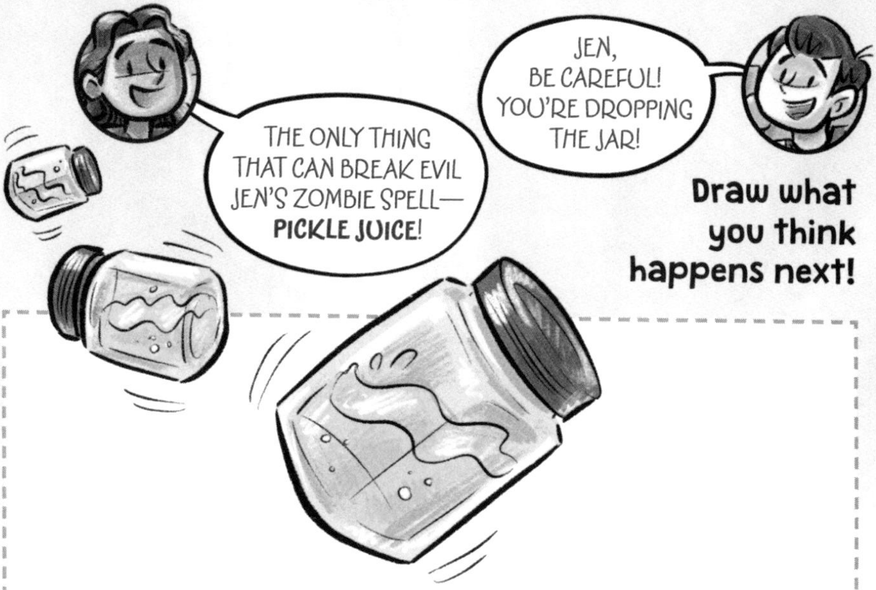
THE ONLY THING THAT CAN BREAK EVIL JEN'S ZOMBIE SPELL— **PICKLE JUICE**!
JEN, BE CAREFUL! YOU'RE DROPPING THE JAR!

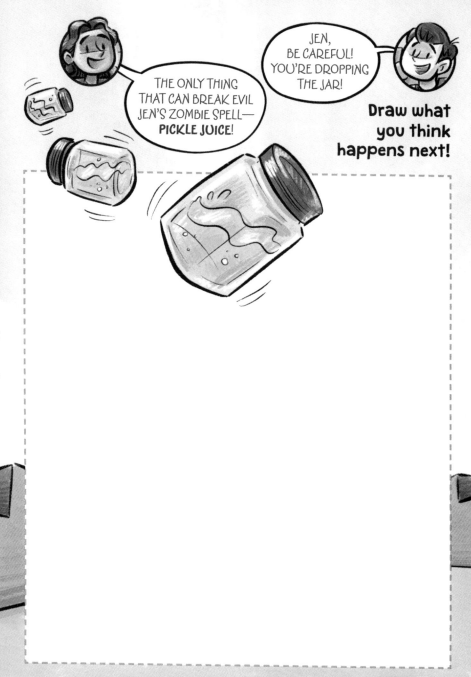

**Draw what you think happens next!**

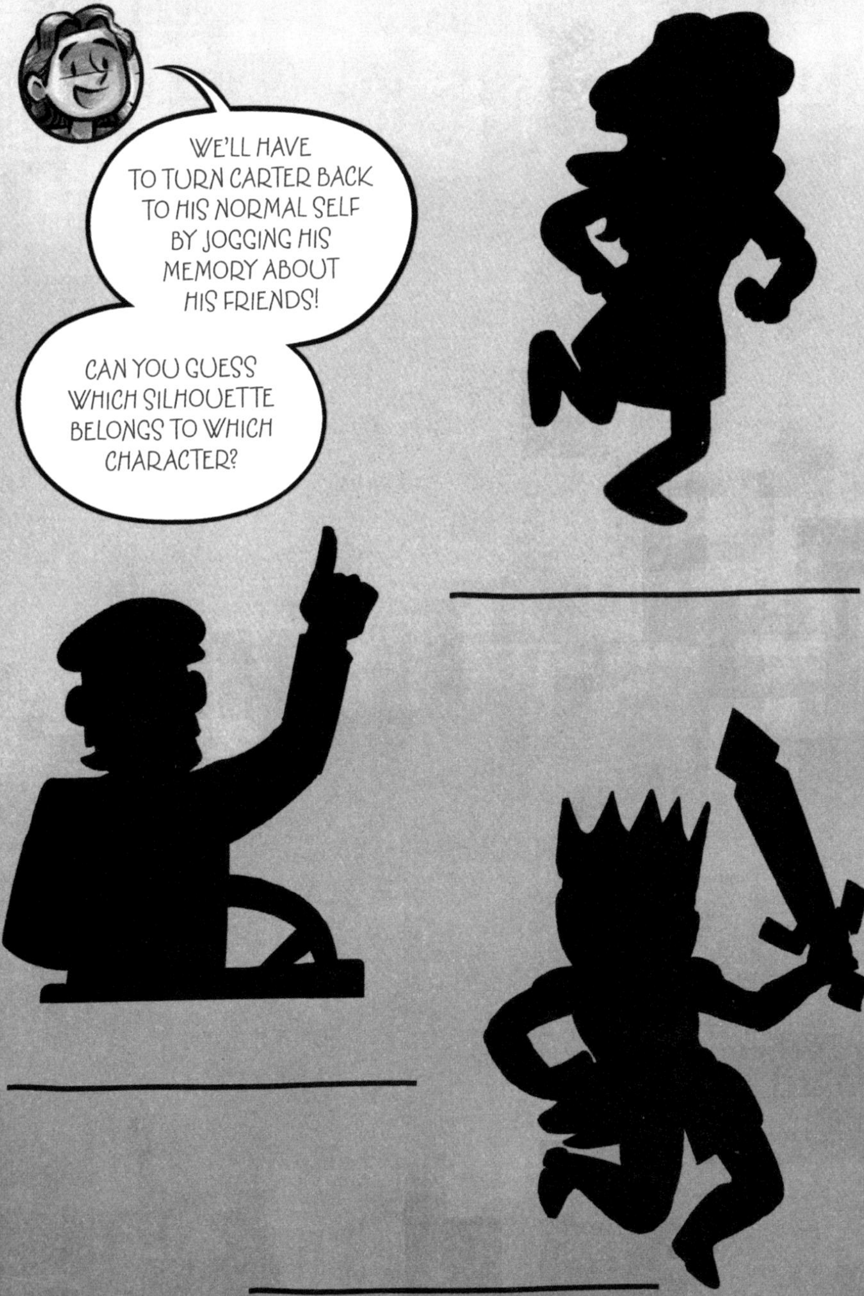
WE'LL HAVE TO TURN CARTER BACK TO HIS NORMAL SELF BY JOGGING HIS MEMORY ABOUT HIS FRIENDS!
CAN YOU GUESS WHICH SILHOUETTE BELONGS TO WHICH CHARACTER?

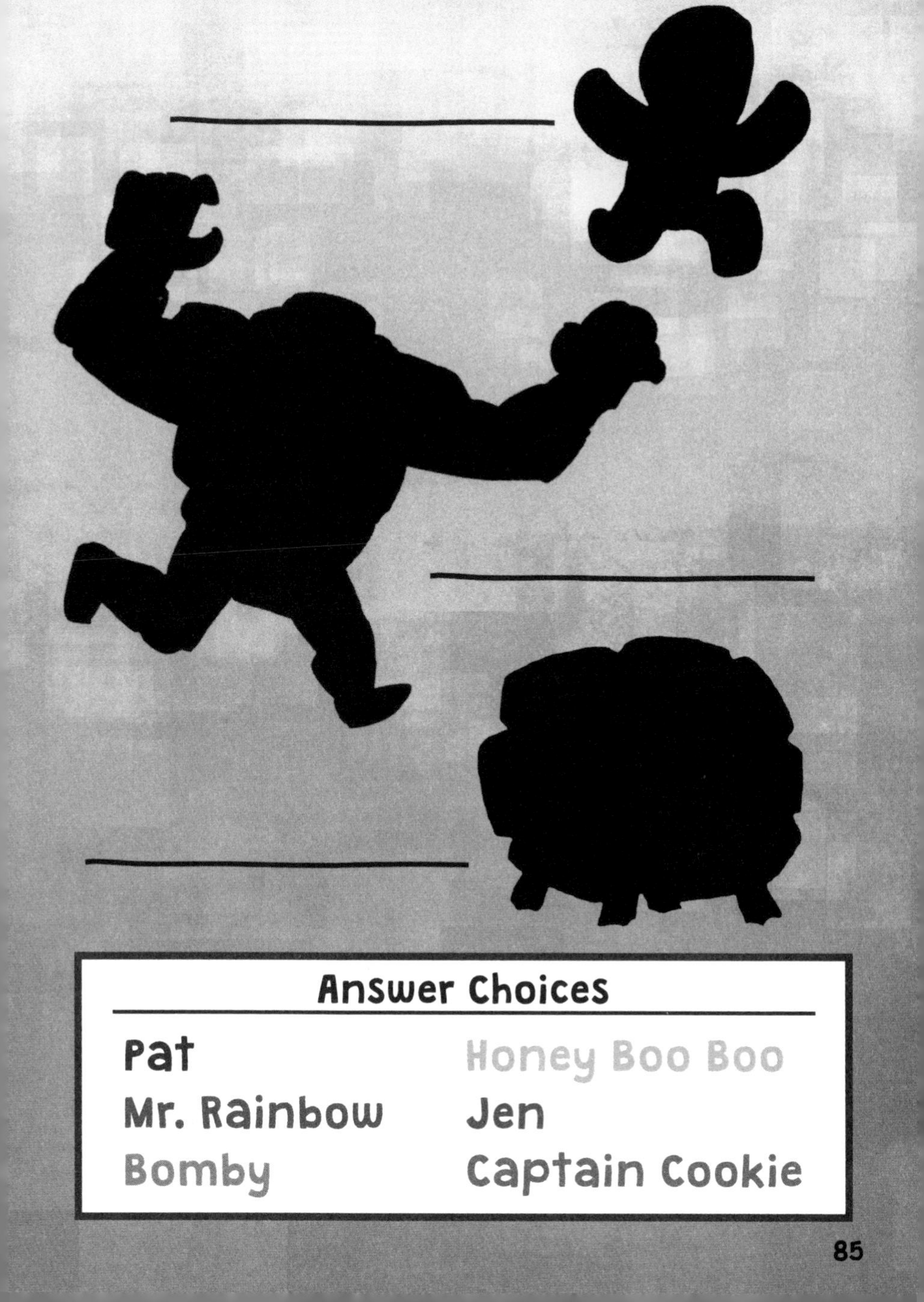

**Answer Choices**

| | |
|---|---|
| Pat | Honey Boo Boo |
| Mr. Rainbow | Jen |
| Bomby | Captain Cookie |

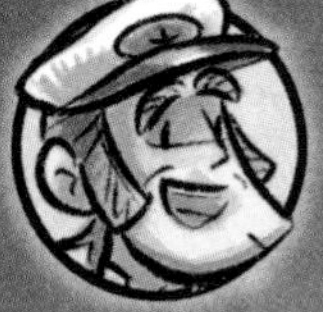

Perhaps Carter will remember his friends if we repeat some of their most famous quotes.

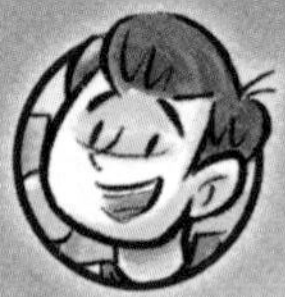

Good idea, Captain! Can you guess which quote belongs to which character?

HONEY BOO BOO!

EWWWW! THEIR BREATH SMELLS LIKE HUMAN FINGER CHEES!

RAB-RAZZLE!

________________

BONJOUR, MY FRIENDS! COME IN! WELCOME!

JEN, CLOUD'S JUST A **CAT**. AND A **SAVAGE**.

________________

________________

I'D BE GLAD TO TAKE YOU, BUT IT'S MY **TEATIME**.

## Answer Choices

| | |
|---|---|
| Pat | Honey Boo Boo |
| Mr. Rainbow | Jen |
| Zombie | Captain Cookie |

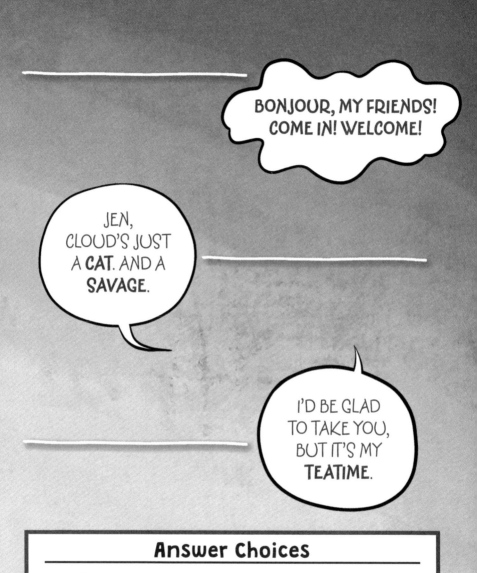

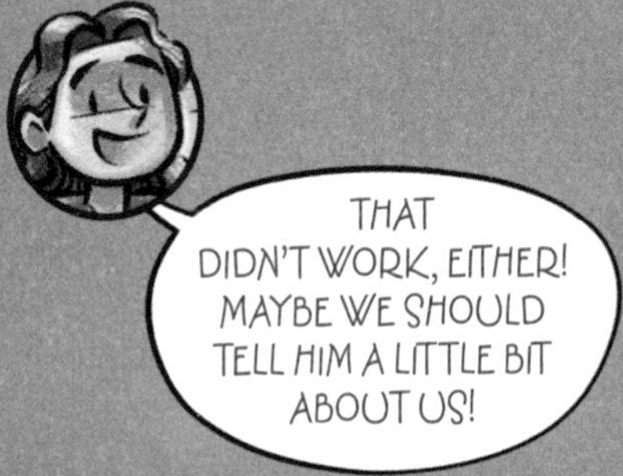
THAT DIDN'T WORK, EITHER! MAYBE WE SHOULD TELL HIM A LITTLE BIT ABOUT US!

Read the character descriptions in the clues below and write the names of the characters in the puzzle to the right.

## ACROSS

3. A magical sheep with mystery boxes aplenty!
4. A sort of pet to Pat who loves making things go boom!
5. He may not be a real sea captain, but he dresses like one.
7. Fluffy on the outside, savage on the inside.
8. This super girly gamer is sweet, but fierce.

## DOWN

1. This magical unicorn leaves a trail of rainbow wherever he flies.
2. An iron golem who's really an old softie.
5. Jen's best friend who carries a pickle for a sword
6. This awesome dude is always looking for an epic adventure!

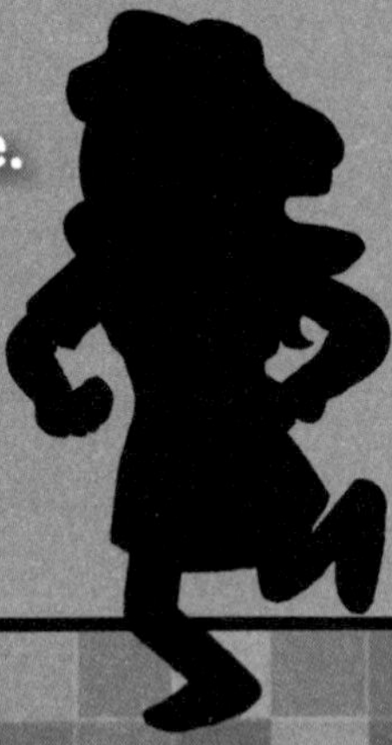

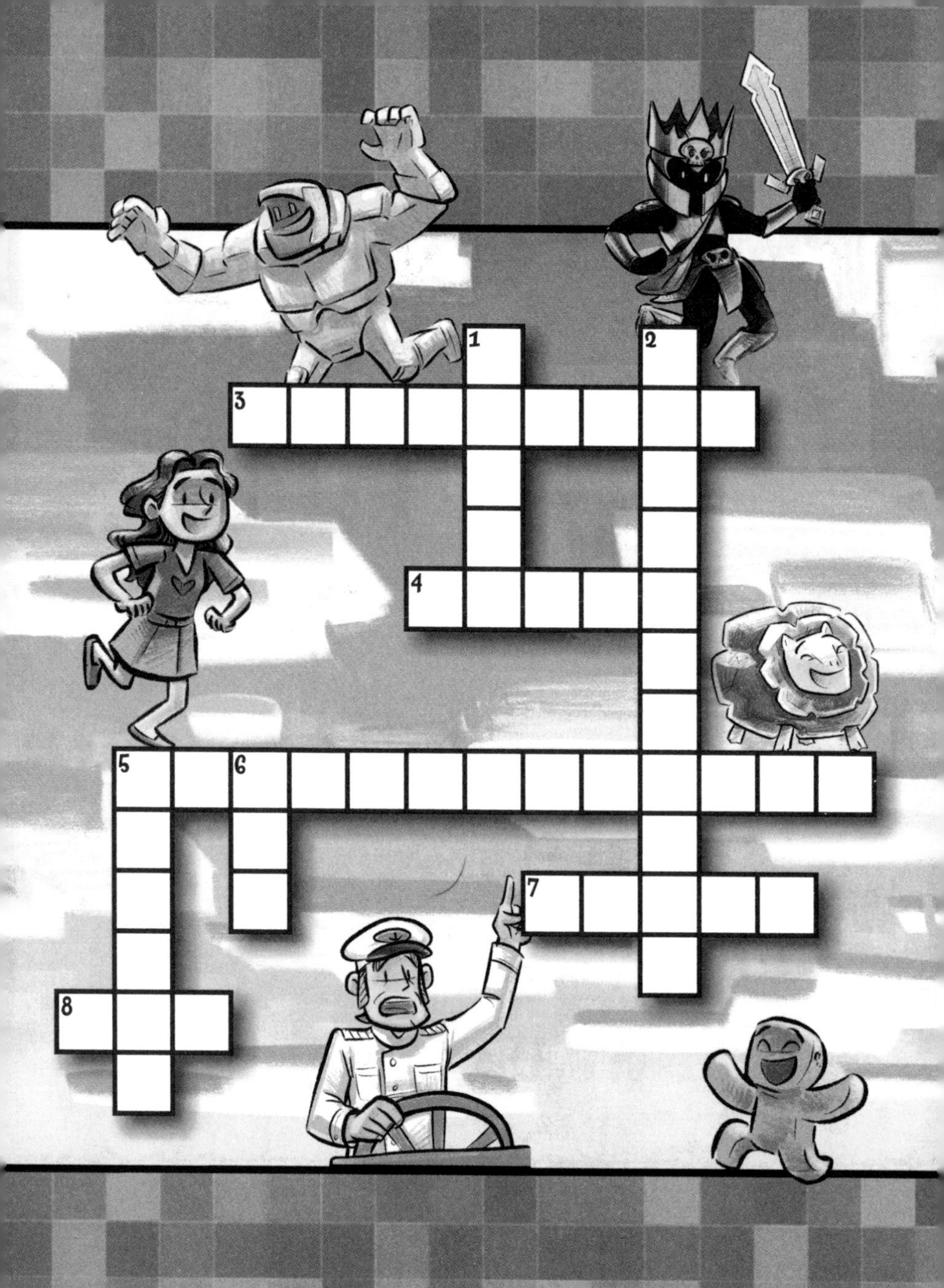
1
2
3
4
5
6
7
8

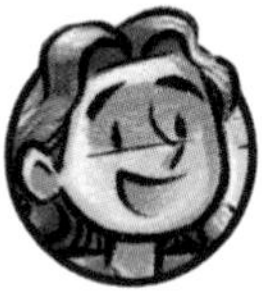

**Have you ever had a friend who needed your help? What did you do to help them?**

# YOU BE THE WRITER!

What are CARTER and JEN saying after Jen helped turn him back to his normal self?

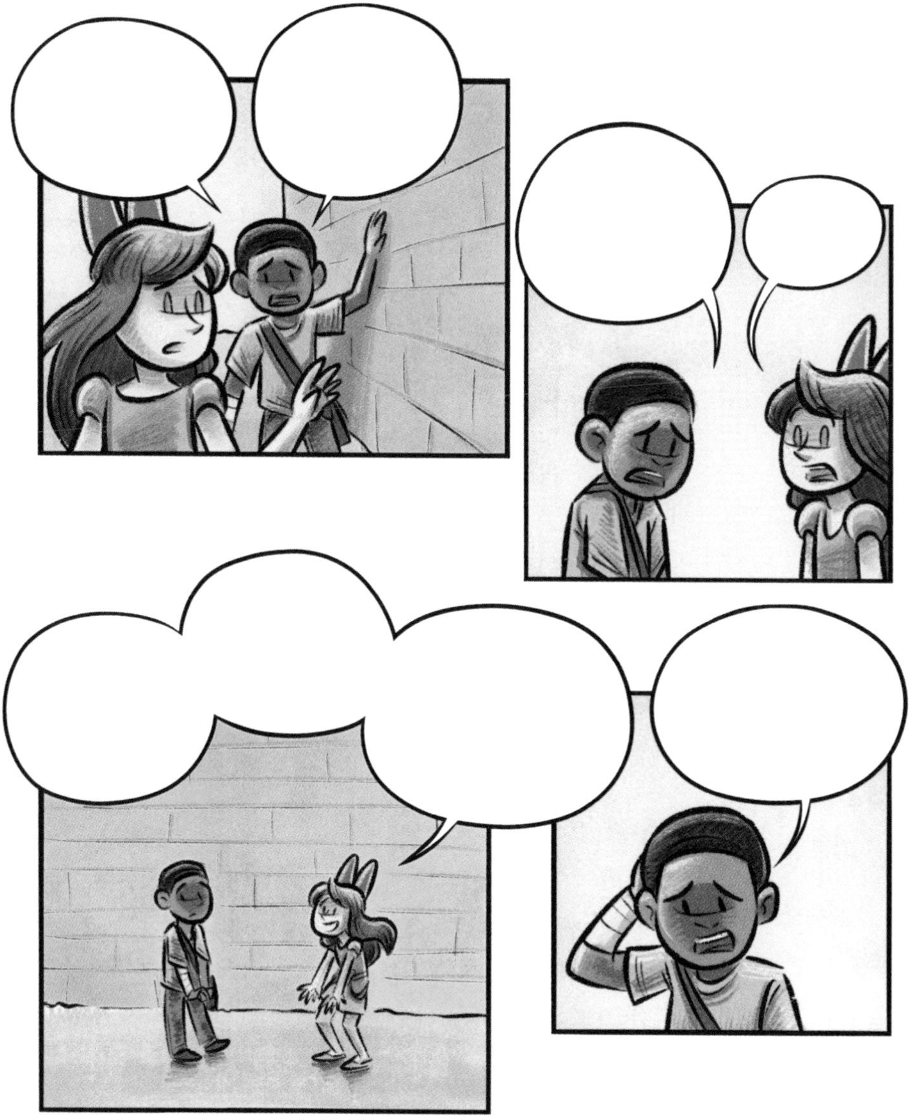

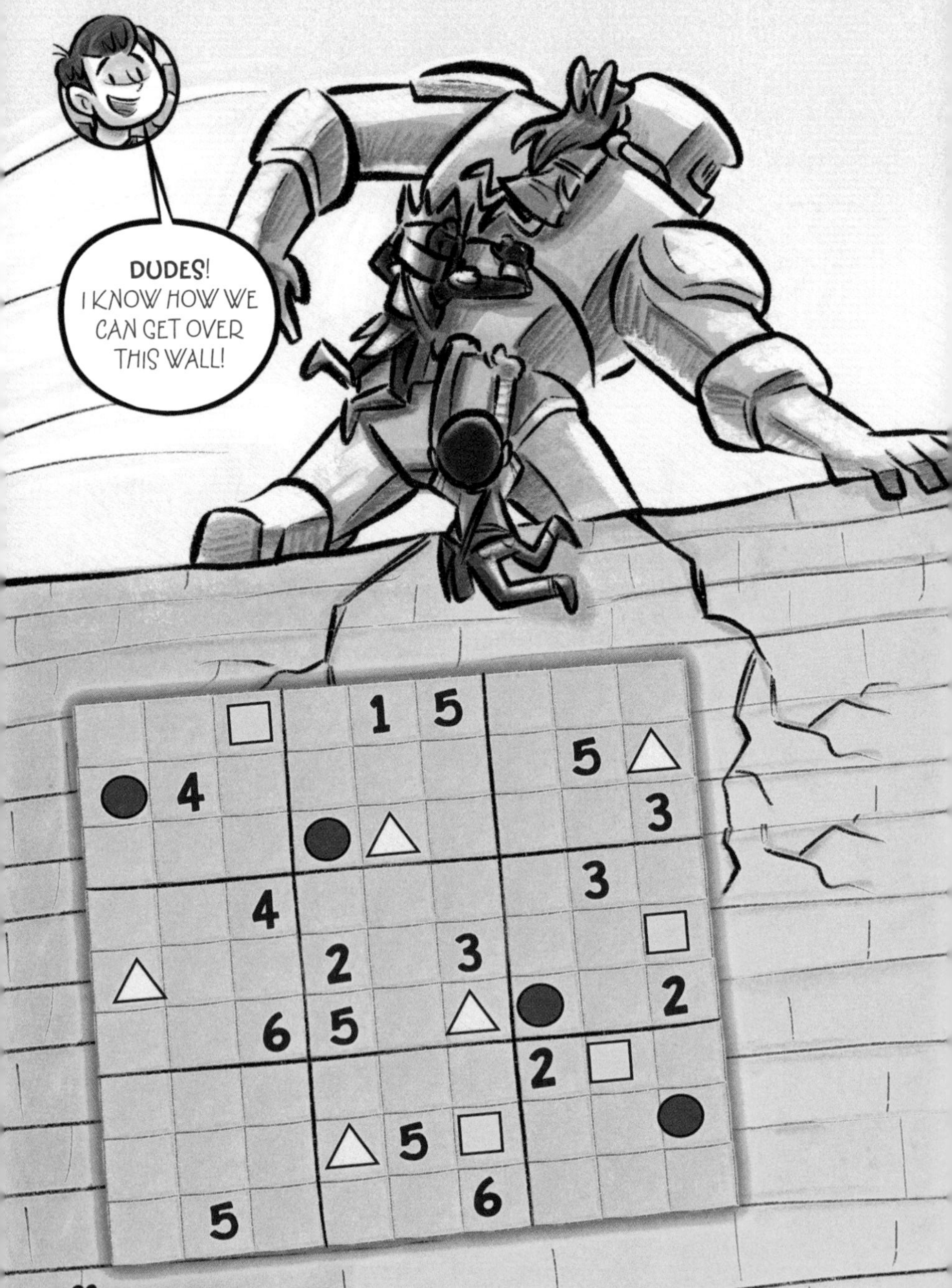
DUDES! I KNOW HOW WE CAN GET OVER THIS WALL!

Help HONEY BOO BOO carry us over the wall by filling in the empty squares with the numbers and icons.

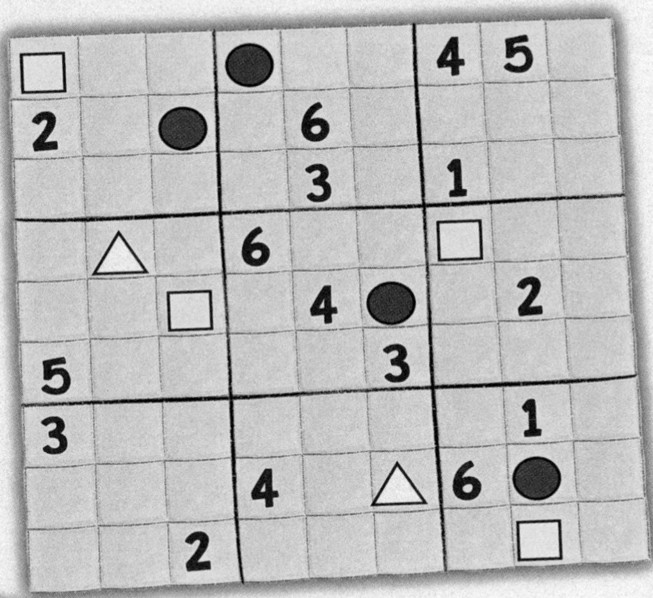

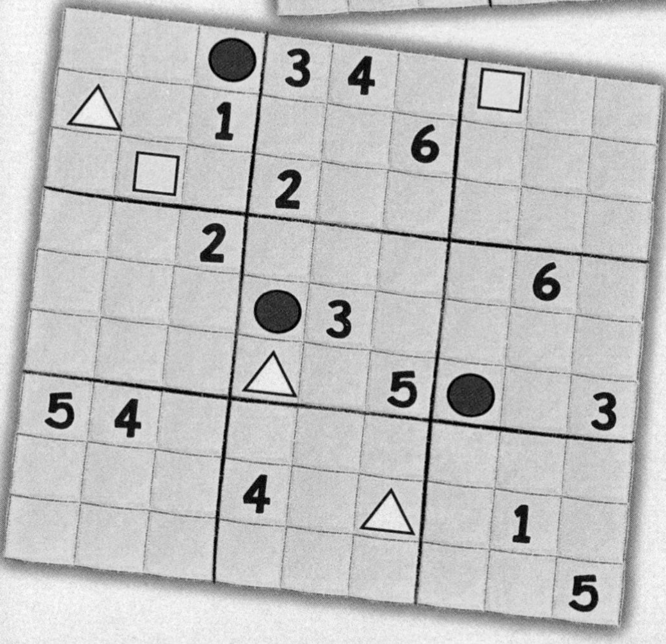

But be sure to use each of them just once in each row and in each column.

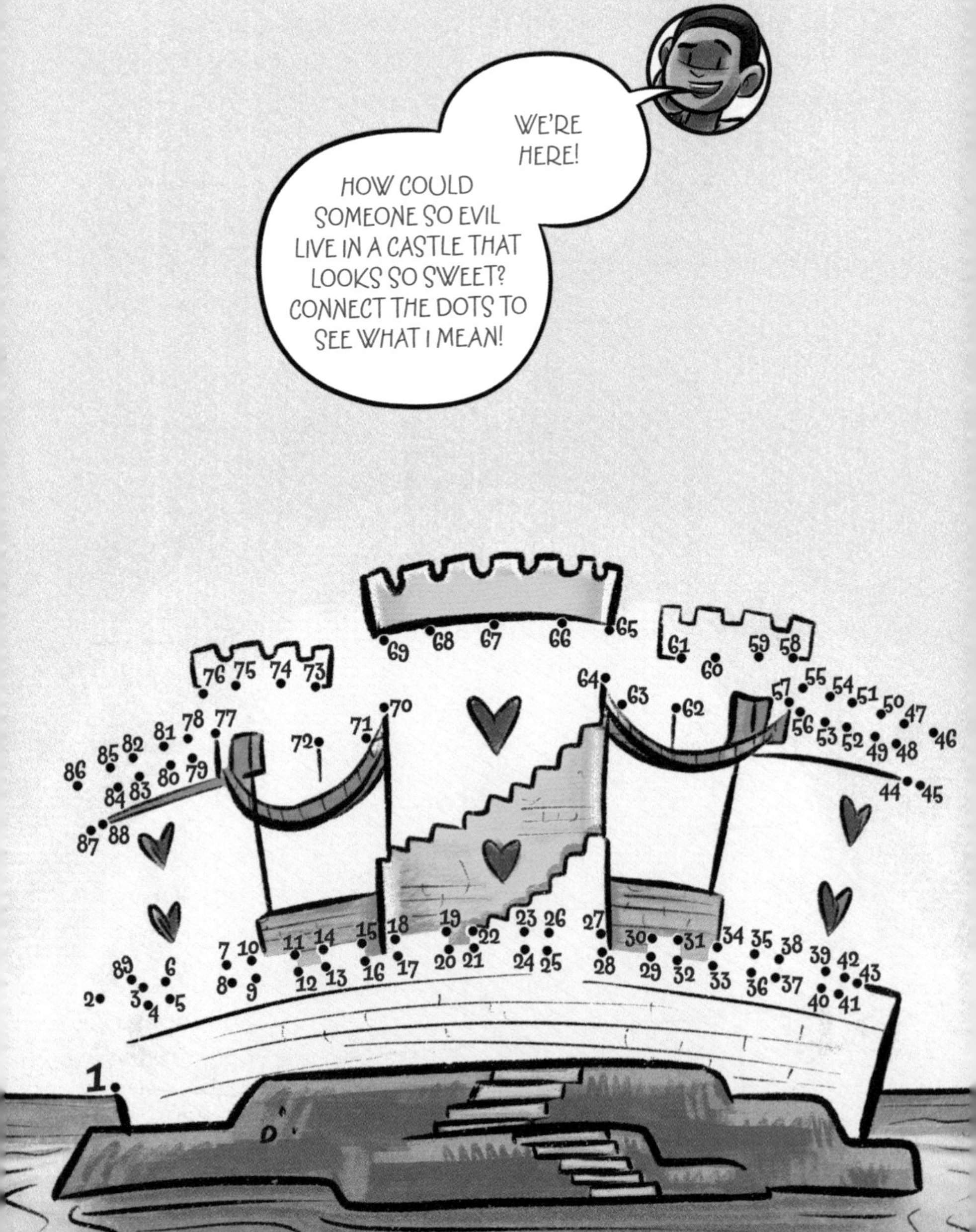
WE'RE HERE!
HOW COULD SOMEONE SO EVIL LIVE IN A CASTLE THAT LOOKS SO SWEET? CONNECT THE DOTS TO SEE WHAT I MEAN!

Help us climb the stairs by writing a word that begins with "A" on the first line. On the 2nd line, write a word that begins with the 2nd letter of your first word. And on the 3rd line, write a word that begins with the 2nd letter of your second word, and so on until you fill the page!

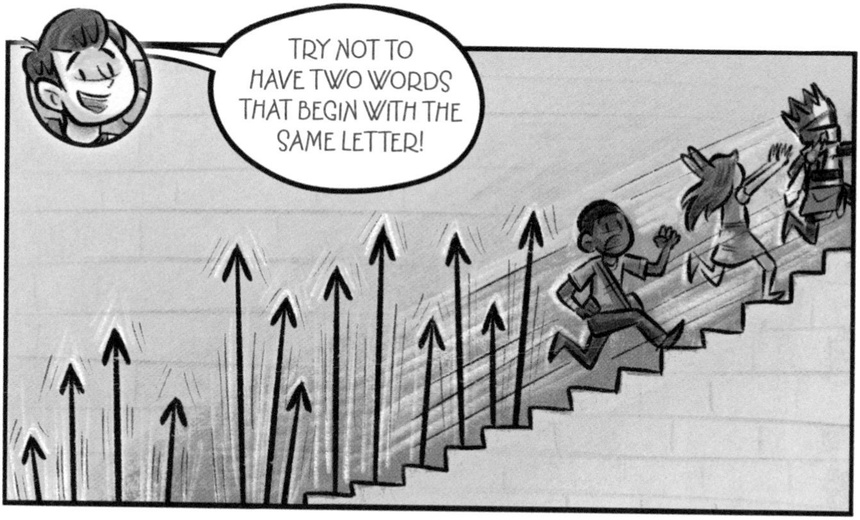
TRY NOT TO HAVE TWO WORDS THAT BEGIN WITH THE SAME LETTER!

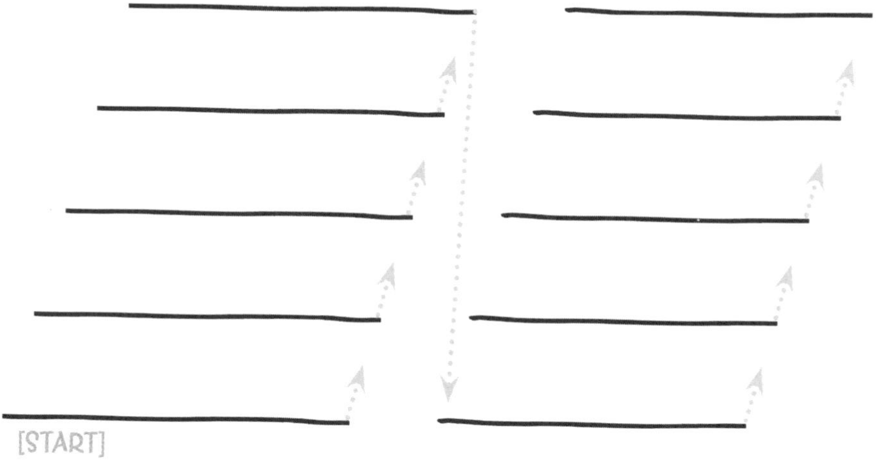
[START]

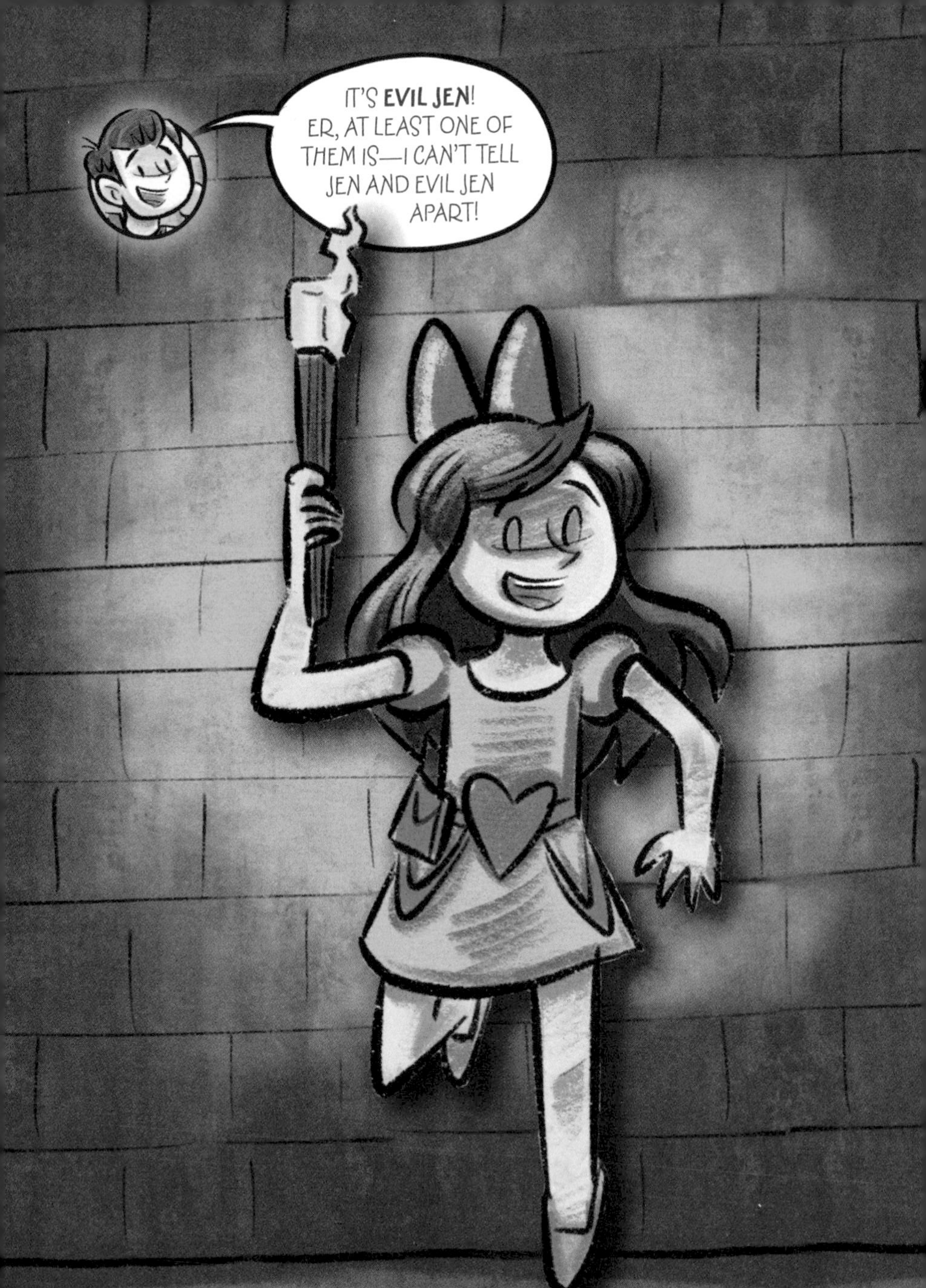
IT'S **EVIL JEN**! ER, AT LEAST ONE OF THEM IS—I CAN'T TELL JEN AND EVIL JEN APART!

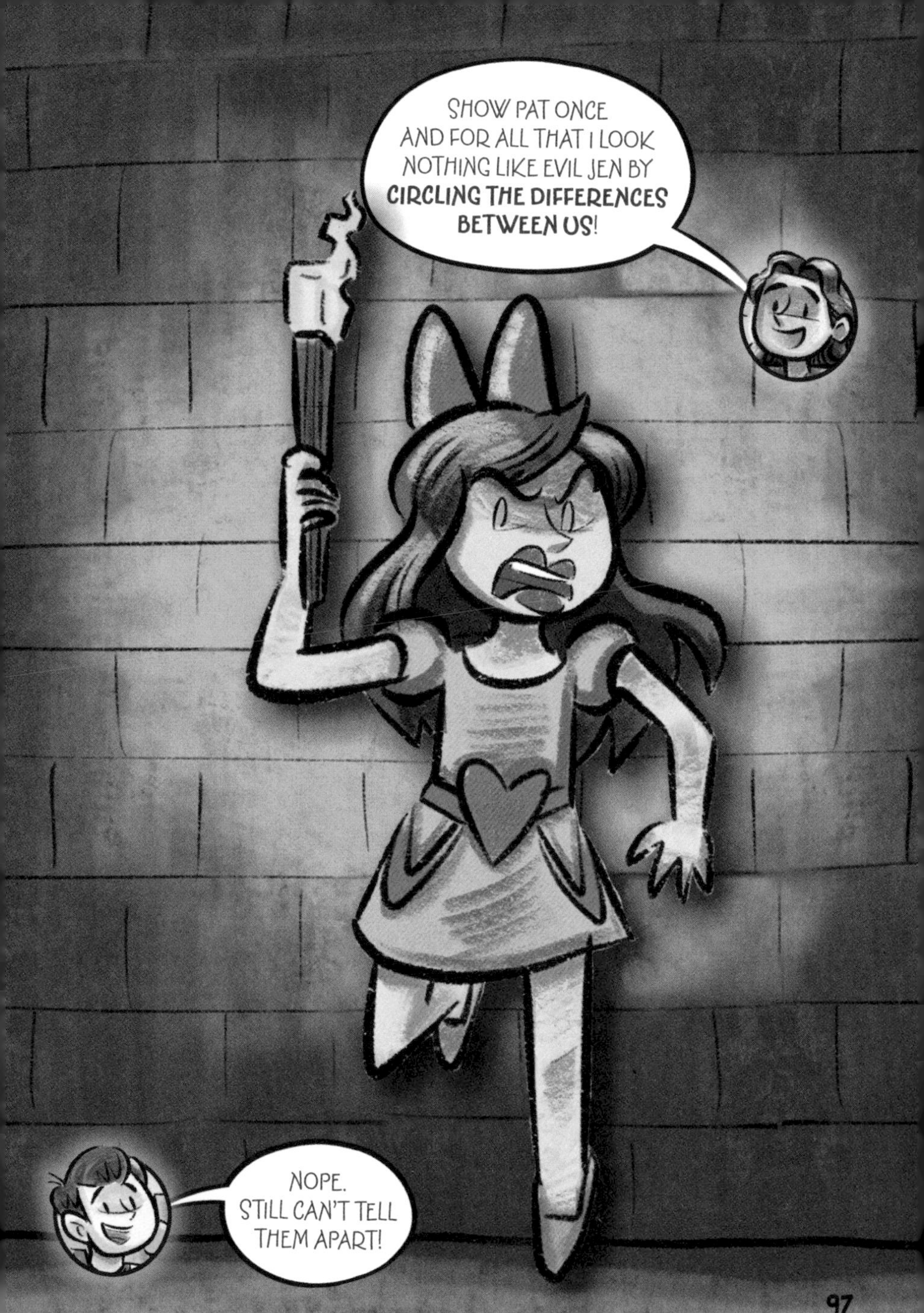
SHOW PAT ONCE AND FOR ALL THAT I LOOK NOTHING LIKE EVIL JEN BY **CIRCLING THE DIFFERENCES BETWEEN US**!
NOPE. STILL CAN'T TELL THEM APART!

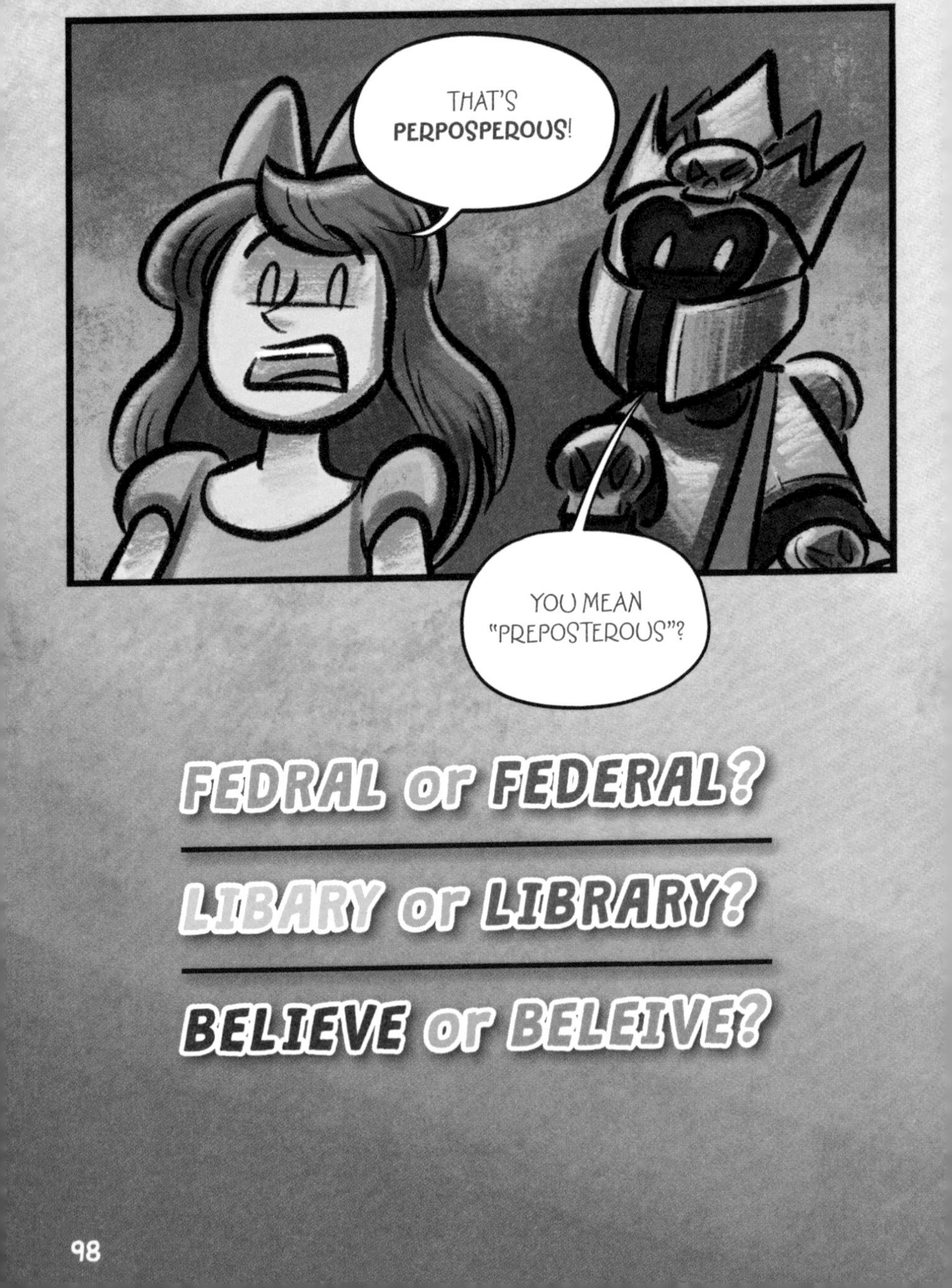
THAT'S PERPOSPEROUS!
YOU MEAN "PREPOSTEROUS"?

## FEDRAL or FEDERAL?

---

## LIBARY or LIBRARY?

---

## BELIEVE or BELEIVE?

HEY! We can tell Jen and Evil Jen apart by Jen's mispronunciations! Circle the word in each pair that's spelled incorrectly.

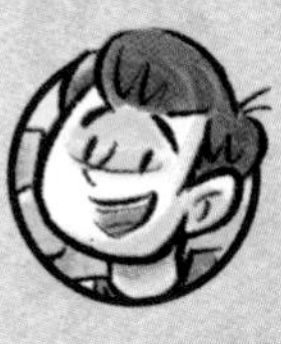

JEWLERY or JEWELRY

PRESCRIPTION or PERSCRIPTION?

RECEIPT or RECIEPT?

FOILAGE or FOLIAGE?

WEIRD or WIERD?

ANTARCTIC or ANTARTIC?

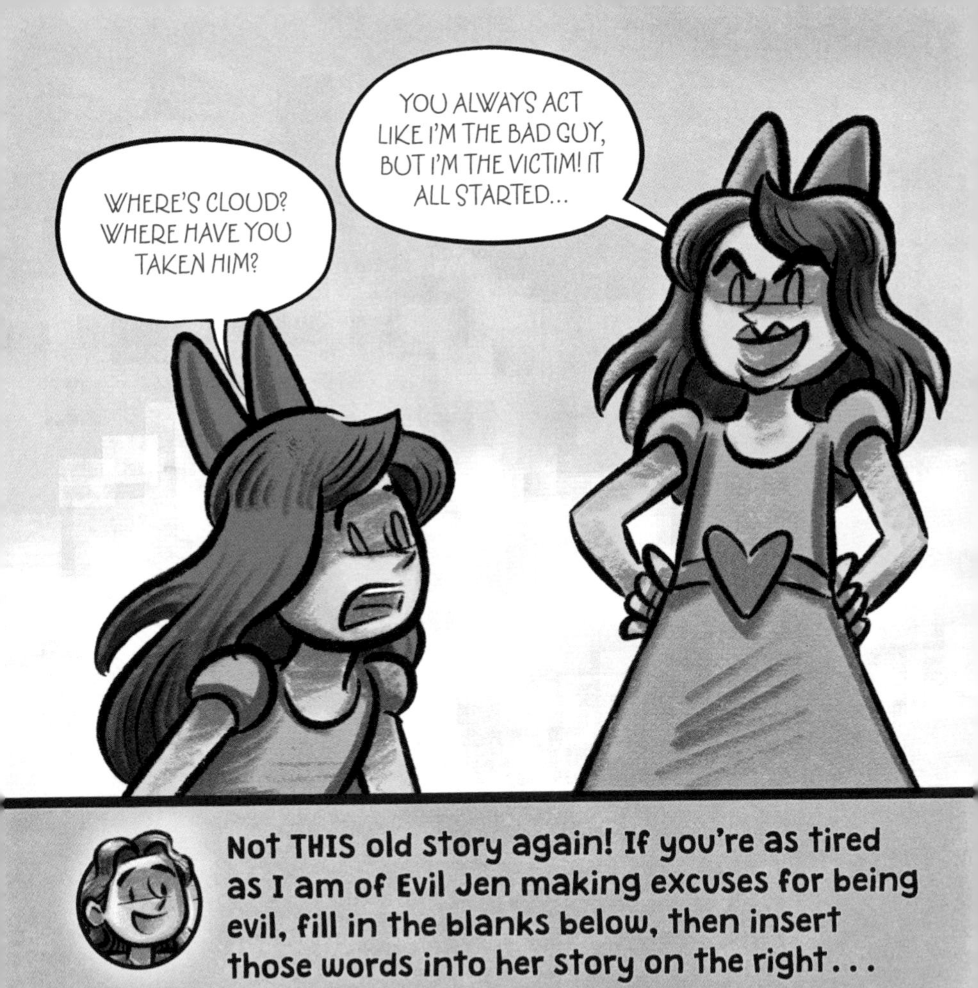
WHERE'S CLOUD? WHERE HAVE YOU TAKEN HIM?
YOU ALWAYS ACT LIKE I'M THE BAD GUY, BUT I'M THE VICTIM! IT ALL STARTED...

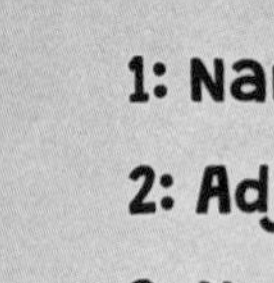

**Not THIS old story again! If you're as tired as I am of Evil Jen making excuses for being evil, fill in the blanks below, then insert those words into her story on the right . . .**

**1: Name a body part** ______________________

**2: Adjective** ______________________

**3: Noun** ______________________

**4: Place** ______________________

**5: Noun** ______________________

**6: Past-tense verb** ______________________

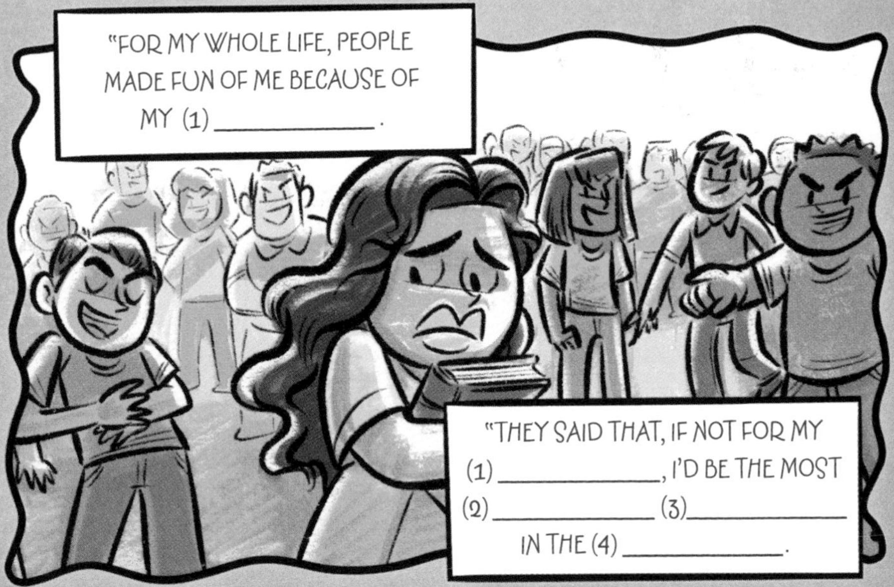
"FOR MY WHOLE LIFE, PEOPLE MADE FUN OF ME BECAUSE OF MY (1) ____________.
"THEY SAID THAT, IF NOT FOR MY (1) ____________, I'D BE THE MOST (2) ____________ (3) ____________ IN THE (4) ____________.

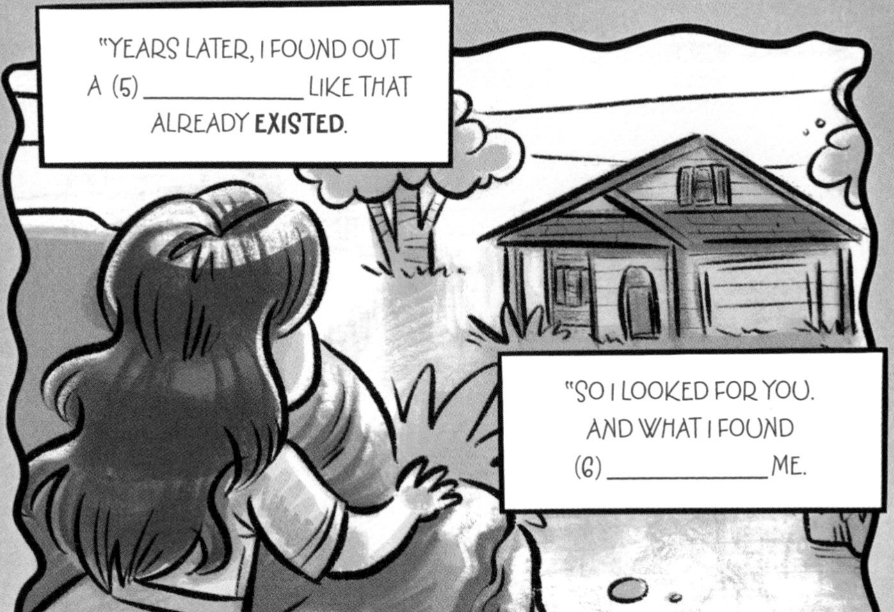
"YEARS LATER, I FOUND OUT A (5) ____________ LIKE THAT ALREADY **EXISTED**.
"SO I LOOKED FOR YOU. AND WHAT I FOUND (6) ____________ ME.

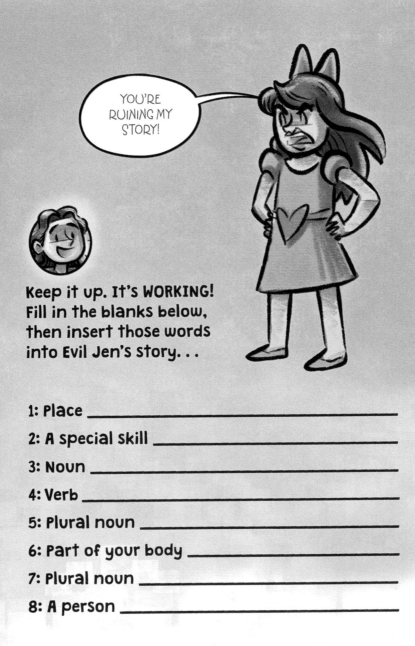

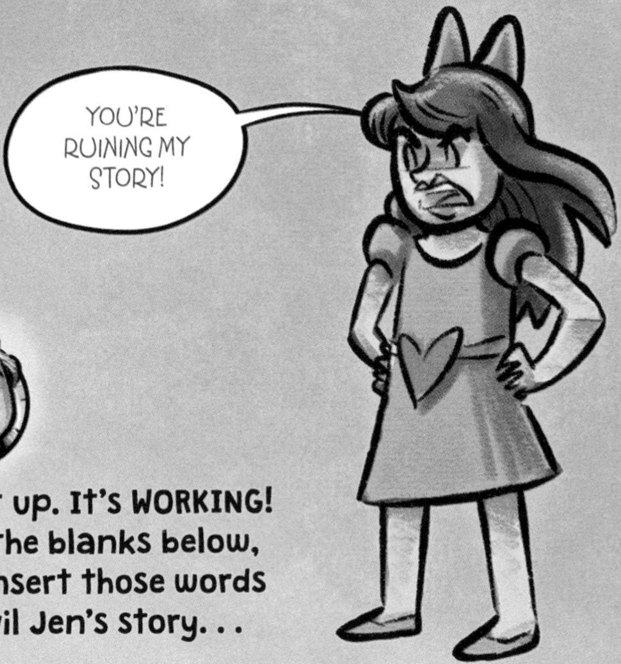
YOU'RE RUINING MY STORY!

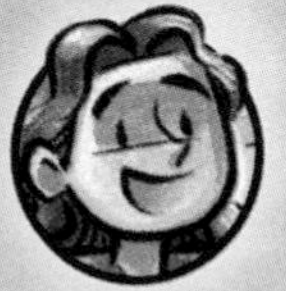

**Keep it up. It's WORKING! Fill in the blanks below, then insert those words into Evil Jen's story. . .**

**1: Place** ______________________

**2: A special skill** ______________________

**3: Noun** ______________________

**4: Verb** ______________________

**5: Plural noun** ______________________

**6: Part of your body** ______________________

**7: Plural noun** ______________________

**8: A person** ______________________

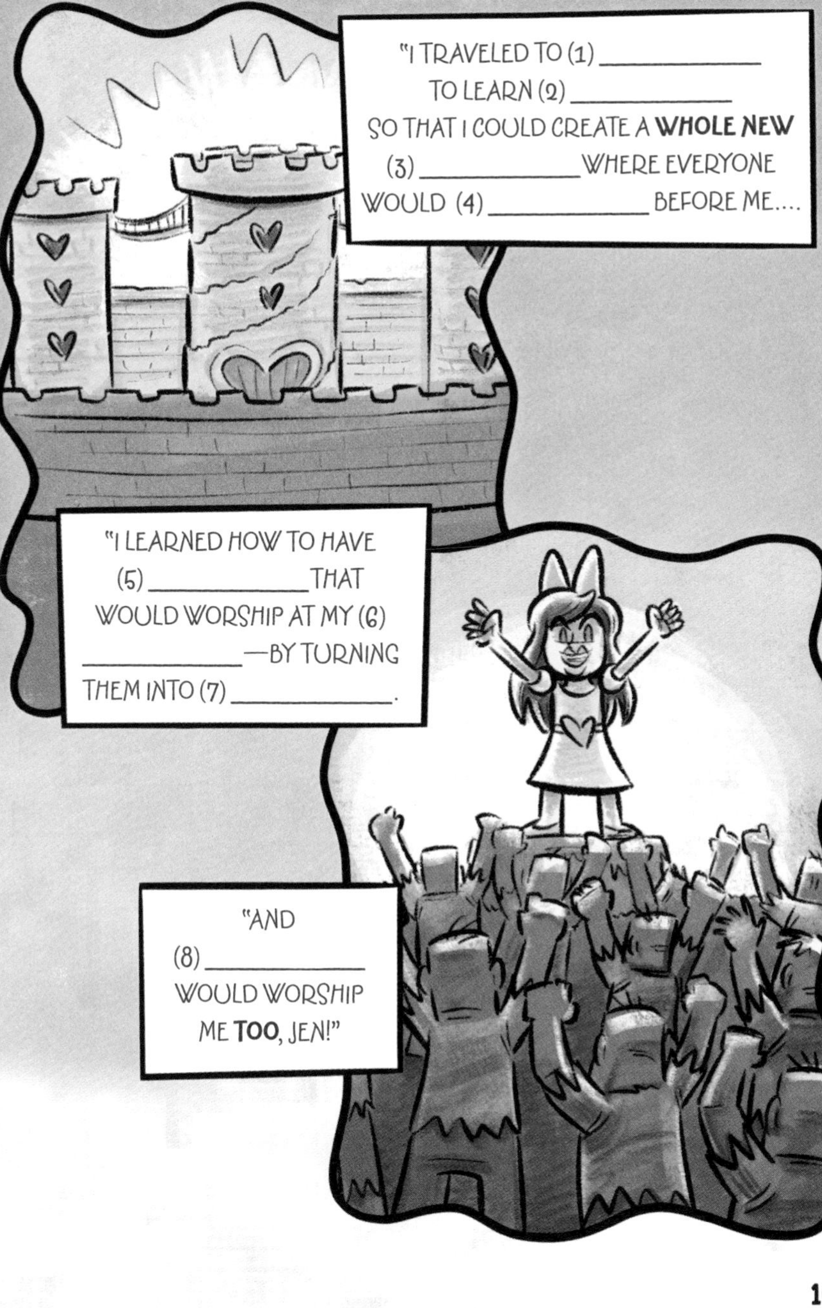
"I TRAVELED TO (1) ____________ TO LEARN (2) ____________ SO THAT I COULD CREATE A **WHOLE NEW** (3) ____________ WHERE EVERYONE WOULD (4) ____________ BEFORE ME....
"I LEARNED HOW TO HAVE (5) ____________ THAT WOULD WORSHIP AT MY (6) ____________—BY TURNING THEM INTO (7) ____________.
"AND (8) ____________ WOULD WORSHIP ME **TOO**, JEN!"

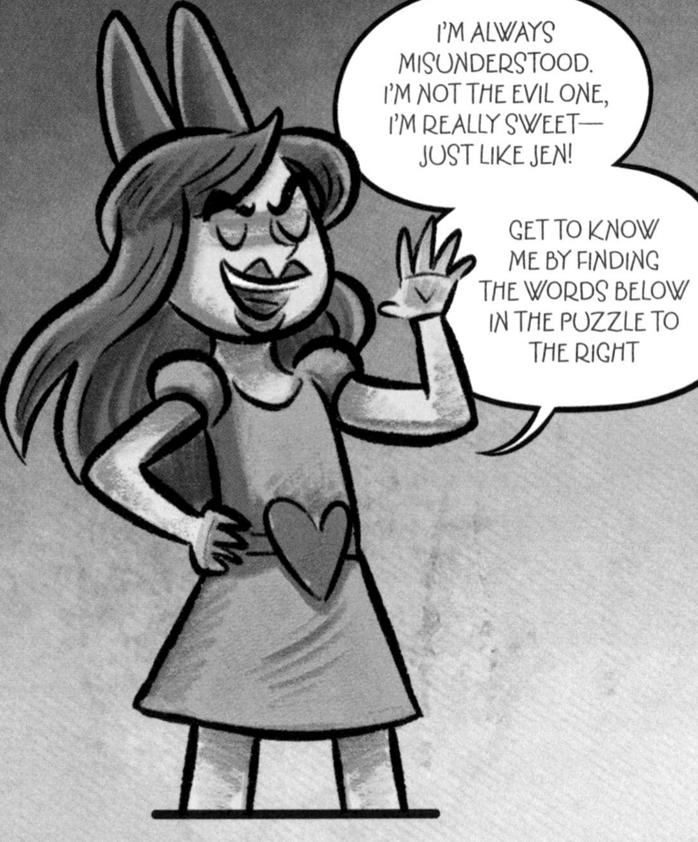
I'M ALWAYS MISUNDERSTOOD. I'M NOT THE EVIL ONE, I'M REALLY SWEET— JUST LIKE JEN!
GET TO KNOW ME BY FINDING THE WORDS BELOW IN THE PUZZLE TO THE RIGHT

ANGRY
BOW
CASTLE
HEARTS
JEALOUS
JEN
KIDNAP
LIPS
RULER
THRONE
UNDERWORLD
ZOMBIES

| | | | | | | | | | | | | | | |
|---|---|---|---|---|---|---|---|---|---|---|---|---|---|---|
| C | N | B | Y | C | A | N | G | R | Y | B | T | E | O | P |
| G | Q | F | K | P | A | M | K | D | T | H | K | C | P | A |
| T | H | R | O | N | E | S | U | R | L | P | A | K | E | G |
| L | A | Z | W | J | X | R | T | F | V | K | J | X | E | J |
| Q | I | M | F | E | C | J | V | L | D | I | Z | Z | L | X |
| T | O | P | L | N | W | S | L | N | E | D | X | Q | S | Q |
| K | Z | I | S | O | F | E | Z | I | W | N | J | W | B | S |
| I | B | Q | B | K | M | I | G | O | P | A | Y | B | T | S |
| G | D | H | Y | E | Y | I | U | H | M | P | Z | R | I | J |
| U | N | D | E | R | W | O | R | L | D | B | A | J | R | E |
| T | Z | I | P | O | I | E | V | E | B | E | I | E | T | A |
| Y | J | Z | U | R | Q | Z | P | B | H | M | L | E | V | L |
| B | C | H | W | B | B | Z | I | Z | K | U | Q | Y | S | O |
| S | O | N | B | L | P | B | Q | F | R | E | V | F | L | U |
| Y | L | Y | S | X | I | X | X | J | J | Z | K | T | R | S |

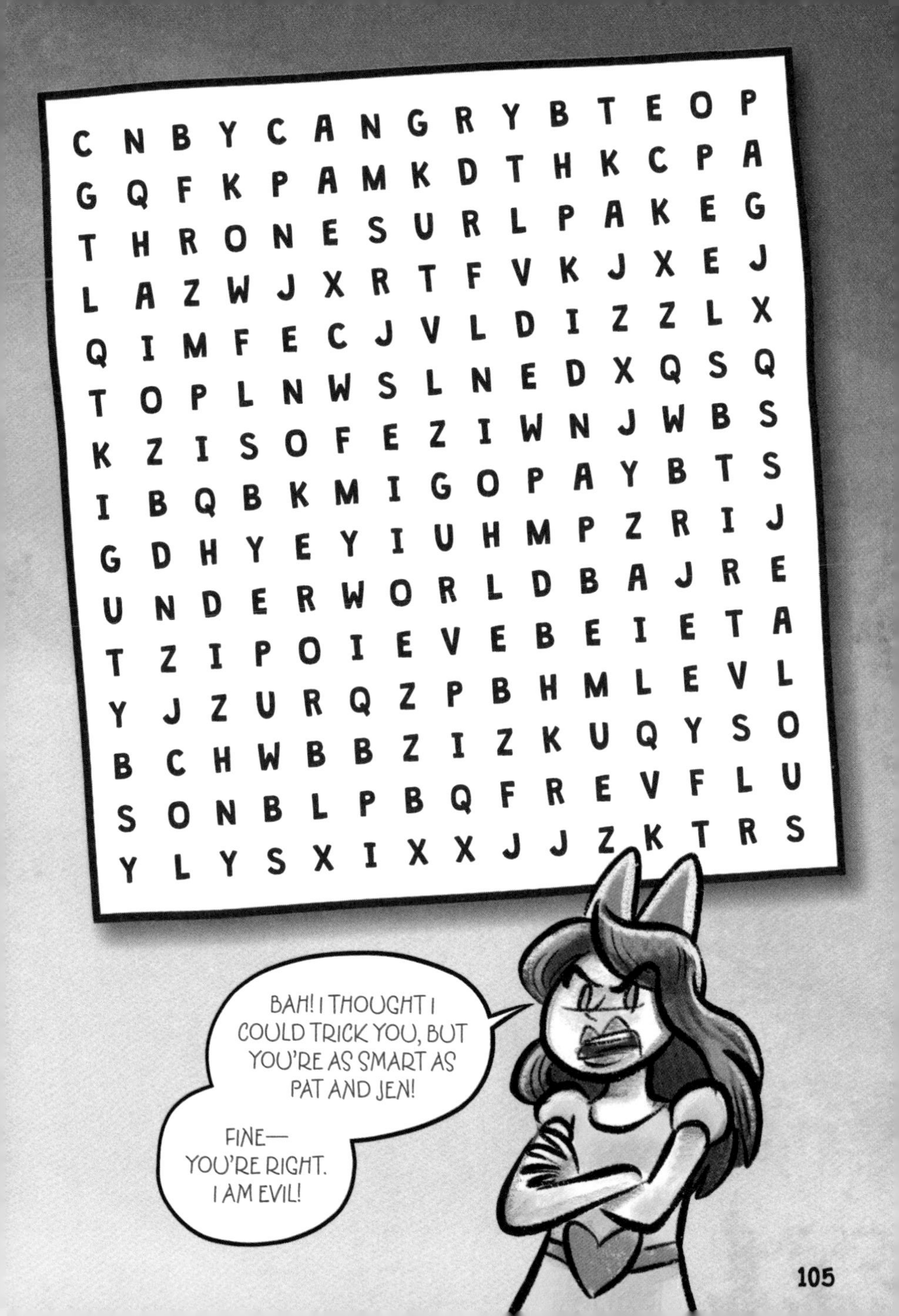

BAH! I THOUGHT I COULD TRICK YOU, BUT YOU'RE AS SMART AS PAT AND JEN!
FINE— YOU'RE RIGHT. I AM EVIL!

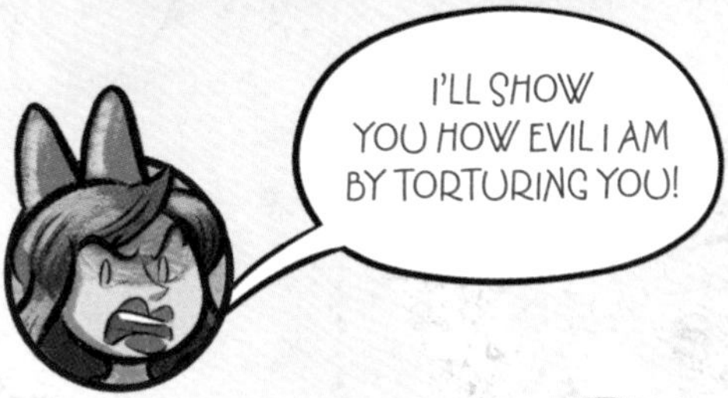
I'LL SHOW YOU HOW EVIL I AM BY TORTURING YOU!

**Draw a sound effect for the most annoying sound in the world!**

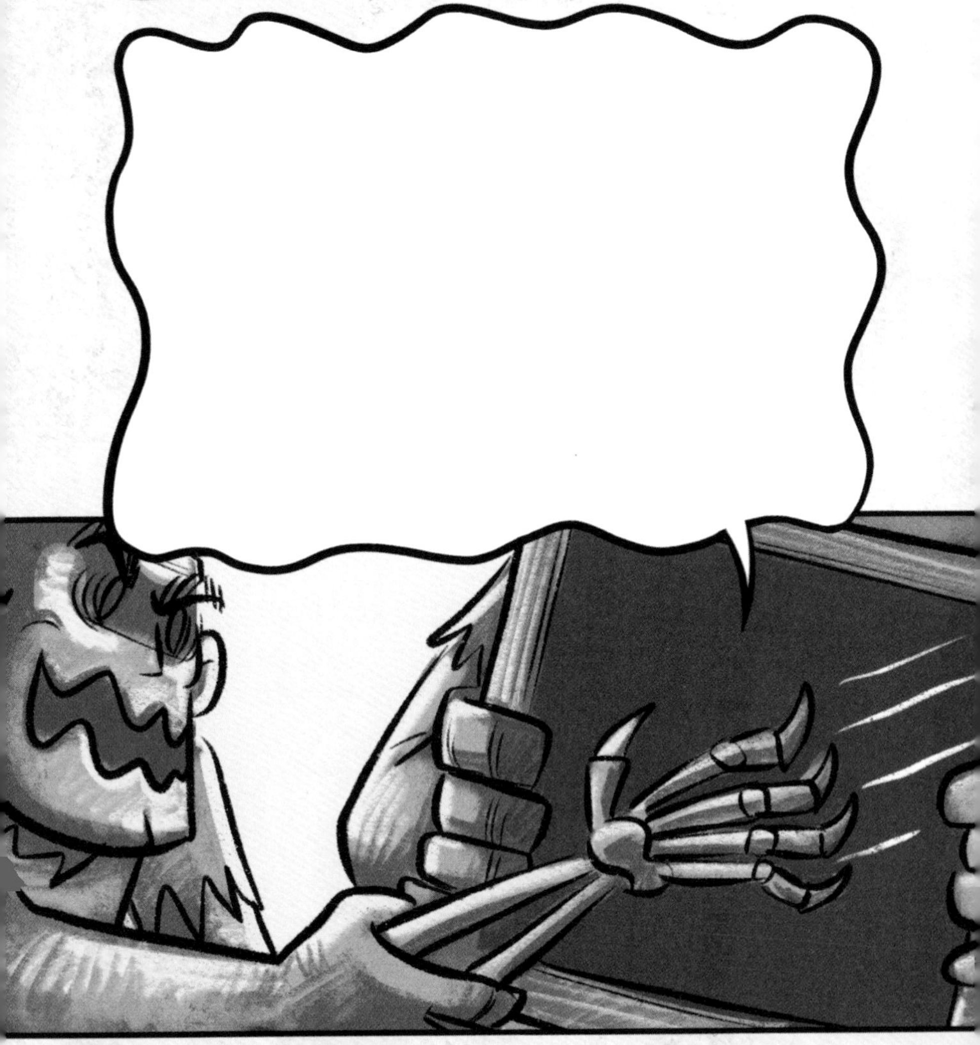

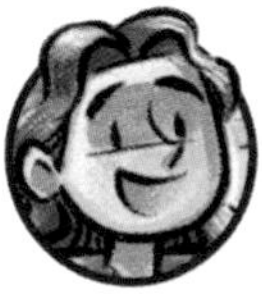

Evil Jen is such a bully. Have you ever been bullied or seen someone get bullied? What happened? How did that make you feel?

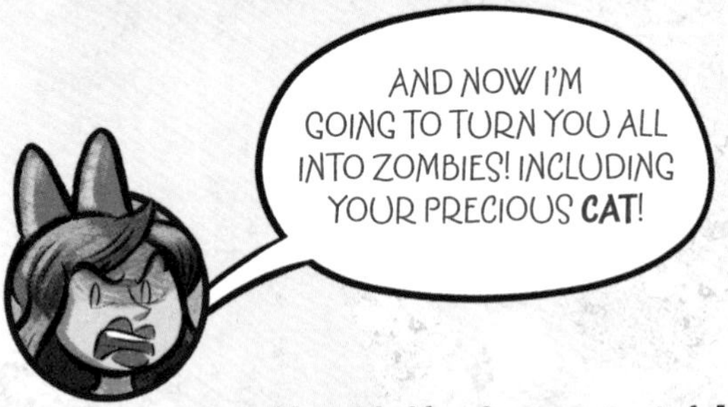
AND NOW I'M GOING TO TURN YOU ALL INTO ZOMBIES! INCLUDING YOUR PRECIOUS **CAT**!

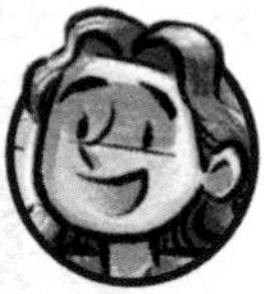

**Don't eat that sandwich! Take it apart by making ten words out of the letters in:**

# HUMAN FINGER CHEESE SANDWICH

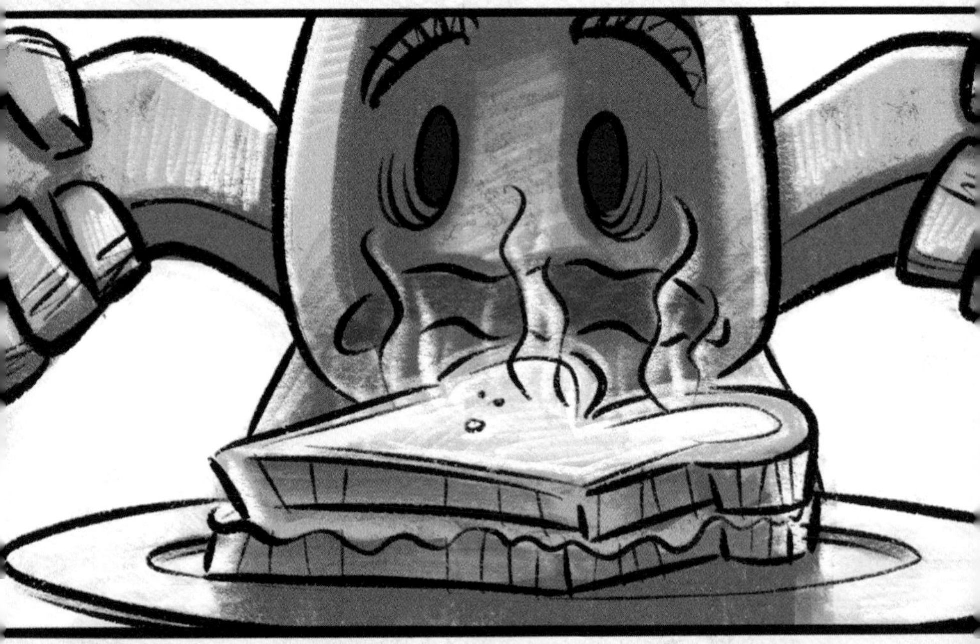

_____  _____

_____  _____

_____  _____

_____  _____

_____  _____

## Connect the dots!

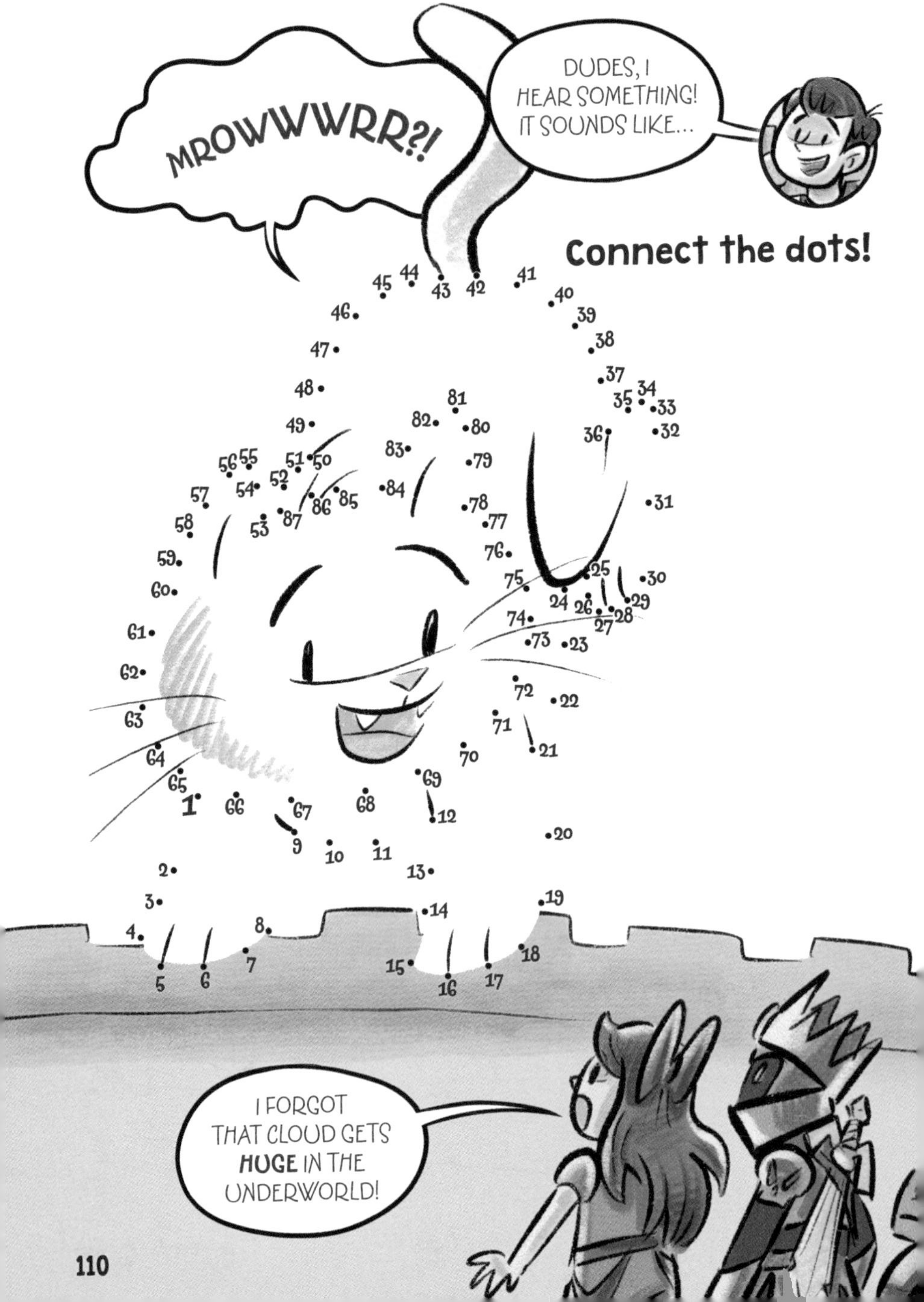
MROWWWRR?!
DUDES, I HEAR SOMETHING! IT SOUNDS LIKE...
I FORGOT THAT CLOUD GETS **HUGE** IN THE UNDERWORLD!

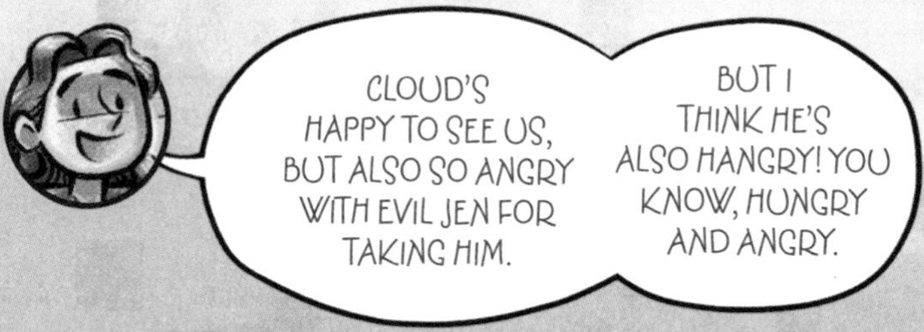
CLOUD'S HAPPY TO SEE US, BUT ALSO SO ANGRY WITH EVIL JEN FOR TAKING HIM.
BUT I THINK HE'S ALSO HANGRY! YOU KNOW, HUNGRY AND ANGRY.

**Draw Cloud's facial expression to match each of his emotions!**

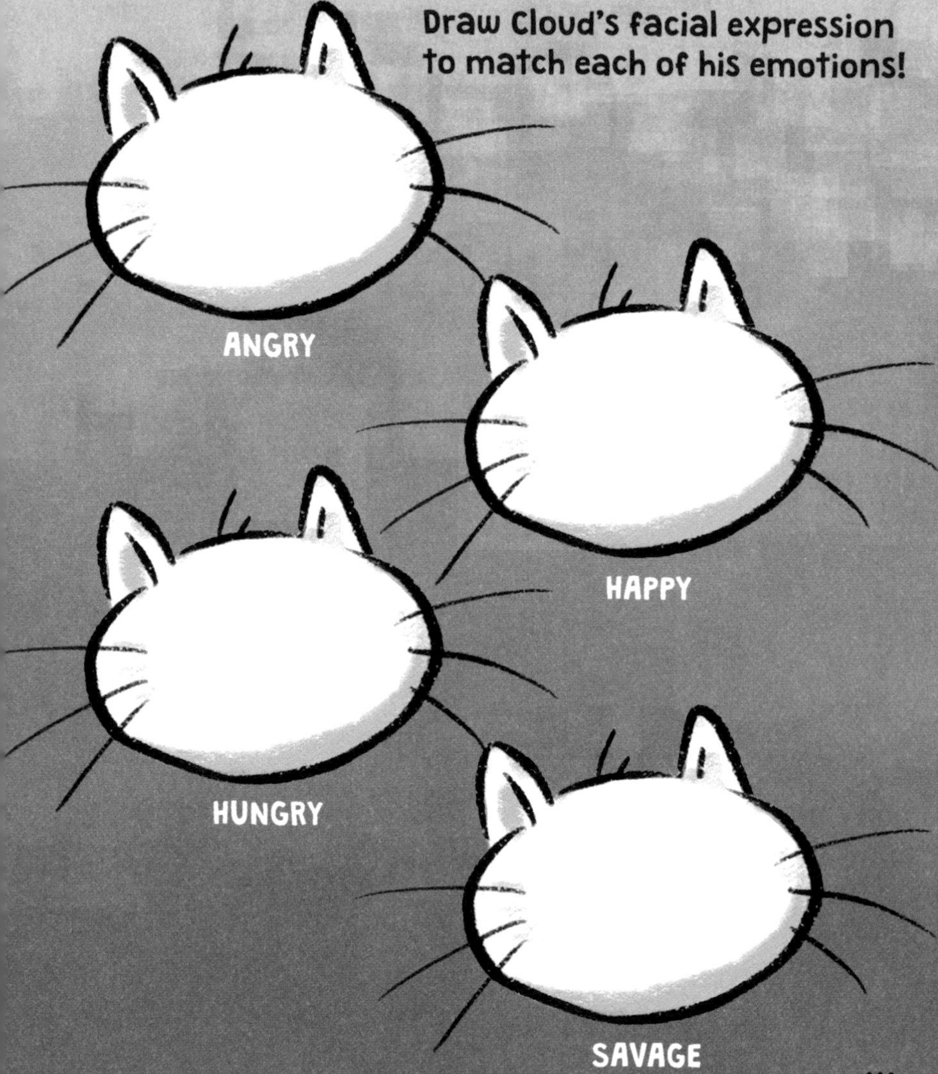
ANGRY
HAPPY
HUNGRY
SAVAGE

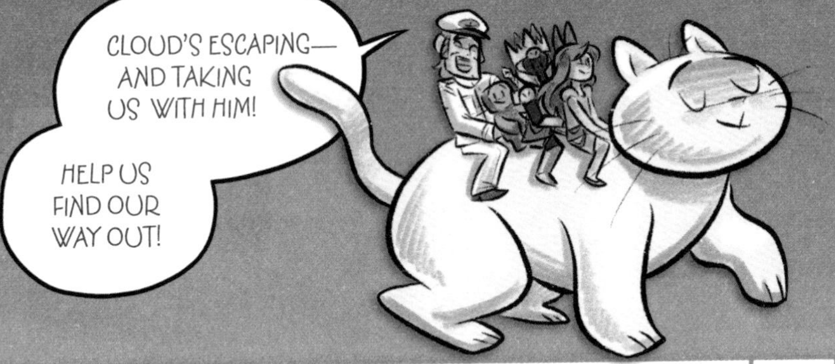
CLOUD'S ESCAPING—
AND TAKING
US WITH HIM!
HELP US
FIND OUR
WAY OUT!

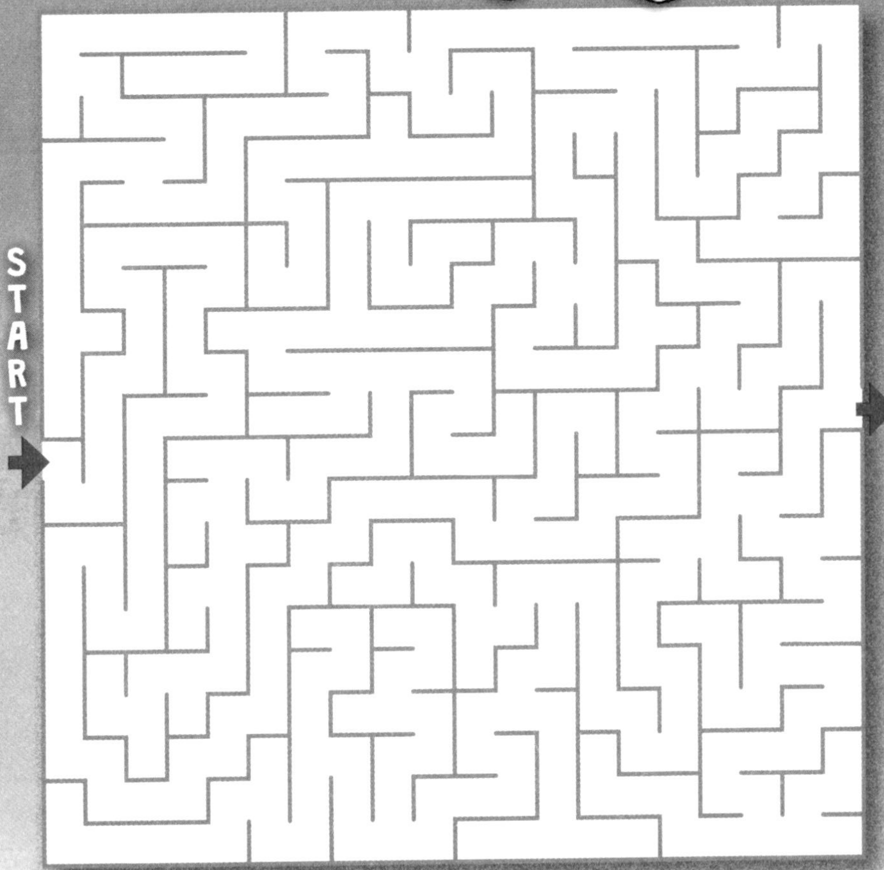
START

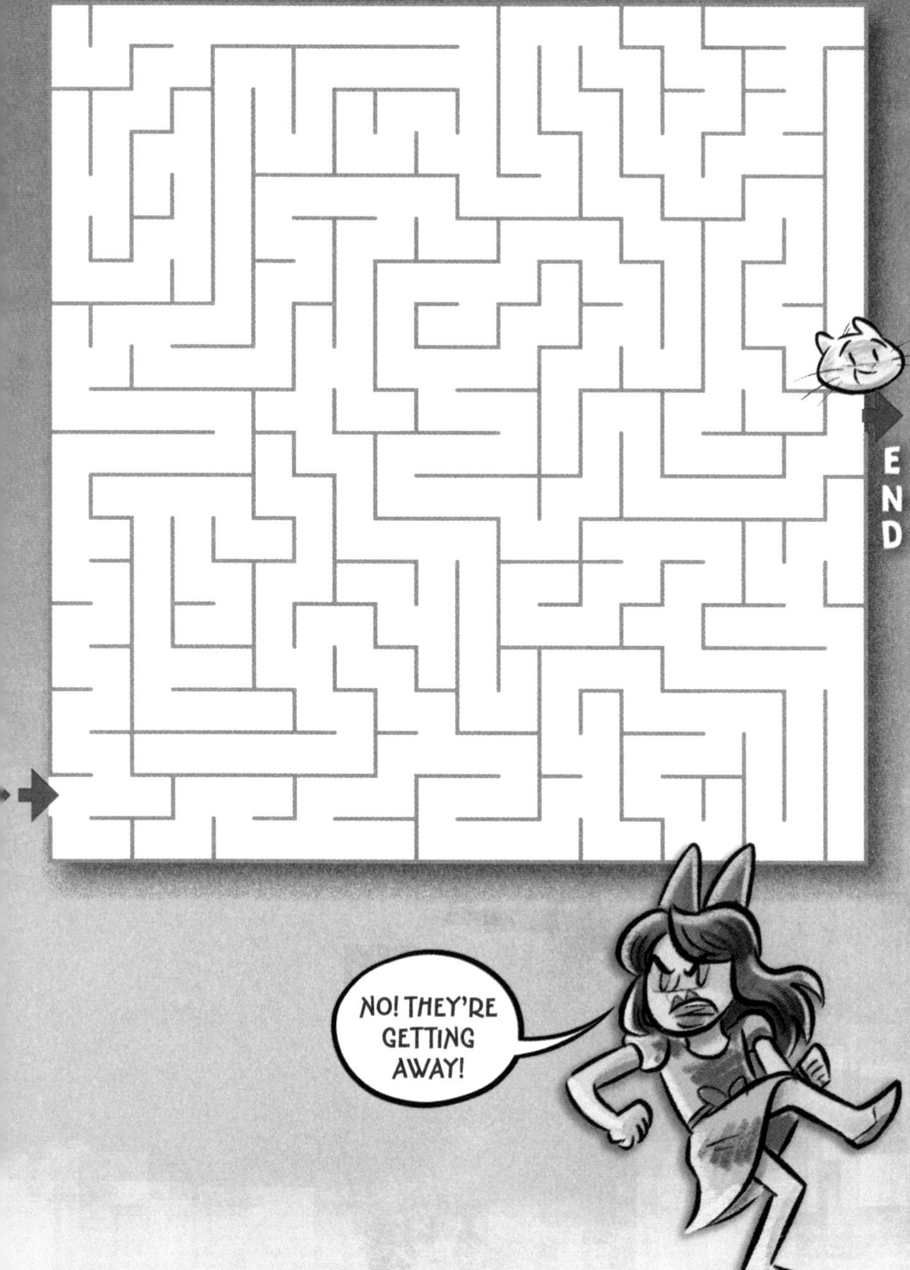
END
NO! THEY'RE GETTING AWAY!

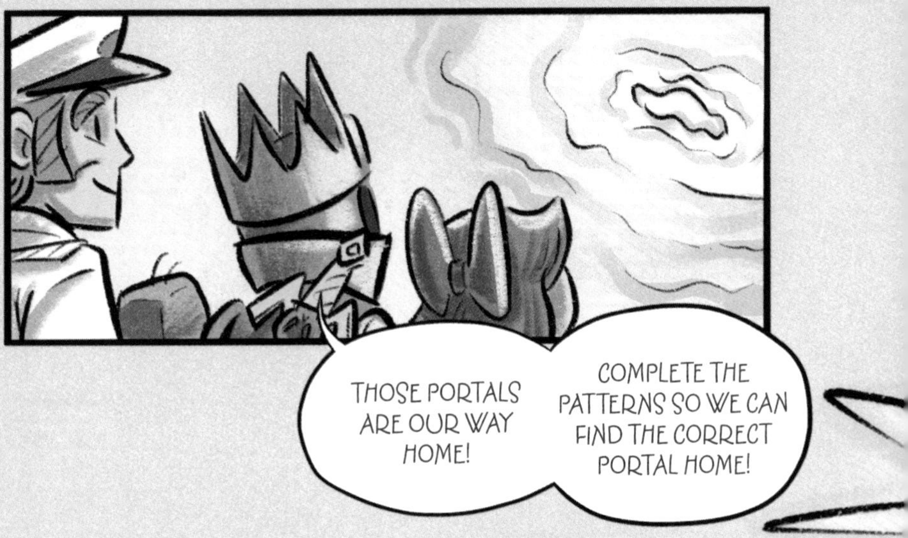
THOSE PORTALS ARE OUR WAY HOME!
COMPLETE THE PATTERNS SO WE CAN FIND THE CORRECT PORTAL HOME!

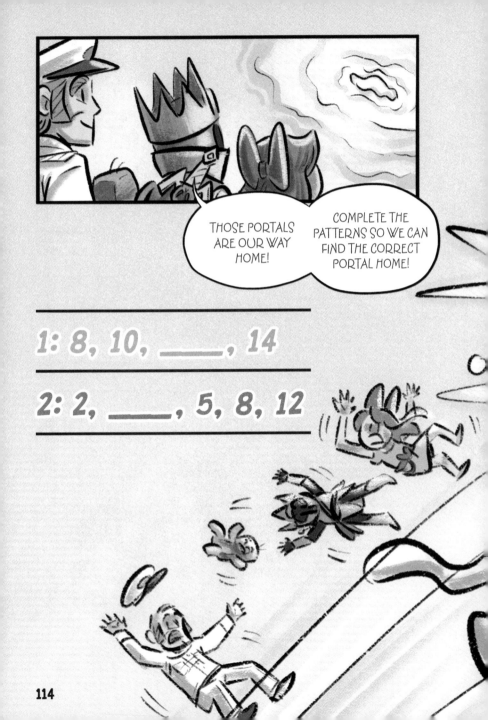

**1: 8, 10, ____, 14**

**2: 2, ____, 5, 8, 12**

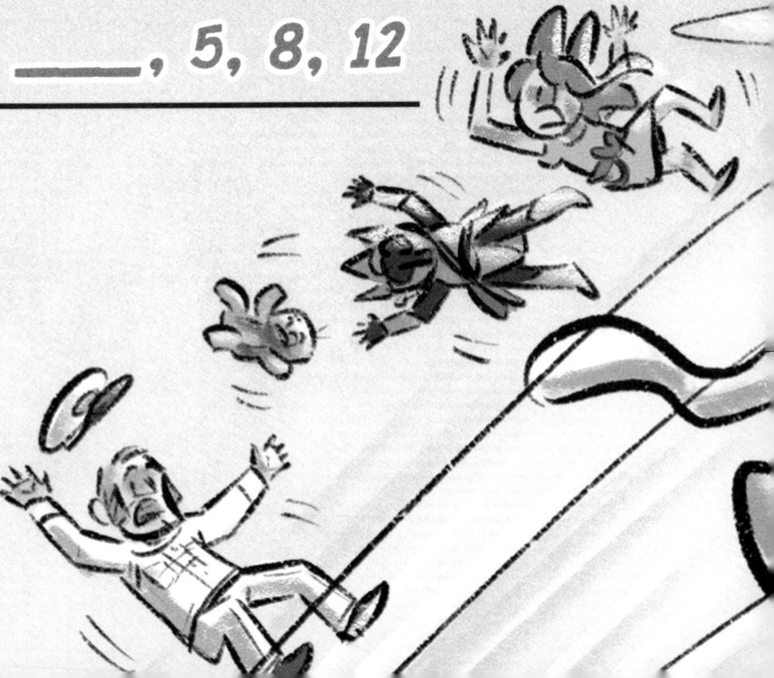

3: ____, 10, 15, 20

4: 37, 36, 34, ____, 27

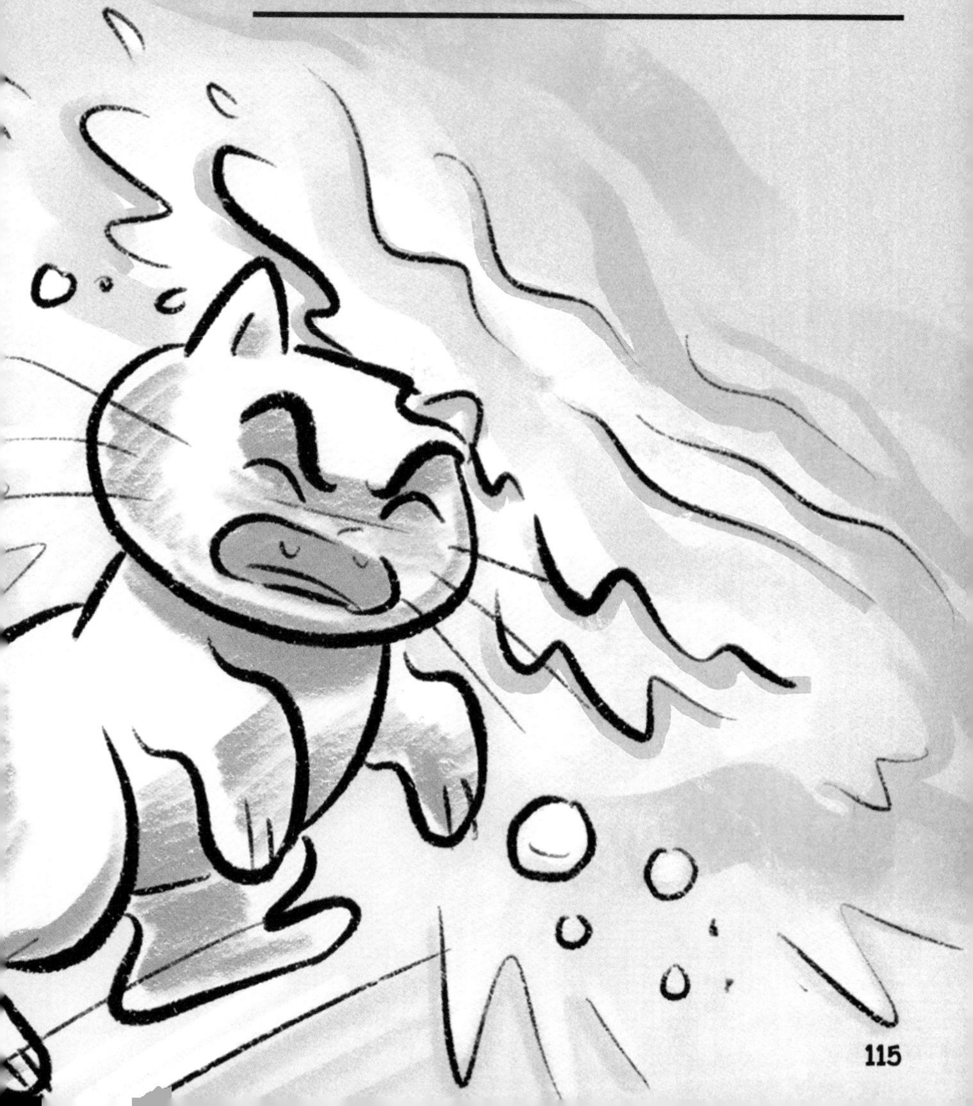

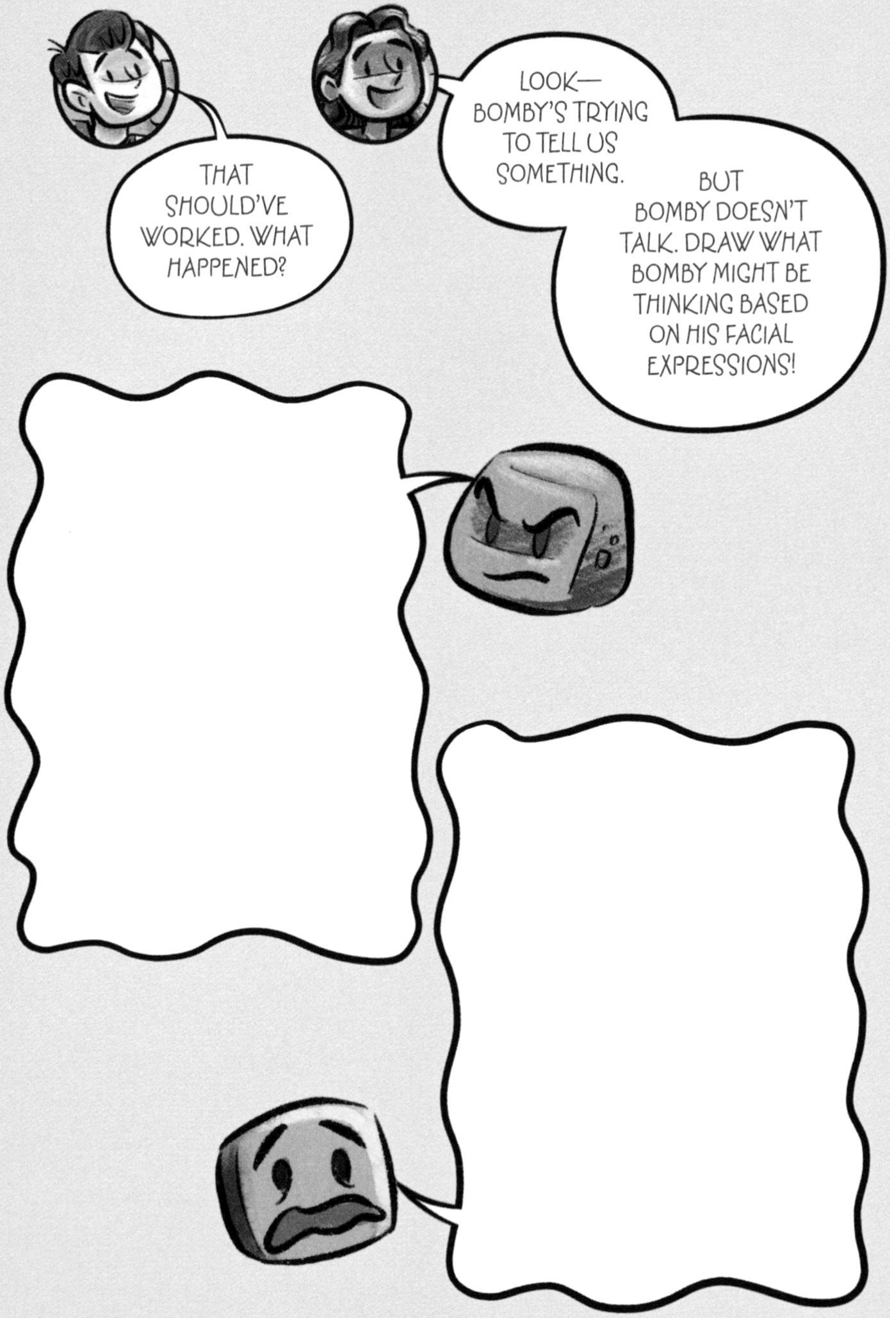
THAT SHOULD'VE WORKED. WHAT HAPPENED?
LOOK— BOMBY'S TRYING TO TELL US SOMETHING.
BUT BOMBY DOESN'T TALK. DRAW WHAT BOMBY MIGHT BE THINKING BASED ON HIS FACIAL EXPRESSIONS!

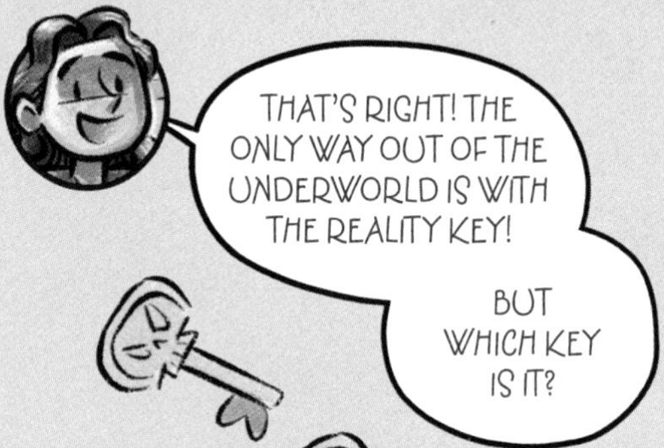
THAT'S RIGHT! THE ONLY WAY OUT OF THE UNDERWORLD IS WITH THE REALITY KEY!
BUT WHICH KEY IS IT?

**Find the key that doesn't match!**

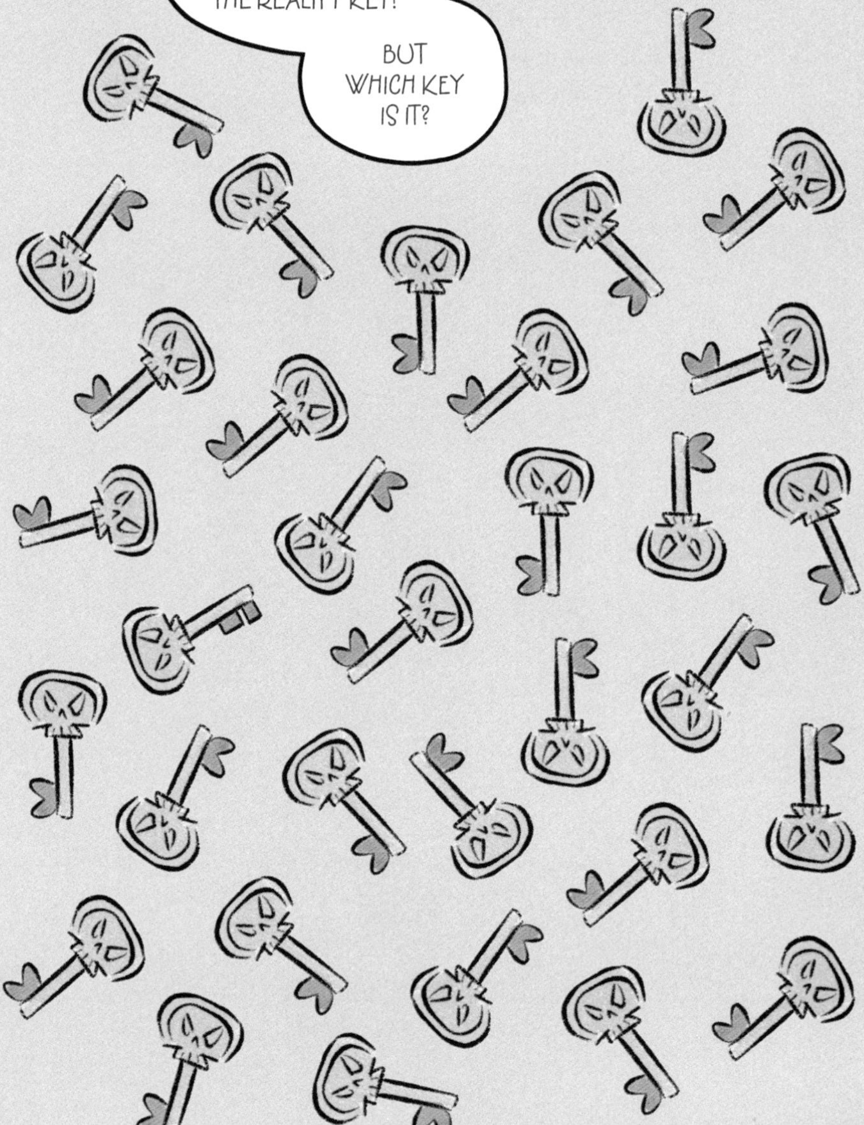

It WORKED! We're HOME!

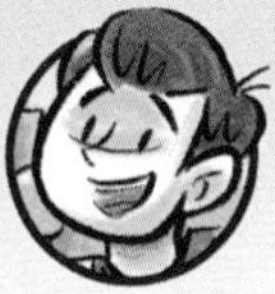

Draw your own home inside of the portal back to the real world!

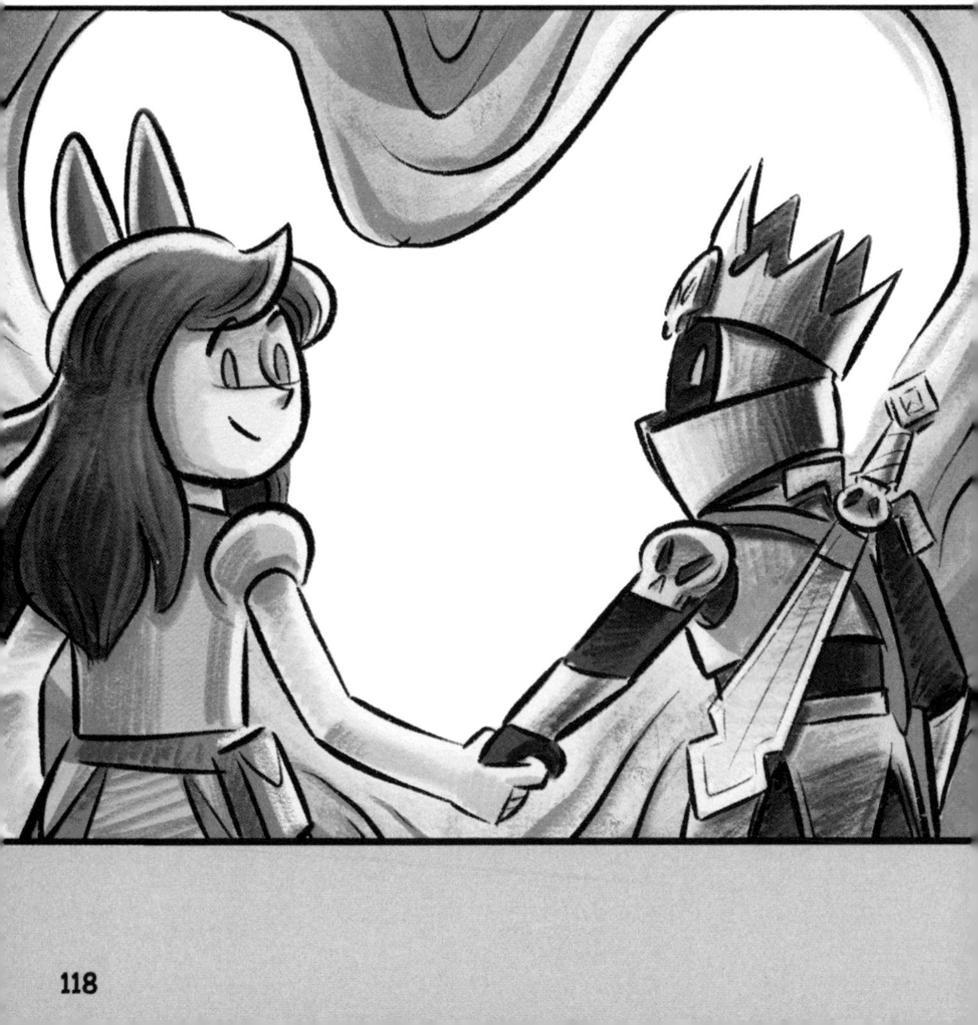

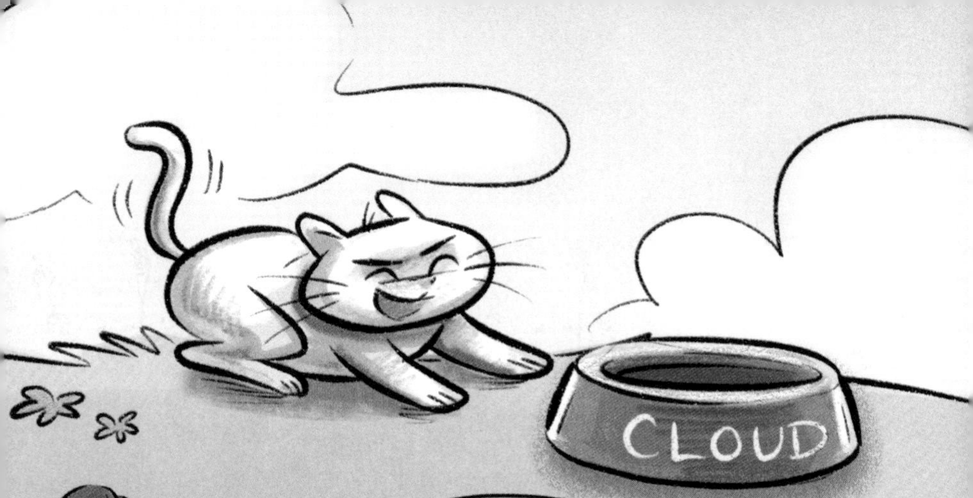
CLOUD

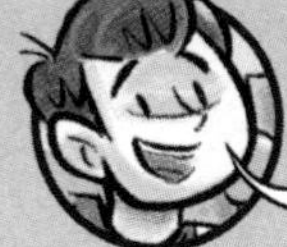

NOW THAT WE'RE HOME, CLOUD'S STARVING.

FILL CLOUD'S BOWL BY CIRCLING THE FOODS BELOW THAT HE MIGHT LIKE TO EAT OR DRINK.

WATER

BRUSSELS SPROUTS

CHICKEN

BANANA CREME PIE

TUNA FISH

TEA

MUDDY FROG SOUP

HUMAN FINGER CHEESE

ROOT BEER

COCONUT

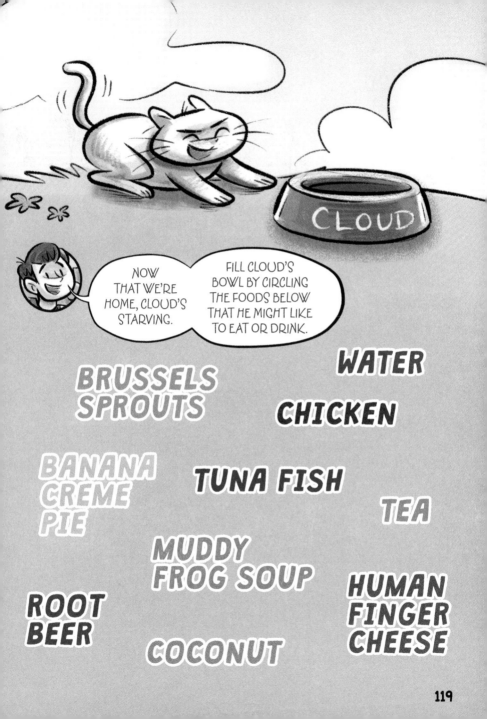

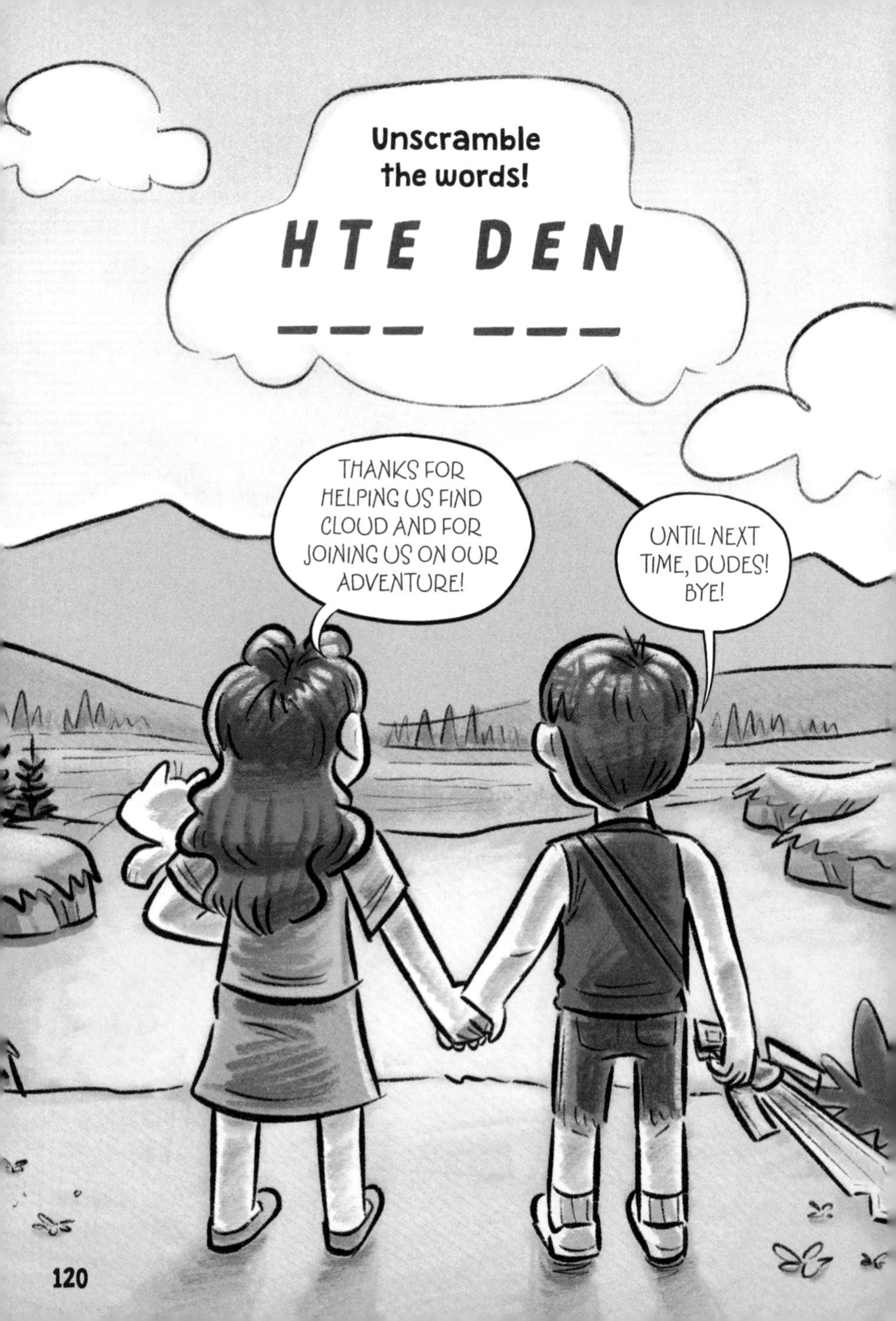
Unscramble the words!
HTE DEN
THANKS FOR HELPING US FIND CLOUD AND FOR JOINING US ON OUR ADVENTURE!
UNTIL NEXT TIME, DUDES! BYE!

# ANSWER KEY

**PAGE 1:**
Connect the Dots

**PAGE 6:**
Word Scramble

**WHITE**
**SMALL**
**SAVAGE**
**WHISKERS**
**FLUFFY**
**MEOW**

**PAGE 9:**
Sudoku 1

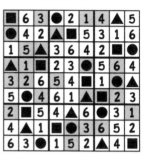

**PAGE 9:**
Sudoku 2

**PAGE 11:**
Crossword Solutions

| Across | Down |
|---|---|
| 2. BLUE | 1. PICKLE |
| 5. JEALOUS | 2. BEST |
| 6. BANDAGE | FRIEND |
| 7. SWORD | 3. SECRET |
| | 4. ZOMBIE |

**PAGE 12:**
Odd Pickle Out

**PAGE 13:**
Math Solutions

$7 \times 8 = 56$
$34 + 17 = 51$
$43 - 15 = 28$
$64 \div 8 = 8$
$6 \times 7 = 42$

**PAGE 14:**
Connect the Dots

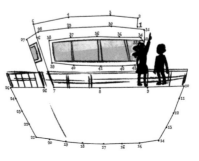

**PAGE 15:**
Choose the Word

**PROPELLER**
**ANCHOR**
**KAYAK**
**OAR**
**CAPTAIN COOKIE**

## PAGE 17:
Word Search

```
F F H L P E N X C I I R P S N
S H O R T B R E A D A A N N K
O O C W B S Y Y F G I I G I A
B W E K Z V F Z U M Y I K C G
I J D U B A J S A L N A I K I
S X P K X L O D J G X A I E N
C H O C O L A T E C H I P R G
O W S H J C B R L H H T H D E
T H H A A B B W A F E R L O R
T R S M N R L R F T O Z P O S
I Z Y W E D C C V Q R W J D N
Y F E A Z Q W Z T Y U L R L A
L D D K H M N I Z P M U K E P
M A C A R O O N C P V Z Q Z S
J K C L I M E O A H F T V N G
```

## PAGE 18:
Choose the Word

**HOT SAUCE
FROG LEGS
FINGER
    CHEESE
MUSHROOM
    SYRUP
BACON
ALMONDS**

## PAGE 23:
Maze

## PAGE 25:
Color Code

**RED
ORANGE
YELLOW
GREEN
BLUE
INDIGO
VIOLET**

## PAGE 28:
Connect the Dots

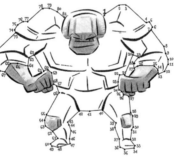

## PAGE 29:
Odd Golem Out

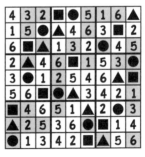

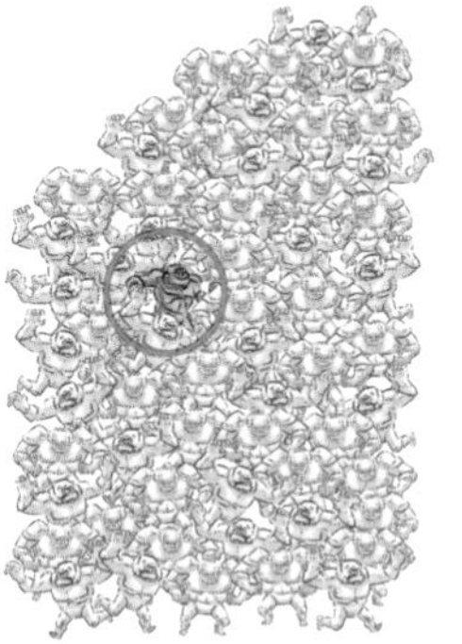

## PAGE 30:
Word Scramble

**HONEY BOO BOO,
DINNER'S READY!**

## PAGE 31:
Match Game

**CLUES:**

|5| Angry

|1| Excited

|2| Disappointed

|4| Sad

|3| Worried

## PAGE 32:
Sudoku

| 4 | 3 | 2 | ■ | ● | 5 | 1 | 6 | ▲ |
|---|---|---|---|---|---|---|---|---|
| 1 | 5 | ● | ▲ | 4 | 6 | 3 | ■ | 2 |
| 6 | ■ | ▲ | 1 | 3 | 2 | ● | 4 | 5 |
| 2 | ▲ | 4 | 6 | ■ | 1 | 5 | 3 | ● |
| 3 | ● | 1 | 2 | 5 | 4 | 6 | ▲ | ■ |
| 5 | 6 | ■ | ● | ▲ | 3 | 4 | 2 | 1 |
| ■ | 4 | 6 | 5 | 1 | ▲ | 2 | ● | 3 |
| ▲ | 2 | 5 | 3 | 6 | ● | ■ | 1 | 4 |
| ● | 1 | 3 | 4 | 2 | ■ | ▲ | 5 | 6 |

## PAGE 33:
### Sudoku 1

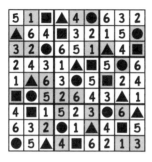

| 5 | 1 | ■ | ▲ | 4 | ● | 6 | 3 | 2 |
| ▲ | 6 | 4 | ■ | 3 | 2 | 1 | 5 | ● |
| 3 | 2 | ● | 6 | 5 | 1 | ▲ | 4 | ■ |
| 2 | 4 | 3 | 1 | ▲ | ■ | 5 | ● | 6 |
| 1 | ▲ | 6 | 3 | ● | 5 | ■ | 2 | 4 |
| ■ | ● | 5 | 2 | 6 | 4 | 3 | ▲ | 1 |
| 4 | ■ | 1 | 5 | 2 | 3 | ● | 6 | ▲ |
| 6 | 3 | 2 | ● | 1 | ▲ | 4 | ■ | 5 |
| ● | 5 | ▲ | 4 | ■ | 6 | 2 | 1 | 3 |

## PAGE 33:
### Sudoku 2

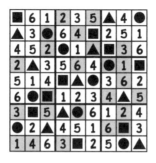

| ■ | 6 | 1 | 2 | 3 | 5 | ▲ | 4 | ● |
| ▲ | 3 | ● | 6 | 4 | ■ | 2 | 5 | 1 |
| 4 | 5 | 2 | ● | 1 | ▲ | ■ | 3 | 6 |
| 2 | ▲ | 3 | 5 | 6 | 4 | ● | 1 | ■ |
| 5 | 1 | 4 | ■ | ▲ | ● | 3 | 6 | 2 |
| 6 | ● | ■ | 1 | 2 | 3 | 4 | ▲ | 5 |
| 3 | ■ | 5 | ▲ | ● | 6 | 1 | 2 | 4 |
| ● | 2 | ▲ | 4 | 5 | 1 | 6 | ■ | 3 |
| 1 | 4 | 6 | 3 | ■ | 2 | 5 | ● | ▲ |

## PAGE 35:
### Crossword Solutions

Across
2. CASTLE
4. SMALL
5. DYNAMITE
6. FRIEND
Down
1. GREEN
3. SANDWICH
4. SPIDER

## PAGE 36:
### Odd Spider Out

## PAGE 39:
### Maze

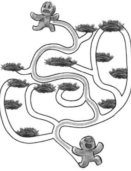

## PAGE 41:
### Math Solutions

| 305 | 287 | 255 | 268 |
|-----|-----|-----|-----|
| T | H | U | P |
| 305 | 287 | 255 | 214 |
| T | H | U | D |
| 220 | 287 | 255 | 214 |
| W | H | U | P |

## PAGE 42:
### Connect the Dots

## PAGE 45:
### Word Search

```
F D K L R U B J V F D W N C W
T N A K E J N A Q A J E G R K
S U K Y N F T D E B E M A E E
P L G F X J Z D E R R L W E A
I Q O S A J N B G R S A S P F
L I Z W P U H C B C W H I Y E
X G Z B S T I N K Y B O Q N P
H O R D E S R Q B Y I I R T S
S O I Q R Z Z X M B T W I L D
M P F B H R D U U D E X F N D
G U A U X X T W Z Y Y I P G A
Q G S W W M P N Y I Y S V T T
H E O A N D D G L L B D Y T G
P S D D X E C E D V M T V S T
Z D D V D U R R C S D L E O L
```

## PAGE 15:
### Odd Zombie Out

## PAGE 51:
Math Solution

**165**

## PAGES 52–53:
Mazes

## PAGE 54:
Connect the Dots

## PAGE 58:
Sudoku

| | | | | | | | | |
|---|---|---|---|---|---|---|---|---|
| 5 | ■ | 6 | 3 | 4 | 1 | ● | 2 | ▲ |
| ▲ | 4 | 1 | ■ | ● | 2 | 5 | 3 | 6 |
| ● | 2 | 3 | 5 | ▲ | 6 | ■ | 4 | 1 |
| 4 | ▲ | 5 | 1 | ■ | ● | 3 | 6 | 2 |
| 2 | 1 | ● | 6 | 3 | 5 | 4 | ▲ | ■ |
| 3 | 6 | ■ | 4 | 2 | ▲ | 1 | 5 | ● |
| 6 | 3 | 4 | ▲ | 1 | ■ | 2 | ● | 5 |
| 1 | ● | ▲ | 2 | 5 | 3 | 6 | ■ | 4 |
| ■ | 5 | 2 | ● | 6 | 4 | ▲ | 1 | 3 |

## PAGE 59:
Sudoku 1

| | | | | | | | | |
|---|---|---|---|---|---|---|---|---|
| 6 | 2 | ● | 4 | ■ | 3 | 1 | 5 | ▲ |
| 4 | 5 | 3 | ● | ▲ | 1 | 6 | 2 | ■ |
| ■ | 1 | ▲ | 6 | 2 | 5 | ● | 4 | 3 |
| ▲ | 3 | 4 | 5 | 1 | ■ | 2 | 6 | ● |
| 5 | 6 | 2 | ▲ | 4 | ● | ■ | 3 | 1 |
| 1 | ● | ■ | 3 | 6 | 2 | 5 | ▲ | 4 |
| 3 | ■ | 5 | 2 | ● | 4 | ▲ | 1 | 6 |
| 2 | ▲ | 1 | ■ | 3 | 6 | 4 | ● | 5 |
| ● | 4 | 6 | 1 | 5 | ▲ | 3 | ■ | 2 |

## PAGE 59:
Sudoku 2

| | | | | | | | | |
|---|---|---|---|---|---|---|---|---|
| 2 | ▲ | ● | 6 | ■ | 5 | 3 | 1 | 4 |
| ■ | 5 | 3 | ▲ | 1 | 4 | ● | 2 | 6 |
| 1 | 6 | 4 | 3 | ● | 2 | 5 | ■ | ▲ |
| 4 | ■ | 1 | ● | 5 | ▲ | 2 | 6 | 3 |
| ● | 3 | 5 | 2 | 4 | 6 | ■ | ▲ | 1 |
| 6 | 2 | ▲ | ■ | 3 | 1 | 4 | ● | 5 |
| ▲ | 1 | ■ | 5 | 2 | 3 | 6 | 4 | ● |
| 5 | ● | 6 | 4 | ▲ | ■ | 1 | 3 | 2 |
| 3 | 4 | 2 | 1 | 6 | ● | ▲ | 5 | ■ |

## PAGE 62:
Word Scramble

**MR. RAINBOW**

## PAGE 63:
Draw A Line

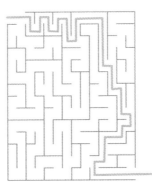

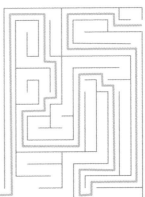

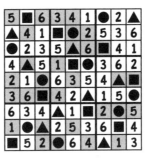

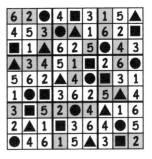

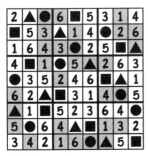

PAGES 64-65:
Color By Number
Math Solutions

174 + 242 = 416
53 - 24 = 29
152 + 132 = 284
295 - 180 = 115
12 X 20 = 240
166 + 89 = 255
22 X 11 = 242
WELCOME

PAGE 69:
Odd Star Out

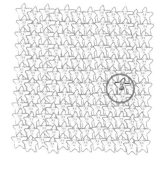

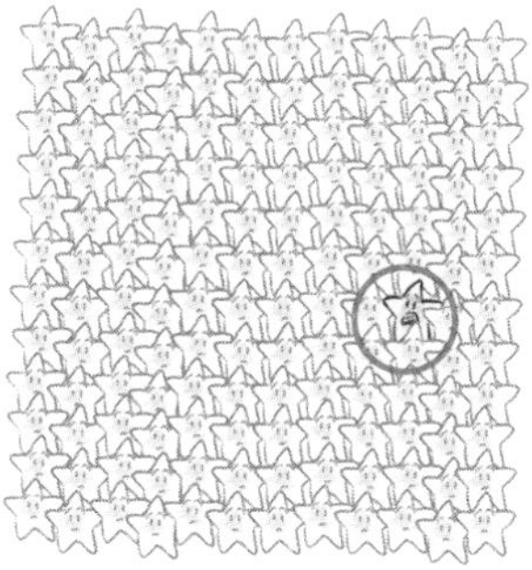

PAGE 71:
Word Search

PAGES 36-37:
Math Game

4.2
2.27
9.82
5.55
4.16

PAGES 74-75:
Word Scramble

MR. RAINBOW'S CAVE
STINKY EYE LAKE
CRUSTY TOE CANYON
ZOMBIE WOODS
EVIL JEN'S CASTLE

PAGE 77:
Odd Splat Out

PAGES 78-79:
Math Game

92 = 45 + 47
98 = 47 + 51
108 = 49 + 59
101 = 48 + 53
181 = 82 + 99
127 = 51 + 76

PAGE 81:
Coded Word Scramble

IF YOU EVER
WANT TO SEE
YOUR CAT
AGAIN COME
TO THE CASTLE
—EVIL JEN

PAGES 84:
Match the Silhouette

JEN

CAPTAIN
COOKIE

PAT

PAGE 85:
Match the Silhouette

BOMBY

HONEY
BOO BOO

MR. RAINBOW

PAGES 86–87:
Who Said It?
Page 86
**HONEY BOO BOO**
**JEN**
**ZOMBIE**
Page 87
**MR. RAINBOW**
**PAT**
**CAPTAIN COOKIE**

PAGE 89:
Crossword Solutions

Across
3. **MRRAINBOW**
4. **BOMBY**
5. **CAPTAINCOOKIE**
7. **CLOUD**
8. **JEN**
Down
1. **GIZMO**
2. **HONEYBOOBOO**
5. **CARTER**
6. **PAT**

PAGE 92:
Sudoku

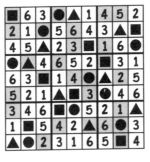

PAGE 93:
Sudoku 1

PAGE 93:
Sudoku 2

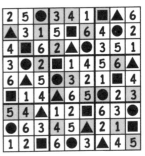

PAGE 94:
Connect the Dots

PAGES 98–98:
Spot the Differences

PAGES 98:
Choose the Word

**FEDRAL**
**LIBARY**
**BELEIVE**

PAGES 99:
Choose the Word Cont.

**JEWLERY**
**PERSCRIPTION**
**RECIEPT**
**FOILAGE**
**WIERD**
**ANTARTIC**

PAGE 105:
Word Search

C N B Y C A N G R Y B T E O P
G Q F K P A M K D T H K C P A
T H R O N E S U R L P A K E G
L A Z W J X R T F V K J X E J
Q I M F E C J V L D I Z Z L X
T O P L N W S L N E D X Q S Q
K Z I S O F E Z I W N J W B S
I B Q B K M I G O P A Y B T S
G D H Y E Y I U H M P Z R I J
U N D E R W O R L D B A J R E
T Z I P O I E V E B E I E T A
Y J Z U R Q Z P B H M L E V L
B C H W B B Z I Z K U Q Y S O
S O N B L P B Q F R E V F L U
Y L Y S X I X X J J Z K T R S

PAGE 110:
Connect the Dots

PAGES 112-113:
Maze

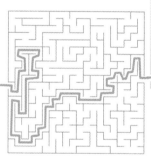

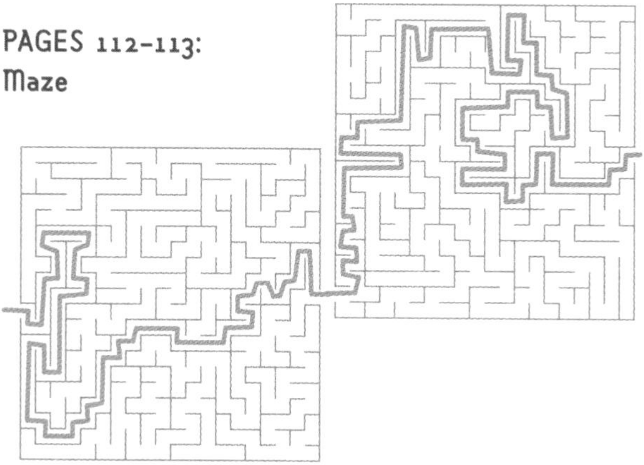

PAGES 114-115:
Math Solutions

1: 8, 10, 12, 14
2: 2, 3, 5, 8, 12
3: 5, 10, 15, 20
4: 37, 36, 34, 31, 27

PAGE 117:
Odd Key Out

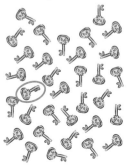

PAGE 119:
Choose the Word

**WATER**
**CHICKEN**
**TUNA FISH**

PAGES 120:
Word Scramble

**THE END**

# POPULARMMOs

## PRESENTS

POPULARMMOs
PRESENTS
ENTER THE MINE
PAT+JEN from POPULARMMOs
DANI JONES

POPULARMMOs
PRESENTS
A HOLE NEW WORLD
By PAT+JEN from POPULARMMOs
DANI JONES

POPULARMMOs
PRESENTS
A HOLE NEW ACTIVITY BOOK
MAZES, PUZZLES, GAMES, and MORE!
PAT+JEN from POPULARMMOs
DANI JONES

**HARPER**
*An Imprint of* HarperCollins*Publishers*
www.harpercollinschildrens.com